Green Flash at Sunset

hardcover ISBN: 979-8-9921516-3-3

paperback ISBN: 979-8-9921516-1-9

e-book ISBN: 979-8-9921516-2-6

Library of Congress Control Number: 2024926290

First Edition

1 2 3 4 5 6 7 8 9 0

Also by Nic Schuck

Native Moments

Panhandlers

Green Flash at Sunset

A Novel

Nic Schuck

To my wife, Julie

"Key West is the place to be if you're looking for immortality."
- Bob Dylan, "Key West (Philosopher Pirate)"

"The days are stacked against what we think we are."
- Jim Harrison, "The Theory and Practice of Rivers"

1

The afternoon storm ended, and as Bobby Drexler stepped from his pickup truck an empty beer can spilled out and rolled across the steaming blacktop of the corner store parking lot. He slammed the door, a mismatched color from the rest of the vehicle, and yelled for his wife, "Janet? You in there?" The cigarette miraculously stuck to his lower lip. A scar ran from just below his left eye to his jawline.

She didn't tell him she picked up an extra shift on her day off. Still, for some reason, she convinced herself that he would understand since he was out of work and there wasn't much opportunity in the Florida-Alabama border town of Sullivan in Escambia County, Florida.

Janet handed the soft pack of cigarettes and the scratch-off lottery ticket to the large woman standing in front of the register. The lady set down crumbled bills and exact change. A fly landed on the counter next to the money.

"Janet!" Bobby shouted again. "What the fuck, Janet!" He glared at the women through the glass as he approached the door.

"I'm sorry about that," Janet said to the lady in a hushed tone.

"Oh, hon. It's okay. I've been there myself."

"He don't mean no harm. He's all bark."

"Most of them are." The lady stuck the pack of cigarettes in her shirt, reaching in from the stretched-out neck of her Molly Hatchet t-shirt and into her bra before heading for the door. As she reached for the handle, the bells on the glass door rang. Bobby Drexler flicked the lit butt on the sidewalk before barging through. Without looking up from scratching her ticket, the lady stepped aside to let Bobby pass and exited the store by squeezing through the door before it shut.

"I thought I told you I don't like you leaving the house without telling me?" Bobby said. He grabbed a tall-boy can of Bud Ice out of the ice-filled standing cooler and popped the top.

"I was asked to come in, and I thought we could use the money," Janet said.

"Yeah? Well, now you ain't working at all no more. Get your shit, and let's go."

"Bobby, you can't do that," she said.

He took a long gulp of the beer and then threw the can across the store, beer flinging out of the opening, before smashing into the opposite wall, and then very calmly looked at Janet and said, "I can't do what?"

She averted her eyes from his. He walked down the potato chip aisle, opened a bag of Funyuns, took one circular chip out, ate it, and threw the bag to the ground. At the end of the aisle, he opened a Slim Jim, snapped off a bite, and stood chewing while staring at Janet.

"Well?" he said. "What're you waiting for?" He walked over to the Slushies, filled a cup, stuck in a straw, and took a long sip of the red frozen drink. "I'm leaving," he said, "and you damn well better be behind me. I'm going to stop at Sally's for a beer to give you time to get home before me and get dinner started."

He left the barely drank Slushie on the stack of Thrifty-Nickel classifieds by the door and picked up the latest Auto-Trader. Janet stood there for a minute, trying to telepathically make him wreck into a telephone pole as she watched his truck drive off, leaving a black cloud dissipating into the already smoggy air polluted by the paper plant just down the street.

She finished her shift, knowing that when Bobby said he was stopping for a beer he would be gone way longer than he implied, and was home well before Bobby. Not only was dinner started, but it was ready when he came stumbling through the screen door. That wasn't enough to keep Bobby from busting her lip and flinging the hot ground beef from the skillet at her.

"Who the fuck eats soft tacos?" he shouted as she slumped on the linoleum floor, holding the dishrag to her lip and using her other hand to try to remove the greasy meat from her hair.

"I'm driving into town to get a Whataburger," he said. "Ain't eating that bullshit that you call food. This kitchen better be cleaned up by the time I get home."

He slammed the screen door of the trailer behind him, and she stayed on that floor until there were no more tears left to cry and the blood on her lip dried.

2

The gray-haired man in a neck-flap fishing cap helped his wife onto the shallow-water skiff. She wore a long-sleeve blouse, a visor, and sunblock that wasn't rubbed in thoroughly on the back of her neck and between her sagging breasts. They booked a charter trip with Randall Greene for the third consecutive year and Randall knew how the trip would go: the lady would drink too much vodka, and the man would land a handful of permit that he could take to a restaurant to have cooked, probably a few bonefish that they would throw back after snapping a couple of pictures, possibly some mackerel, and hopefully a tarpon. Randall would get a larger tip if he could get them to land a tarpon. Tips were his beer-drinking money while the amount paid for the trip barely covered the bills.

They motored out of Cow Key Channel between Key West and Stock Island toward the Jewfish Basin. A cormorant sat perched on a channel marker with its wings spread wide. It was early, but the sun and humidity were nearly unbearable. The sun behind them reflected off the water into brilliant sun glitter. Birds close to shore sang their songs of caws and laughter. Randall stood at the helm and relished in the steady bouncing of the boat and the rushing wind on his face. It reminded him of his youth. He thought back to the warm Lake Okeechobee mornings, hauling seines for catfish or gigging for frogs, or some mornings out stalking boars knee-deep through the swamps or riding full-speed in an airboat hunting gators. He thought of the days showing up to school in camouflage gear and blood from that morning's kill still drying on his pants. He thought about standing on the football field with his teammates and wrestling in the locker room. He thought of sitting out under the power lines and drinking from kegs. He thought of the girls that he slept with and how often his teammates slept with the same girls, sometimes simultaneously. He thought about those high school years and how all of it made him feel like a fraud.

Mostly, he thought about Jared Baker. How someone tied him to that fence post, and how that poor migrant worker went to jail for it. The memory of Jared Baker never entirely left him. At any moment, the image of drunken Jared in the rearview mirror as Randall drove away from the party that night, knowing damn well he shouldn't have left him there alone. And then driving back toward the party the next day to be turned away by the cops surrounding Jared's beaten, sunburnt, and bug-eaten body, barely alive. All those images seemed to be able to sneak up on Randall at the least expected time. Nearly always in dreams.

He tried to shake the thought as he stopped the boat at the first island, positioning the skiff into a section of vegetation to get a couple of mangrove snapper—something to start the trip, so if they didn't get the ones they wanted, they still had something to show. They cast their lines, and after pulling only one snapper aboard, Randall moved to another spot. The man was getting agitated. He paid to catch fish, not to sit on the boat and reflect on nature. He needed something tangible to show for his money and time.

Randall zipped to the next mangrove island. He cut the motor and stood on the platform above the motor and poled the boat in closer to the mangroves. Cassiopea jellyfish floated upside down in the clear water. As he approached a little nook of another spot that served him well in the past, he saw what looked to be bluish-greenish, bloated feet floating just below the surface. He slowed the boat and saw another foot, maybe a fourth. The adipocere on the limbs looked avulsed and gnawed by sea creatures. Randall felt bile rise. He set the boat in reverse, motored around to another area of the mangrove island, and set an anchor. After tying the lines for his guests, they cast out, and he said he needed to check on something and would be right back.

"What the hell you talking about?" the man said. "You leaving us on this boat alone?"

"It's just for a second. I'll be right back."

"I don't like that idea," the man said.

"Let him go," the lady said. "Not like you'll catch a fish that quickly."

Randall stepped from the boat, leaving the two bickering, and waded to the small patch of sand. He worked his way through the mangroves to where the submerged bodies lay piled on one another—three swollen, naked bodies. One face up, the eyes missing as if fish feasted on them, and the hair majestically floating in the rolling tide. He unsnapped his buck knife from his belt and poked at the bloated flesh. A putrid gas emitted from the small hole created by the tip of the blade. He vomited, wiped the spit with the back of his hand, and headed back to the boat.

3

After the sunburnt, drunken crowd at Mallory Square in Key West finished watching a performance of a hunched, gnome-like man who somehow trained cats to jump through fire-lit rings, they migrated over to another performance area of a metal teepee-looking structure where a black man stood in an unfastened straight jacket. The sun hung low heading toward the horizon. Passengers from the cruise ship boarded, exhausted from the day's excursions.

"Sir," the man in the straight jacket said to a well-groomed onlooker. "My name is Eli. Have you ever put a man in a straight jacket?"

"No sir," the gentleman replied.

"How about a black man?"

Most of the crowd laughed. Others looked uncomfortable. Some seemed too comfortable.

"Well, it's easy. Do you mind helping me out?"

The man said he would help.

"Do you mind looking at my good eye when you talk to me?"

"Sorry," the man said. He looked directly at Eli's clouded, yellowed blind eye, which looked more like it belonged to a dead fish than a human.

"It's this one," Eli said, pointing to his good eye.

After the man fastened the straight jacket, Eli asked for more participants. A few men raised their hands.

"You, sir, with the Cubs hat, what do you do for a living?" Eli asked.

"I'm a bail bondsman," the Cub fan said.

The crowd oohed. "So I take it that you know how to use a chain?" Eli would have said that no matter the man's occupation.

"You bet." Eli knew most men would have said something along those lines, no matter their occupation, especially if their woman stood next to them.

"There. On the ground." Eli motioned to two chains coiled next to him. "Take the shorter one, that's the one in the smaller pile, and place it around my neck slowly."

The man did.

"Grab the lock, too, you genius."

The man laughed and picked up the padlock.

"Now put the chain around my neck, slowly."

The man did.

"Slowly," Eli said. "You look too damn eager to be doing this. You know we ain't in Mississippi, right?"

The crowd laughed. Eli called for another fellow in a Magnum P.I. Aloha shirt. "You, sir, if you would now stand on the other side of me and grab ahold of the other end of the chain." The gentleman did. "Now, gentlemen, simultaneously - that means at the same time."

The crowd laughed. Some kids inched their way to the front of the group as more people filled in. Behind Eli, the sun slowly made its way toward the horizon. A pirate ship set sail, and a catamaran followed. A cruise ship blasted its horn. Seagulls squawked overhead. The smell of grilled fish wafted from the neighboring restaurants.

"At the same time, I want you guys to pull the chain at each end below my elbows," Eli continued. The men did. "Now, back up towards my neck. Behind my neck, Forrest," he said to the Aloha shirt man. "Use some torque. Give these people what they paid for. They want to see a black man get strung up? Then by golly, we'll string up a black man." The crowd laughed. One person hooted. "Easy now," he said to the crowd, "that was just a joke. We ain't really hanging a brother. I'm going to be getting out of this shit. It's my job, you know. You are going to pay me to escape from this thing. Some of you don't want to see me escape, but I will. I do it every day." The crowd cheered and laughed some more.

"All right, gentlemen," Eli said. "Now cross those chains. And pull it down over the shoulders and tight to the chest. Come on, pull it tight, fellas. You gotta make the ends touch so we can put a lock on it." The men were pulling hard. "What's the matter, lady?" Eli said to a lady in the audience. "You acting like this the first time you have seen two white guys chain up a black man." The crowd oohed. "Oh, did I take it too far?" Then, the crowd laughed.

The men got the chain tight, and the ends touched together. "Now, sir, pick up that other chain. Grab one of the end links and lock it with these other two." The men did. "Now, just start winding me up in the chain, tight, like a mummy." They started. "Come on, make it tough on me. Go over the shoulders and under the elbows. Mix it up a bit."

Finally, the men finished chaining him and secured the lock. "Ladies and gentlemen," Eli said. "Harry Houdini once said, 'Give people a good enough thrill, and they'll come back again and again.' And I've been doing this a long time, and you guys keep coming back again and again. So, to that, I say thank you."

The crowd cheered. He took a bow of gratitude. He then asked the two men to help him lay on the ground. When they did, he asked the Cubs fan to get the pair of ankle chains and place them on him.

While the man was doing so, Eli again addressed the crowd, "Now, before I do this, I want to hear by applause if you have truly, so far, been enjoying yourself here at the beautiful Mallory Square Sunset Celebration."

The crowd roared and clapped and whistled.

"Good. After the show, as is the tradition, I will pass the hat for tips and donations. And if they ain't good, I gotta return to my old job: jacking your cars."

The crowd laughed.

"Now, sir, hook my ankle chains to those wires you see there and then slowly pull until I say stop." Then he whispered, "And don't let go of that rope when I'm halfway up either, mother-fucker."

A few of the folks near him heard and roared with laughter. Once lifted, he instructed the Cubs fan to secure the rope's end to the designated spot. And there he dangled to the crowd's delight.

"There you go, folks. That's it. That's the performance. You get to pay just to watch a brother hang upside down in chains."

Some people laughed uncomfortably, and some laughed in a way that made Eli know that they did still like to see a black person strung up.

"I'm kidding. Like I said earlier, I'll be escaping from these chains. My ancestors didn't put up with four hundred years of chains for me to not be able to stand out here and not break free. Now, on my mark, I will begin." He took a deep breath. "Here I go."

And he began slithering to remove the bondage from him subtly. His snake-like movements were slow and deliberate, and it didn't look like much was happening at first, but then he made a quick jerking motion, and a layer of chain slid off his elbows and down around his head. The crowd clapped. He then started swinging slowly back and forth and flopping just a bit like a man hanging onto his last breaths after execution, and another layer of the chain came down. The crowd clapped louder. And then, with one quick expansion of his arms, the rest of the chains tumbled to the ground. The crowd clapped and hooted, and a few folks simply said, "Wow."

"I can't hear you," Eli said, and the crowd roared excitedly. "With joy, there is pain," he shouted, wiggling a bit more, his shoulders twisting and turning in odd directions. His shoulders seemed to collapse into his chest, and then he straightened, and his left arm came over the top of his head. His left arm slithered toward his right shoulder, and he inhaled deeply before exhaling. Somehow, he slid both arms whipped around in front him and the jacket fell to the ground. The crowd erupted.

Eli held his hands out to his side like an inverted crucifixion, and he stayed like that as the crowd cheered louder and louder. As he hung there, the sun inched closer to the horizon, a silhouette on a dying day.

4

S tacy Ringling stepped onto the stage at an East Nashville
music venue that was originally built as a laundromat. After tuning her guitar, she sat on the stool and stared through
the fallen strands of hair from under her worn straw cowboy
hat. She stubbed out her cigarette, sipped her beer, and then
strummed the opening A-minor chord of a song she worked on
for nearly five years and was playing for the first time in public.

She knew a music executive from a major label in the audience waited to hear what she played and was willing to sign her if
he thought it would sell. He listened to her cover songs that the
crowd loved, proving she provided something special. He was
impressed with the small but loyal following she gained after a
few short years in a city overrun with musicians wanting to be
a star. He could take her to the next level if all went well. She
began her song, a narrative set in the Panhandle of Florida about
crystal meth, dogfighting, and a bingo parlor robbery. A life she
escaped but knew all too well.

She sang:
He was only eight years old
When his brother took his dog
And he never could recover
From the sight of all that blood

His daddy used to clean swimming pools
When he wasn't out getting drunk
His momma had been dead for years
When her breasts grew them lumps

During a short stint in New Orleans playing on street corners and an occasional gig at the Tropical Isle or Kerry's Irish Pub, she recorded a four-song EP, usually giving away more than she sold. She spent two years slumming it in the Big Easy, sleeping with men that she quickly tired of, she stuck it out with them because they gave her a place to stay, but eventually wanderlust was too strong.

Other musicians told her she needed to go to Nashville on more than one occasion. The last guy she lived with for six months, the one that said he loved her in the first week, hinted at marriage, so she packed her one bag and snuck out in the early morning hours on a Greyhound Bus to Music City Row. Left him with a one-line note: "You're a good guy." She may have been no good for him, but he knew he would never have sex with a woman like that again. And for that, he was heartbroken.

She spent a couple of years on Lower Broadway playing country cover songs for drunken bachelorette parties and what many call the "Woo-Woo Girls" and sloppy businessmen who thought because they tipped her $20 to play current radio hits, she would hangout with them once her set ended. On stage, she flirted. She smiled, she winked, and she gave those guys hope, and that hope usually turned into dollars dropped into her tip jar. But once the set ended, she packed up without a smile and was out of there. Sometimes she was called a "slut" or a "bitch" because she turned down having a drink with them.

On one of the occasions, she didn't turn down a drink from a wealthy businessman who showed interest in her. She used that interest to get him to invest in her music. He paid for her to get some studio time, and she chose ten songs from the seventy-five or so she had written and pressed two hundred CDs. And then she left him.

She performed a solid first set. Didn't forget any lyrics. All twelve or fifteen people in the bar bobbed their heads or attempted to talk quieter as she sang. A few laughed as she told stories about how she created each song. The buzz was good from the two whiskies prior to the show and the High Life that the bartender never allowed to empty during her set. She tried not to make eye contact with the music executive for too long. He didn't wear a suit or cowboy hat but blended with the crowd in a trucker hat and flannel shirt. She saw him clap a few times and tried not to get excited. Instead, she focused on the red neon Schlitz sign floating above the whiskey, gin, vodka, and tequila bottles.

She set down her guitar, and the music over the speakers drowned out the murmur of the patrons. She stepped from the stage and slowly walked through the haze of smoke on her way to the executive who stood with his elbows on the bar. She shook hands with the few people who stopped her to say they enjoyed her songs. She bowed in appreciation and told them to stick around until after the next set when she would sell t-shirts, CDs, and the four-song EP she spent way too much money recording.

The executive bought her a whiskey and said he thought she was phenomenal. He liked her raspy voice, felt her stories were engaging, and appreciated her music's originality and novelty. It reminded him of some of the old country sounds nostalgic for so many listeners. She sipped her whiskey and didn't respond. She stared at him, waiting for what she knew he would say next. Praise didn't interest her.

Praise didn't pay the bills. And her bills piled up. If something didn't happen soon, she was pretty sure she would have to leave Nashville. If she was going to sleep in the streets, she damn sure wasn't going to do it in the Tennessee winters. She would pack up her van and drive south until it warmed up. She would drive south until she couldn't drive south anymore. Key West, a city that worked for many others: Jerry Jeff Walker, Jimmy Buffett, Shel Silverstein, and Thomas McGuane.

"I just don't think we can sell your songs," he said. "They are so good, but it's not the kind of thing that will get radio play. If you could maybe turn down the violence and drug references, maybe we could work with you. Maybe some love songs that don't end with the woman siccing her dog on her husband's balls. You understand, right? That I really enjoy..."

"Yeah," she said, cutting him off. She smiled her gap-toothed smile. "I get it." She downed the rest of her whiskey. "Thank you for coming out and listening."

5

Randall considered getting back on his boat and radioing in his discovery, but that would mean hours of interrogation and postponing the rest of the trip, if not canceling it altogether. He needed those six hundred dollars. He hadn't run a tour in over a week. The charter boat business became saturated with new captains every day, and then that goddamned *Victory Watersports* pretty much swallowed up the market in three years with their thirty-five person catamaran, two six-pack charter boats, jet skis, and parasailing. Everyone knew where that kind of money came from. Hell, it was where everyone got their cocaine. It was common knowledge on the island who was behind the rise of *Victory Watersports*, but because of who was behind it, no one contested it.

So instead of doing what he knew he should've done, Randall did what was necessary. He stepped back in the boat, scribbled the coordinates on the back of a gas receipt, stuck the receipt in his pocket, and motored off into deeper waters. They landed a permit for the man to take to a restaurant to have cooked, and they hooked a tarpon to get a picture and have a story for his co-workers back home. The woman got drunk and strolled off into the sunset on her man's arm, and they were happy. That was what Randall needed to do to keep his customers returning.

He arrived home, tired and sunburnt. He drank a shot of vodka and showered off the smell of fish the best he could, knowing that smell never entirely disappeared. He drank another shot of vodka and then took a nap, having about four hours before his night-shift bartending job. Before falling asleep, he pictured those naked bodies floating in the water, and as sleep overtook him, Jared Baker joined those three bodies.

He woke up for his night-shift bartending job, snapped on his silicone-breasted bra, and slid on his sequined dress. He fluffed his wig, smeared on lipstick, and paraded out the door—a spectacle most locals were used to seeing, and the tourists were happy to see as he rode his moped to the bar, his high heels dangling from the handlebars.

6

J anet Schroeder sat in the back of Mrs. La Fluer's third-grade class at Sullivan Elementary School. Mrs. La Fleur, in her floral print dress and her long gray hair that hung to her waist, stood at the chalkboard and attempted to teach multiplication over Bobby Drexler's armpit fart noises and the snickers of the class.

Janet looked up from under her tangled web of matted hair as the principal walked in and introduced the class to the new student, Stacy Ringling. This new girl walked in with shiny brown hair pulled back in pigtails, the ends dyed green. She wore a suede frilled jacket, a long, flowy skirt, and cowboy boots. When asked to tell the class about herself, unlike most third graders, Stacy took command of the spotlight, and Mrs. La Fleur gladly stepped aside.

"Hey y'all," she said and waved to the class. "As the principal said, I'm Stacy Ringling. I come from New Orleans. We moved here because my dad is a correctional officer, and he got a job at the new jail."

"Your dad's a cop?" little Bobby Drexler shouted out. "I heard they like donuts." Bobby was older than the other kids. Held back once in first grade and then again in third.

The kids laughed. Mrs. La Fleur scolded Bobby, but Stacy continued as if nothing happened. "Oh, he does. I don't know too many people who don't love donuts. You know what I like even more though? King Cake. Do y'all know what King Cake is?"

"Why don't you tell us," Mrs. La Fleur said.

And Stacy did. She told the class all about Mardi Gras and said she heard that down in Pensacola, they celebrated it too but not to the extent of New Orleans.

"I ain't ever been to Pensacola," Bobby said.

"You've never been to the beach, Bobby?" Mrs. La Fleur asked.

"Nah. My momma ain't got no car to drive us to no beach."

"Well, you'll get there one day. You'll swim in the gulf, Bobby. Don't you worry." She pronounced "gulf" like "guff."

The kids walked through a line, and the ladies with hairnets and aprons placed chicken nuggets, mashed potatoes, and a fruit bowl on yellow plastic trays. The kids then grabbed a white or chocolate milk from a cooler. While in line, Bobby stood behind Janet and pulled her hair. Janet didn't acknowledge the annoyance.

The children squeezed three aside in the booths, and the teachers sat at a long table in the center of the cafeteria. Janet sat alone. Stacy sat across from her.

"What do you want?" Janet said, slurping the syrup out of her mixed fruit cup.

"Can I sit with you?" Stacy asked. "I don't know anybody else."

"I guess," Janet said. "Looks like you're already sitting." Janet looked down at her food tray.

"Well, aren't you going to tell me your name?"

Janet didn't say anything.

"I'm Stacy."

"Janet."

"I'm from New Orleans."

"I know. I heard everything you said." Janet looked up. "I'll give you my potatoes for your fruit cup."

Stacy handed over her fruit cup. Stacy slid her tray over so Janet could scoop the potatoes from one tray to the other. Janet pulled back the clear plastic lid and slurped the juice.

"Why do you sit all alone?" Stacy said.

Janet looked at her. She shrugged.

"Don't the other kids talk to you none?"

Janet shrugged again.

"Can we be friends?" Stacy asked.

Janet hesitated and then nodded.

A few days later, Bobby threw a dodgeball at the girls who were jumping rope and hit Janet in the side of the head. Janet wasn't jumping rope but sitting cross-legged off to the side of the basketball court. The boys laughed and so did most of the girls. The coach, a fat-bellied man in gray gym shorts, sat under an oak tree chewing tobacco and too far away from the kids to see if any conflicts arose. Even if conflicts did arise, Janet knew not much would happen because she remembered last year when a kid named Wesley, a kid with a large burn scar on his forearm, peed on himself after not being allowed to go to the bathroom, and the kids started laughing at him. The coach yelled "dogpile," and Wesley was face first in the dirt with soiled pants as a wild pack of heathen children climbed on top of him. Janet couldn't believe what she witnessed. She couldn't believe that an adult would encourage such behavior and couldn't believe how easily children participated in such behaviors.

When the dogpile ended, the image of Wesley's dirty, tear-streaked face and the darkened area of his jeans around his crotch haunted her for days. So much so that she decided she would never cry at school, no matter how mean the kids or teachers could get. She often wondered what happened to Wesley. He stopped coming to school shortly after that, and the kids simply moved on to the next kid to bully. Janet was lucky enough not to get the full-on bullying. It was primarily verbal stuff. Stupid things like saying her house was so dirty that the cockroaches rode dirt bikes or that they were so poor her mom slept with dogs to keep the lights on. Things that didn't make sense because they were in the third grade, and if she attempted to explain to them that the insults didn't make sense, she would then get made fun of for being too smart. She learned that the kids left her alone if she didn't react. She started to appreciate going unnoticed. It became like a game for her to pretend she was invisible and try to sit as quietly as possible.

The ball bounced to the ground and rolled away from the basketball courts, and Janet sat there with her hair hanging in her face, her dingy dress, and dirty fingernails and waited for the laughter to stop and the attention to be diverted to something else.

Stacy picked up the ball and walked it over to Bobby. "Did you drop this?"

"Yeah, it was an accident," Bobby said. The other boys laughed, too.

"You want it back?" Stacy held it out to him. He reached for it, and she fake-tossed it toward his face. Bobby raised his hands and flinched, thinking Stacy let go of it. The boys laughed at Bobby. That never happened before. No one ever attempted to make Bobby look like a fool.

Stacy smiled. "I thought you said you wanted it?"

"Give me the ball," Bobby said. "Stop playing." He reached for it. Stacy made him miss again. The girls joined in the laughter. Stacy then turned and punted the ball further than anyone ever punted a ball on that field.

"Whatcha go and do that for?" Bobby Drexler said.

"Next time," Stacy said. "I'm going to kick the ball up your butt."

The kids laughed. And the laughing didn't let up. So, Bobby did the only thing he knew to do: hurt the person who embarrassed him. He drew back his fist, but before he could hit Stacy, she lifted a foot between his legs. Kids often threatened to kick one another in the balls, but none of them ever actually had the balls to follow through with it. Stacy did without hesitation. The coach slow-jogged over to the commotion and grabbed Stacy by her upper arm, way up near her armpit, to walk her away from the other kids and sat her down on his crate before going over to check on Bobby who continued squirming on the ground.

The principal suspended Stacy from school for ten days. Bobby was called "one-nut strut" for the remainder of the year because the coach said that's how you walk after getting kicked in the nuts.

7

Around the community pool deck of a neighborhood in Cudjoe Key that branded itself as a "resort," kids gathered around a converted hotdog cart filled with ice water in one tub and melted wax in another. In reality, the neighborhood was a mixed-use facility with RVs, trailers, and a handful of houses no larger than eight hundred square feet.

Children of servers, bartenders, plumbers, oil changers, and roofers waited their turn somewhat patiently as the kid in front of the line dipped his hand in the ice water past his wrist and then into the melted colored wax. Some shaped their hands like peace signs, some into the sign language for "I love you," some into the "shaka" sign, and a couple did the heavy metal devil horns. After dipping their hands into different colors, they waited for the wax to dry. The young girl working the wax hand cart, maybe still a senior in high school, helped them slide their hands out so they would have a cute souvenir from Helen's eighth birthday party.

The fathers, the few there, hovered around the grill flipping hot dogs and drinking from cans of Coors Banquet, and the mothers stood waist-deep in the shallow end of the pool with their vodka cranberries in plastic red cups. The boombox on one of the tables blared rock tunes, and the crows perched on the rails squealed and waited for an opportunity to move in and steal crumbs of hot dog buns or the coveted pizza crust.

While their wax hands dried, the kids settled around the concrete tables as the moms passed around food and waxy paper cups of Coca-Cola or Sprite, all awaiting the big event of the day: Eli the Great. Magic tricks and balloon animals, and once he finished, they would sing "Happy Birthday" and eat cupcakes before finishing the day in the pool until sundown while parents turned that kid party into an adult party with more alcohol and passing around joints in the dark.

Helen's parents never heard of Eli the Great before, but when Freckles the Clown said he didn't have availability on his schedule, they asked for a recommendation. Freckles said another guy who worked out of Key West was pretty good but sometimes could be abrasive. For some reason, they were not expecting a black clown. And not a black clown with an eye patch.

Eli rolled his trunk of props to the pool deck, stopping just before opening the gate to smush out a cigarette butt on the bottom of his boot and flick it into the grass. The children cheered as he entered. The fathers snickered at a grown man working as a clown for a living, and Eli could see the smirk on some of the white women's faces who fetishized tall black men.

The children sat in a semi-circle at Eli's feet, and the parents stood behind them, drinking and smoking. Eli started his show by blowing up a long black balloon into the shape of a hot dog. "Fucking balloon animals," said the one dad with shoulder-length, feathered-back, blond hair. A cigarette hung from his mouth, and as he spoke, it bounced around underneath a hefty mustache as if glued to his lower lip. His name was Dean, and he often wore a shirt that said, "Mustache Rides - $5."

"My man," Eli said to the father. "Is your wife here?"

A young girl raised her hand, and as she said, "Right here," her unreserved gap teeth lay bare from behind her red lips. She rested her arm on top of her head before quickly removing it, as if she realized she may have messed up her teased bangs, which remained unmoved with enough hairspray to single-handedly widen the hole in the ozone layer.

"What's your name, sweetie?"

"Cheryl," she said, and as quickly as she made eye contact with him, she averted her eyes.

"Good," Eli said. "Cause this one's for you." He held up the long, black balloon. The men gave Dean a ribbing. Dean's wife blushed, and a couple of her friends woo-hooed. The kids did not get the humor.

"You're lucky there are kids here," Dean said.

"No. You're lucky the kids are here. Otherwise, they may start to question why she calls me daddy." Before the game of "the dozens" could continue, Eli blew up another balloon, a white one. He stopped it before it was fully inflated and compared it to the black balloon. The adults laughed. Eli smirked and winked before combining the two balloons to make a zebra that he handed off to a little girl.

"I thought the black one was mine," Cheryl said.

"I ain't forget about you, baby. I'll give you one after the party," Eli said.

"All right now," Dean said. "You're taking this shit too far for a children's party, and I suggest you start acting like you're at one."

"Loud and clear, big guy," Eli said before winking at Dean's wife.

"Goddamn it. I ain't ever killed a clown before, but it ain't too late to start," Dean said to the men beside him. They laughed. Eli heard it, too, and he smiled his big-toothed smile right at Dean before blowing up another balloon and turning it into a sword to hand to another kid.

After the balloon animals, the real dazzle began. Eli unfolded and set up two birdcages on either side of him. He lit a cigarette, using that as a form of distraction, doing a series of sleight-of-hand parlor tricks to make it look like he stuck the cigarette in his ears and nose, and then he lifted the patch and showed his eye. The kids screamed in horror.

"Want to know why it looks like this?" he asked the kids. He then made it look like he shoved the cigarette in his eye. This time, the kids and the adults hollered in horror. Even Dean, knowing it was a trick, turned his head.

Just as the excitement settled, he pulled out the lit cigarette from his ear, and to end that set and transition from the cigarette tricks to the next trick, it simply looked like he used his tongue to flip it around and eat the burning butt. The kids were amazed.

Dean said, "Fucking animal" to his friends. The women clapped.

"You ought to see what I can do with a cherry stem," Eli said, winking at the adults.

He bent down, scrambled around in his chest of props, and pulled out a small fish bowl filled with water. Removing the lid from the bowl, he stuck his hand in and caught one of the swimming fish. He held the fish by the tail for everyone to see before holding it above his opened mouth. The screams grew louder the closer the fish lowered toward his opened mouth until he dropped it in and swallowed. He poured water from a thermos into a plastic cup and drank it all.

Silence fell over the crowd.

"If I can get the birthday girl to help me with this next trick. Come right here, young lady." He handed a separate fish bowl to the girl. This one emptied. "Do you have a pet?"

She said that she did not.

"Well, I've brought you a goldfish as a gift."

She looked in the bowl and then at Eli.

"Is there a problem?"

Shyly, she said, "I don't see a goldfish."

"What do you mean? Look in there."

She did. "I still don't see one."

Eli looked down into the bowl. "I'm so sorry. That is embarrassing. Ummm. Let me try something. What are some magic words that you know?" He asked her.

"Abracadabra," the girl said.

"Okay, we'll try that. Abracadabra," Eli said, flung his arms around, producing a dove from under his sleeve that sat in his hand in dazed wonderment. The kids shouted with excitement, and the adults laughed.

"That is definitely not a goldfish," Eli said. He placed the dove inside one of the cages. He then revealed four more doves. The girl still stood with the fishbowl.

"We still don't have your fish, do we?"

"No," the girl said and let out a sweet laugh. Those laughs helped him get out of bed every morning. Those innocent laughs told him that he was more than a minstrel act. There were times, many times, when he felt ashamed about the profession he chose. But the laughter of kids and the sincere astonishment of some adults told him differently—that it was a noble calling. He participated in something larger than himself.

"And you really want a goldfish, don't you?"

She nodded yes.

"Let me think," Eli said. "I feel something tickling my throat."

He then coughed. "Oh man," he said. He then pulled his shirt tight around his torso and made his stomach do a wave-like dance. The girl stood confused. "I think I found that goldfish," Eli said. He started making movements like a cat about to hack up a hairball and then regurgitated a goldfish and spit it and a mouthful of water into the fishbowl. The kids laughed while saying, "Ewww." Some women turned their heads in disgust but also laughed.

Dean and his friends said, "How in the holy fuck?"

The birthday girl looked down at the fish and saw it swimming around and looked up at Eli and said, "How?"

Eli shrugged his shoulders. "Magic."

For his final trick, he told Dean to place him in a straight jacket and chain him up before he walked into the pool's deep end and sank to the bottom. He was trained to hold his breath for two minutes and could escape from the chains and jacket in less than one minute. The screams coming from outside the pool sometimes frightened him, and other times made him want to fail the trick purposefully. But he would never fail the trick at a child's birthday party. At the bottom of the pool, removed from the world, time slowed. Houdini performed water escape tricks in front of thousands in Coney Island, and Eli the Great did it for tens of onlookers in the pool of a trailer park.

He broke free from the chains and jacket and rose to the water's surface to sheer panic, mayhem, and a few children crying. He forgot to warn the parents of his grand finale.

"For fuck's sake, man," Dean said. "I thought you fucking offed yourself at my kid's birthday party."

Dean gave him two one-hundred-dollar bills and a beer and told him to get the fuck out.

Two hundred dollars to swallow a goddamn fish and entertain some white folks, he thought as he walked back to his faded baby blue, rust-splotched, dented, rattling pickup truck, a tiny little thing that looked like a miniature truck when sitting next to a full-sized pickup. He lifted his trunk into the bed and slammed the tailgate several times until it stayed shut. Still enough time to return home before going to Key West for the Mallory Square sunset celebration. Eli drank the beer in three gulps.

8

U nderneath the bleachers of a high school near Okeechobee Lake, Randall Greene, the junior backup quarterback, sold Jared Baker, a junior wide receiver, an eighth of
pot, mostly sticks and stems. Instead of paying cash, Jared gave
him a blowjob. Often, unless drunk, Randall couldn't finish
because he wasn't gay.

"Alright, cut it out," Randall said as he stared down at the
fire-red head of hair crouched before him.

Jared stood up. "Something wrong?"

"No. Just get the fuck out of here," Randall told him. Jared
stood, wiped his mouth, and walked toward the school. Jared
was a sweet kid, and he didn't belong at this honkey-ass school in
this honkey-ass town in this honkey-ass state, Randall thought.
He belonged with the rest of the freaks in New York, Vegas, or
Los Angeles.

That afternoon at practice, Randall wouldn't throw the ball
anywhere near Jared, even if he was open. The one time he did,
he threw as hard as he could to make sure Jared couldn't catch
it, and it bounced right off his hands, and the team mocked
him. Called him a faggot. Called him a cocksucker. Called him a
butt-bandit. The coach grabbed him by the facemask and shook
his head so hard that Randall thought Jared's head would snap

off. Then, the coach hollered for the linebackers to circle up around Jared. Everyone knew that meant the "bull in the circle" drill. Probably the most diabolical drill in sports history.

The rest of the team gathered around and were permitted to remove their helmets and drink water as they watched. Randall removed his helmet and swatted gnats from his eyes as linebackers took turns running full strength to the center, hitting Jared and knocking him to the ground. As he stood, turning like a dazed bull looking for where the next banderilleros would be coming from, another linebacker charged at him, knocking him to the ground.

When getting to his feet slowed, the coach instructed the linebackers to lift him under the guise of helping your teammate to his feet, but Randall and all the others knew it was so the next linebacker could destroy this kid's ego with another hit. The coaches joined in on the cheers and the high fives and backslaps. Randall stood near the back, not wanting to watch but also unable not to watch. The kid who sucked his dick just hours ago was now getting his ass kicked because of what Randall did.

While it made Randall feel horrible, as if he ingested something rotten, Randall knew that if the others even so much as suspected that he allowed Jared to do something like that, what he would endure would be worse. And he wasn't prepared for that. He would never be ready for that and hated himself for it. His stomach soured, watching Jared take the beating for him. Randall stepped off the field and vomited.

9

Forty-one of the forty-seven students of the Sullivan Junior High eighth grade class gathered in the cafeteria for the last school dance before moving on to high school. The only kids absent were the three Nelson kids because they were Jehovah's Witnesses and not allowed to participate in school functions and the three kids in the special-ed class—one with no cognitive issues but was in a wheelchair from an ATV accident while riding on her dad's lap on the way to pick up some beer and canned sausages. Although she was fully functional mentally, the teachers decided it was best if she did not interact with the "normal" kids so she wouldn't get bullied. The other two kids didn't have to be told not to attend because they didn't want to be around crowds anyway.

Janet Schroeder attempted to befriend the wheel-chaired girl while in the fifth grade, and Bobby Drexler and some other kids told her that if she liked playing with the retarded kids so much, they could break her legs for her so she could ride in a wheelchair alongside her friend. From then on, whenever Janet saw Crippled Lily, she looked away, too embarrassed to make eye contact. After eighth grade, none of the students would see her again. Her family moved down to Pensacola so she could attend a high school that practiced inclusion, where the non-normal kids were allowed to interact with the normal kids and even be in the same classroom.

Stacy danced with multiple boys, making sure her pink ruffled skirt spun around to show the boys her short shorts underneath. Teachers asked her not to dance so close a few times. Janet stood off to the side. When "I've Had the Time of My Life" rang out through the speakers, Stacy performed a choreographed dance with another girl that ended with a lift, and the students cheered. For weeks leading up to the dance, Stacy tried to get Janet to learn the steps so they could do it together, but Janet said she didn't want to do it. Standing to the side and watching the class cheer, she regretted not doing it. She always felt she was Stacy's pity friend. That's what some of the kids called her in the past.

The class sang in unison to "Livin on a Prayer," and Stacy dragged Janet out on the dance floor. Stacy shouted the words as loudly as she could, and Janet lip-synched along.

The crowd slowly dispersed toward the night's end, and Stacy and Janet walked out to the front of the school to wait on their ride home with the older sister of another classmate. Bobby Drexler stood to the side with another boy, sharing a cigarette butt they picked from the ground. Janet watched him eyeing them. He wore a Four Horsemen Metallica shirt and a mullet hairdo greased back on the sides. Wispy hairs grew over his lip and on his chin. At fifteen, he looked like a young man, no longer that child's face or demeanor. He was already earning money cleaning pools on weekends and skipped school as much as he attended. He walked over to the two girls, his dumb-looking friend followed behind in a stoner-like shuffle, laughing about nothing and everything.

"You ladies need a ride home?" Bobby pointed to the two four-wheelers.

"No, thank you," Janet said quickly.

"Maybe," Stacy said. "What's in it for us?"

"Besides my protection?" Bobby said. "I've got some Mad Dog 20/20."

"What flavor?" Stacy asked.

"I got red and purple."

"We'll take the purple."

"All right," Bobby said. "This way then, ladies." His buffoon friend laughed again and punched Bobby in the arm.

Janet looked at Stacy with her eyes wide, trying to convey a message of concern through telepathy.

"It's fine," Stacy said. They were behind the boys, and Stacy opened her clutch purse and showed Janet a container of mace. "We'll drink their alcohol and then leave."

"What's that?" Bobby said, turning to the girls as they approached the vehicles.

"I said that I forgot to tell April we didn't need a ride anymore," Stacy said.

Stacy hopped on behind Lucas, and Janet sat behind Bobby.

"You hold on real tight now, ya hear," Bobby said. Janet felt her heart pound and a little flutter in her crotch as she wrapped her arms around Bobby's waist. She was pleasantly surprised to feel the ripples of muscle in his midsection.

They pulled next to April, standing with a handful of other girls.

"April," Stacy said. "Bobby is going to give us a ride home. Will you let your sister know?"

April said she would.

The two boys and two girls sped off into the Spring night along the darkened two-lane road. Bobby led the way, and he turned off a side street and a rutted-out dirt road. They continued until the borrow pit, where in the day time the pooled water reflected blue from the limestone underneath the clay and the kids often swam there, but at night it looked like obsidian. Only the four-wheeler lights broke the darkness and showed the girls where they were. Termites swarmed in the rays shining from the headlights. Cicadas rang out and seemed to get louder every few seconds.

Bobby retrieved from underneath his seat two bottles of MD 20/20. He unscrewed the cap of the purple one and handed it to Janet. He then unscrewed the cap of the red one, flinging the cap over his shoulder and taking a long gulp before passing it on to Lucas.

"Whatchu waiting on?" Bobby said.

Stacy took the bottle from her, turned it up, and returned it to Janet.

Janet held it to her nose and sniffed and scrunched up her face. She then took a sip and coughed. The boys laughed.

"It's all right," Stacy said. "You don't have to drink it if you don't want to."

"That's bullshit," Bobby said. "Drink that shit."

"Hey, asshole," Stacy said. "If she don't want to, she ain't got to."

Bobby looked at Stacy, which frightened Janet, but Stacy didn't notice. She took the bottle back from Janet, took another drink, and walked down to the pond's edge.

Lucas followed her. When those two were out of earshot, Bobby handed Janet the bottle of red MD 20/20. "Take a drink," he said. "You'll get used to it."

She hesitated, and Bobby grabbed her by the wrist, his fingers overlapping either because of his gangly fingers, her slenderness, or both. He lifted her hand to the bottle, and she gripped it by the neck.

"Won't hurt you," he said with a crooked smile.

She put it to her mouth and drank, watching Bobby over the top of the bottle. Her eyes shifted to see Stacy and Lucas's silhouette skipping rocks in the pond. She started putting the bottle down, but Bobby put two fingers underneath it and lifted it again, making Janet drink more. Her eyes watered. He smiled. For the first time, she noticed a missing tooth on the side of his mouth.

"Pretty good, huh?" he said.

She shook her head no. He blew out his nose in a half-hearted laugh.

Stacy removed her shirt and skirt and waded into the pond in her underwear. Jupiter and Saturn shone brightly over the nearly full moon.

"Go join her, faggot," Bobby yelled out to Lucas.

"I'm not getting in that water," Lucas said.

"Won't hurt ya," Bobby said. "It's just rainwater."

Lucas took off his shoes, shirt, and shorts.

"I like them whitey-tighties," Bobby said. Lucas lifted his middle finger and carefully stepped into the pond without turning around.

"Watch for them snakes," Bobby yelled out. Stacy and Lucas both raised a middle finger.

Bobby then turned to Janet, "Get you another drink."

"I don't think I should," Janet said.

"I think differently," Bobby said.

Stacy kept wading further out. She was near her waist as she squished her toes in the clay bottom. Lucas reluctantly followed.

" I think I'd like to get on home," Janet said.

"Yeah," Bobby said. He took a long pull from the bottle. "We ain't going home just yet. You ought to take a drink instead." He handed the bottle to Janet and held it steady until she finally grasped it and put it to her lips. "There ya go," Bobby said when she lowered it from her lips and wiped her mouth with the back of her hand.

Bobby stepped closer, put his thumb to her mouth, and wiped off a bit of the malt liquor that she missed on her upper lip. He didn't stop. Instead, he rubbed his thumb harder on her cheek, moved his hand around to the back of her head, and grabbed a fistful of hair, pulling her face close to his. He grabbed the bottle in his other hand while almost simultaneously sticking his tongue in her mouth. When Janet tried to tear away, he bit her lower lip.

Janet tried to turn away, but he bent her over the four-wheeler. His one free hand cupped her mouth while he pressed hard into her from behind, keeping her pinned down. He drank the rest of the Mad Dog 20/20 with his other hand and tossed the bottle to the side. Janet made a muffled attempt to yell, but Bobby gripped his hand tighter on her mouth and put his mouth right up on her ear.

"Don't you fucking try to yell," he said. While holding her mouth shut tight, he reached his other hand around and cupped her crotch.

She could feel a part of the seat jabbing into her ribs. She tried to adjust her body to take some of the pain away, to make herself a bit more comfortable. Bobby mistook that slight adjustment as an attempt to break free and applied more pressure on her crotch. Tears welled in her eyes. He moved his hand from her crotch to her breasts, squeezing one and then the other. He then pushed his hand down again, fumbling to get inside the waist of her pants.

Tears rolled down her cheeks, but she stopped fighting him. His hand found her virgin flesh, and his knuckly, chewed nails prodded to find a way inside her. Janet closed her eyes tight and listened to the night sounds.

Bobby looked up and saw Stacy and Lucas stepping from the water, and he eased off of Janet and said, "Stop that crying. And you better not tell a goddamn person about this."

Stacy and Lucas put their clothes over their wet bodies, and when they came closer, Stacy said, "Didn't want to leave you two alone for too long." She noticed Janet looking away. "Everything okay?"

"Everything's great," Bobby said. "You just interrupted us. If you know what I mean." He laughed and walked toward Lucas.

Janet shot a quick look at him and then at Stacy.

"You wish," Stacy said. "Janet has better taste in men than to do anything with you."

10

E li returned to his inherited two-bedroom conch cottage on Fleming Street, which he shared with two other people—a female country music singer and charter boat captain drag queen.

The line of conch houses, painted in different pastels, was home to a mix of blue-haired retirees and younger folks who couldn't afford to live in Key West, although many worked there.

Eli knew that Randall was in his room sleeping after a morning of fishing and did his best not to disturb him. He disrobed in the tiny bathroom they all shared, and make-up covered the counter, whether Randall's or Stacy's, Eli couldn't say. A silicone-stuffed bra hung on the back of the door belonged to Randall. He stood next to the pile of clown clothes on the floor and brushed his teeth while waiting for the shower water to warm. He clenched the toothbrush between his teeth to tear away a square of toilet paper and wipe away some specks of toothpaste that splattered the mirror. He shook his head, knowing Stacy may be the sloppiest woman he ever met. After three years of living together, there were some things they accepted of each other.

As the water washed over him, he imagined the act he was planning for some time. While the classic straight-jacket-in-chains act was a hit, he wanted something that put his name in the papers. He wanted an act that people would talk about for years, a disappearing act that made people believe in magic again, make him believe in magic again. He would become an urban legend for those tourist spectators who were present for his final show and the locals who expected to see his nightly performances. Eli believed that the best magic tricks left people in wonder for the rest of their lives. Not even his roommates knew of his plans. He planned the ultimate disappearing act. After sixteen years as a staple of the sunset celebration, he would be gone, and some may even call the police to search for him, but if executed correctly, he would be gone for good.

He stepped from the shower and stood facing the mirror, staring with his one good eye at his one bad eye, the one clouded, yellowed, and frightening to little children. It brought him back to a moment in his childhood that he often tried to forget.

"Where is he?" the man shouted as he held the woman's head on top of the desk covered in cigar leaf rolling papers and scattered tobacco. Little Eli peered around the backroom corner to see this man standing over his mother. Flipped desks and more tobacco than usual on the floors throughout the shop explained the noise he heard. Another man with a rifle stood guard at the front door.

"Where is he?" the man said again, a loose strand of his otherwise slicked-back hair hanging over his eyes.

Eli's mother said she didn't know. The man grabbed a handful of her hair and lifted her from the chair before slamming her face down again.

Eli wasn't aware that he made a noise, but the man turned to look at him, and Eli didn't move. In his child's brain, he knew he was about to die, but it didn't elicit the kind of terror he expected. Having never contemplated death before, Eli didn't have a frame of reference to scare him. Instead, he stood there looking at the man and wondered why he was being so mean.

"Come here, boy," the man said. The mom whimpered but didn't lift her head.

Eli slowly walked toward the man and his mom. He thought it odd that the only sound he heard was his shoes hitting the flooring. It sounded like he wore high heels, and he didn't like that sound. He wanted his shoes to be quiet.

He stood next to his mom and placed a hand on her heaving shoulders. She let out a heartbreaking sob, heartbreaking even to the man standing over her, but he had to do what was required of him.

"Is this your mother?" the man asked Eli.

"Don't speak to him," his mother whimpered while Eli nodded.

"No. You don't speak to him," the man said. He removed a pistol from his waistband and pressed it behind her ear. "I hear you say another word to him, and he'll be an orphan."

He then turned back to Eli.

"Do you know where your father is?" the man asked Eli.

Eli shook his head.

"That is most unfortunate," the man said. "Have a seat, young man."

Eli sat in the wooden chair next to his mother. The man lifted the woman's head by the hair.

"Look at your boy," the man said. "Such pretty eyes." He smiled. Four golden teeth shone from the right side of his mouth.

41

The woman began to sob harder.

"Momma?" Eli asked.

"No, no, no," the man said. "Shhh." Then, with the barrel of the gun, he directed her to look away from her son, and the man said, "Roll me a cigar. And while you do, think about if you would like to tell me where he is."

She rolled him a cigar slowly, deliberately. He watched her, licking his lips as she licked the tobacco paper. Eli watched the man watching his mother, confused as to why the man seemed to enjoy what she was doing.

"Light it for me," he said. She did. The man replaced the pistol into his waistband, took the cigar, placed it in his mouth, and puffed. Everything happened very slowly. Even the smoke from the man's mouth seemed to hang in front of his face instead of drifting away. The man by the front door stood like a dummy. He may as well not have been there. Very few people walked into cigar shops anymore. Some shops, like the one his mother worked, became covers for illegal activities—drugs, Jai Alai gambling and fixing the games, prostitution—the blight and decline of Ybor City caused by urban renewal. Tampa was yet to become a Community Redevelopment Area. Still a time of uncertainty about how to move forward. Still years away from the bohemian artists moving into the vacant lots, gentrification, and the emergence of cultural tourism. It was a time ripe for criminals to cash in on the lawlessness. And that's what this man did. This was what Eli's father attempted to do, but lawlessness against the lawless proved more difficult than against those who followed the law. The man took another pull on the cigar and reached a hand down into the neckline of Eli's mother's blouse and cupped a heavy breast.

"You are very good with your mouth," he said.

She took a deep breath and turned her head, refusing to look at either the man or Eli.

"Come closer, son," the man said to Eli. Eli stood and inched closer. The man removed his hand from the woman's shirt and gently touched the kid's chin, lifting his face to look at him. The boy looked at the man and had never seen someone like that before. His meanness was calm, frightening young Eli, but not how he thought he should be frightened.

"When is the last time you have seen your father, son?"

Eli didn't know. His father was always out late and rarely home. When he was, he was loud, drunk, mean. A different meanness than what this man carried. It was as if his father didn't believe in his capabilities of meanness and oversold it. But this man exuded confidence in his meanness, and the subtlety made it worse.

"I don't see him very often," Eli said.

"Such a well-mannered kid," the man said. "Your father was not so well-mannered." The man's hand still rested under Eli's chin.

The man stared down into Eli's face. His wet lips drawing on the cigar, lighting up the end, only a few inches from Eli. He removed the cigar and blew out a cloud of smoke.

"When was the last time?"

"You don't have to answer him," the mom said.

The man slowly returned the cigar to his mouth and then with a quick hand, drove a fist into the back of the mother's head. Still, he held Eli's face steady with his other hand. She let out a wail and fell to the ground. She held the back of her head as she looked up from the ground, her skirt high around her thighs, her neck shimmering with sweat. The man slowly removed his cigar again and said, "Son, you do have to answer me. Do you understand? Your father has betrayed me. I thought he was an honest man, but I was mistaken. Don't be like your father. Now, tell me when the last time you saw your father was."

Eli thought back. About a week before, his father burst through the front door excitedly. "I did it, babe," he said. Eli's mom looked at her husband and asked what he did. He pulled out more cash than Eli had ever seen and spread it on the table.

"What did you do?" she asked.

"The opposite of what I was supposed to. Don't you see, baby, we've done it."

"No," she said. "They won't be happy about this."

"Look here, now, don't start that. We are going to be okay."

Eli knew his father spent his days at the Jai Alai games. He took Eli there on several occasions, saying he was swinging by real quick to get something. Smoky auditorium. Seats partially filled with flabby-skinned old people. Women with blue hair and men with brown shirts and pants pulled too high over their paunched bellies. His father sat Eli down once in the yellow, plastic fold-down chairs and bought him a hot dog and a Coca-Cola in a small waxy cup, whispered in his ear which team would win, and then said he would be back.

A few minutes later, an usher told Eli that children weren't permitted. A man a few rows back said, "That's Sergio's boy."

"Very well then," the usher said.

Eli's father was right about which team would win. Many of the people in the stands were not happy with the match's outcome. They all seemed to have bet on the other team. At the time, his father reappeared with a few other men, and they seemed very happy about the game's outcome. Eli saw one man put some cash in his father's shirt pocket.

"Come on, boy," his father said to him. Eli stood up, and the man beside his father pinched Eli's cheeks. He said, "Your father's a good man."

Back in the car, Eli said, "What do you do for work?"

Eli's father looked at his son, one hand on the wheel, the other hanging out the window, a cigar dangling from his lips, and a beer between his legs. His hair blew in the wind as they decided to ride that day with the top down and the Tampa sun beating down on them.

"Many things, son. Many things."

"Do you work at Jai Alai?"

"You could say that."

"But what do you do there?'

They pulled to a stop at a red light at the foot of the Gandy Bridge. His father downed the rest of his beer and tossed the can on the side of the road. He lightly brushed Eli's chin with a fist and winked. "I fix things," he said.

But the day his father walked in with handfuls of cash was the last day Eli saw him. He said he was leaving, and in a few days, they

would hear from him. He would send word where they were to go to meet him. He never sent word, and now those other men were looking for him.

"So you aren't going to tell me?" the man said to Eli.

Eli looked at the man. His mother was still on the floor, her crying subdued.

"I don't know when I last saw him."

"Is that so?' the man said. Within a breath, the man held Eli's face, squeezing him so tight it was as if he would crush his cheekbones. His mother tried to stand but was quickly seated again with a boot to her nose. Blood streamed from her nose and lip.

The man held the cigar out, looking at the thick cherry glowing red hot from the end. He blew on it, and it glowed redder. Then, he slowly stuck that red cherry into Eli's eye. The hissing sound and smell of burnt flesh stayed with Eli for much longer than the pain.

11

In Friday night's game, the starting quarterback injured his knee early in the third quarter. It was nothing serious, but he hurt it enough on a three-yard run that he wouldn't go back in, especially since it wasn't a district game, and they were up by twelve points. Randall stepped in, but things were not looking good by the fourth quarter. They were now down by two. Randall could sense the coach's frustration having blown that lead, but with fifty-two seconds left, all their timeouts, and only eight yards from field goal range, he felt confident they would pull off the victory.

His nerves calmed, even after throwing the interception that led to them trailing. Jared joined the huddle. With it being first down, the coach told them to run it up the middle for the first two downs to try and pick up those eight yards. He looked at Jared again and then called the coach's play. Six yards. Time out. The crowd's noise sounded distant. Insects swarmed around the lights. In South Florida, football season didn't conjure up memories of cool temps and chili on the stovetop. It was just as swampy as any given Friday.

Two yards away from field goal range. The defense looked defeated. On the sidelines, Gordan Byrd practiced field goals into a net. Everyone in the stands and on both sidelines knew he never missed from that distance. The game was just as good as won.

"Just give me the ball," Austin, the running back, shouted, spit flying in the faces of teammates in the huddle. "I'll ram that ball straight up their assholes," he said.

The offensive line shouted in unison. The huddle broke.

"Jared," Randall called out. Jared looked at him. Randall waved him over. He whispered in his ear.

"Hell no," Jared said.

"You don't have a choice," Randall told him. "I'm the goddamn quarterback. I'm going to drop that ball right into your goddamn hands. All you have to do is catch that motherfucker. And you better catch that motherfucker too. Understand?"

Randall didn't look over at the coaches. The center snapped the ball, and Randall turned as if to hand it off to Austin, but he rolled out instead and held the ball close to his body. The other team knew, as everyone in the entire stadium knew, that they were running it right up the middle to pick up only two yards. When the coaches and defense realized what happened, Jared sprinted three yards past his defender, and Randall let the ball fly. He heard his coach yell out, "You stupid motherfucker."

He watched the ball sail over the defense, and for a minute, it seemed suspended in time. He then saw Jared look over his shoulder while still in his route and the ball landed perfectly into his hands. They couldn't have drawn up a better play. The crowd's noise caught up in real-time. The scoreboard changed. The clock showed three seconds left in the game. His teammates ran and congratulated Jared on his first touchdown in four years and his only catch of the season. The coaches didn't have the same reaction, but Randall barely heard a word that they yelled at him, barely felt the smacks to his helmet. The entire time, he watched his teammates revel in Jared's jubilation. And while the coaches threatened to bench him for the rest of the season and nearly ripped his head off by grabbing the facemask and jerking his head around, Randall smiled, knowing he did the right thing.

Underneath the powerlines, a circle of pick-up trucks surrounded a beer keg—the after-party of the Friday night game. The beer flowed easily. There were not enough girls for the team. The testosterone and alcohol were never a good mix. Some of the boys began questioning why Randall threw Jared the ball. One of the boys suggested they were lovers. Randall laughed it off. Jared, not so much.

"I'm heading out," Randall said. "Does anyone need a ride? Jared, do you need a ride?"

Randall tried giving him an out. The boys jeered. "Your boyfriend wants to take you home," one said. Randall laughed and said, "Nah. We're just going to fuck your mom while you're out playing grab ass with a bunch of dudes." Now, the boys were back on Randall's side. They all liked him. The girls liked him. The teachers like him. Jared liked him. But Jared couldn't handle being the butt of jokes and hoped, by sticking around, that the team would finally accept him.

"I'm going to hang out a bit longer," Jared said.

"Hell yeah," #63 said. "Let's get drunk." He put his arm around Jared's shoulders. This lineman, larger than most grown men, looked like a giant next to Jared. He then winked at Randall and said, "Don't worry. I'll take care of him."

Randall drove off in his pickup truck while Jared stayed behind and did too many keg stands. He was not his brother's keeper. As much as he hated it, Jared needed to make his own decisions. Randall looked in the rearview but knew he didn't want to be near them and what they planned to do to Jared.

12

S tacy Ringling, wearing moccasins, a brown mini skirt, and a tank top that showed her midriff, stood at the baggage claim of the Miami International Airport, awaiting the arrival of Janet Drexler, her best friend from high school whom she hadn't seen in seven years. Her blond pigtails hung from beneath her well-worn straw cowboy hat.

Last month, Stacy received an unexpected letter from her childhood friend. Janet needed help. No one ever asked Stacy for help before. It seemed urgent. Janet's husband served his time and was soon to be out of jail on parole. She filed for divorce, sending the papers to the jail and he refused to sign them. In a letter, he responded that he recognized his mistakes and since broke it off with his younger girlfriend and said he wanted to move back in with Janet and her mother. Make their marriage work. The idea frightened Janet. Stacy called Janet immediately after reading the letter and they spoke nearly daily for the next two weeks. Every conversation ended with Stacy closer to convincing Janet to come to Key West. It wasn't safe to stay in Sullivan. Start her life again. Janet couldn't afford it. Stacy said she would pay. Janet agreed with her mother's insistence. Stacy booked her a plane into Miami because the drive through the Keys was part of the experience.

"Is that you?" Stacy shouted as she saw Janet shuffling through the crowd. "Holy shit," she said. "Janet?"

Janet walked through the corridor in a floral pink ankle-length dress. Her brown hair long and frazzled, not cut in years. She looked more like she belonged at a mennonite commune than a tourist in Miami. She lifted her eyes slightly when she saw Stacy, and her lips seemed to have curled upwards into a semblance of a smile. She then put her head back down.

Stacy held in her arms a dozen roses she bought off the side of the street on the way to the airport, and a buzz in her head she picked up at the airport bar from three Vodka Tonics while waiting on the delayed flight. Her cheeks were rosy from the four-hour drive from Key West on her motorcycle in the seventy-eight-degree autumn sunshine. Her heart beat with anticipation at the thought of rekindling a lost friendship.

Stacy grabbed Janet in a bear hug, wrapping the roses around the one lady in that airport who needed it most. Janet's arms stayed straight by her sides.

"Look at you," Stacy said, pulling away a little from her friend. Tears rolled down Janet's cheeks, and Stacy hugged her again, this time tighter. Janet sobbed and lifted her left arm slightly in a weak attempt to return the hug. "Girl, it's been way too long. We are going to have some fun," Stacy said as she let Janet cry on her shoulder. Janet cried for a good three minutes.

On the way to the parking lot, Stacy looked at Janet and said, "First thing we gotta do is cut that hair off."

"I don't know," Janet said in a feeble voice.

"What?"

"I don't know if I want to."

"It wasn't a question."

Janet stood looking at the electric blue motorcycle. "You drive that?"

"Yep." Stacy took a helmet from the bike and handed it to Janet.

"I thought you were picking me up in a car?"

"Nope."

"I don't want to ride in that," Janet said, pointing to the sidecar.

"Get in."

Stacy strapped the suitcase with a bungee cord to the back of the bike, squishing the roses on top of it. She helped Janet buckle the helmet and climb in. The motorcycle rumbled alive. Janet could feel the low grumble in her stomach that caused a slight bit of nausea. She closed her eyes as they rolled out of the parking lot.

For fifty minutes, they sped along the Florida Turnpike. Janet looked down at the many neighborhoods on either side of the turnpike, not knowing so many houses could be crammed so close together. So many cars on the same road going so fast. And then farmland on one side and neighborhoods on another. Then into Homestead, a name she remembered from Hurricane Andrew nearly wiping it flat some years before. Already rebuilt, but the memory of such destruction was alive among the citizens.

Stacy turned off US 1 on Card Sound Road, and they entered the edge of the Everglades. Such a vast difference in such a short distance.

They stopped off Card Sound Road in Key Largo at a well-known watering hole called Alabama Jack's. Stacy parked inline with other motorcycles out front and entered with a sway that attracted men's attention, even the ones on vacation with their wives, who gave them a smack on the arm for looking too long. Janet shuffled behind, a bit embarrassed about the scene Stacy created. Although half the folks there were upper or middle-class staples of society just looking for some good food and cold beer, Janet couldn't help but focus on the few squatters and boat dwellers that frequented the place, also looking for some good food and cold beer. Three of them sat at the bar and Janet hoped that wasn't where they were going.

The original owner, Jack Stratham, a construction worker from Georgia, somehow ended up with the nickname Alabama and purchased the lease in 1953. Through many hurricanes and rebuilds, the bar looked pieced together, barely staying afloat, hovering over a canal no longer a part of the Everglades drainage basin after the federal removal of the wetlands began erasing millions of acres. The smell of sulfur remained and blended beautifully with the scent of fried seafood. A smell that Janet did not appreciate. Seagulls squawked overhead and perched on the railings, hoping for a french fry. An egret waded in the mangroves on the other side of the canal. Plastic tables and plastic chairs made up the open-air dining area.

"How are you doing, babydoll?" Stacy said to the bartender, a weathered, overweight fifty-something. Janet stood back and focused her eyes to the floor when she noticed the three grizzly men at the bar looking there way.

"Well, if I ain't having a flashback," the bartender responded. "Holy shit, girl, what are you doing way up here in these northern parts? Didn't think you traveled up this way anymore." She leaned her big breasts over the bar and kissed Stacy on the cheek, leaving a faint smear of lipstick.

"I normally don't, but I came to pick up a good friend of mine. Janet, this is Momma." Stacy pulled up a bar stool. Janet remained standing and looked up at Momma's tiger claw tattooed cleavage. She then met Momma's wide eyes, shaded in blue eye makeup.

"Hi," Janet said.

"Now, how in the world does such a innocent-looking lady like yourself happen to know such a floozy like Stacy?" Momma asked. The men at the end of the bar laughed.

Janet paused for too long. Stacy and Momma exchanged questioning looks. "School," Janet finally managed.

"She's tired," Stacy said. "Been traveling all morning. We've known each other since what? Fifth, sixth grade?"

Janet nodded. It was third grade, but she didn't want to correct her.

"I guess we'll have..."

"A double shot of Jack, a Bud Light, and conch fritters," Momma said the order first.

"You know me too well," Stacy said. "But not today. I have to drive the bike home tonight. Better just make it a single."

"What about your friend? What would you like, sweetie?"

"A water," Janet said.

Stacy looked at her. "You don't like peach schnapps anymore? Remember how we used to drink that all the time? Oh, we had some good times. I remember that one time, we must've been fifteen or sixteen years old, and we drank so much walking around the neighborhood, and by the end of it, we were puking in every neighbor's bushes all the way home. You remember that?"

Janet nodded. "I haven't drunk since my honeymoon. Bobby said..."

"I ain't listening to shit Bobby said, and you ain't either anymore," Stacy said. Then, she told Momma, "Throw a lemon in there for her in a rock glass." Momma went in the back to put the order in.

Stacy looked at Janet. She looked on the verge of tears. "You all right, hun?"

Janet nodded. But she wasn't. Remaining silent kept her from crying. She didn't know why, but a cloud of despair hovered over her. Maybe she feared what Bobby would do when he found out she left and knew that she visited a place like this. When she blinked, her eyes stayed shut for a second too long, causing a shiver as if she could feel Bobby behind her, remembering a time that he punched her in the back of the head before dragging her out of the bathroom by the hair because she took too long doing her makeup.

"You ever had conch before?" Stacy smiled at the innuendo.

Janet shook her head.

"Big, fat conch. I just love it. And this place makes the best. Wait till you see it. It isn't like all those other bullshit places. This place gives it to you in just one big chunk. Not all those little balls. I don't like little balls. I want to be able to get a good handful of conch."

"Girl," one of the men said, "You better stop talking like that around here. Going to give one us old men a heart attack."

Stacy winked at them and blew them a kiss.

"I'm going to the lady's room," Janet said. She rushed in, slid the lock, sat on the dingy toilet, and cried, asking Bobby's forgiveness.

Tears streamed down, and the snot bubbled just above her upper lip. She wanted his forgiveness for contacting Stacy again, knowing how much Bobby disliked her. She knew better than to hang out with somebody who spoke so crass and made such lewd jokes and who carried herself like such a whore. She cried because she wanted to go home, but the return flight wasn't for another two weeks and left from Key West. She didn't have enough money to make an exchange.

She cried because she was irrational. A problem Bobby accused her of anytime she tried to express her frustration with him, and now she could see he was right. He was right about everything. She feared that when he came back for her, he would see that she abandoned him. She abandoned their marriage. She prayed to God and Bobby for forgiveness and for her to return to the path of righteousness, the path back to Bobby.

13

E li finished cleaning up his area at Mallory Square, slowed by a few people stopping to say how much they enjoyed his performance. He remained cordial but spoke little. Enough being a clown for one day. He walked with his folded-up scaffold under his arm, set it in the bed of his pickup, and tossed his duffel bag, filled with his straight jacket and chains, in the back. He drove his truck back home, unloaded his equipment, and without showering this time, set out to have a drink or three.

He would eventually end up at Randall's bar, but he first needed something quiet and dark, a place to prepare for pulsating disco music and drag queens.

He greeted the old man at the door. The old man said hello and then returned to entertaining the young tourists with his stories of gunrunning and shipwrecking and taking pictures with the ladies and telling their boyfriends that the girls would leave them for him. "They all do," Captain Tony said. "But don't worry. I'll send them back when I'm finished." The girls feigned offense while their boyfriends laughed.

Eli sat at the end of the bar. The bartender popped the top on a beer bottle and set it before him. Eli nodded.

The darkness outside, thick with humidity, but inside Capt Tony's Saloon, the air-conditioning blew cold, like walking into a cave, a cave with walls made of dingy one-dollar bills and faded business cards for businesses that were more than likely no longer in existence. Signatures and drawings in pen and marker like ancient hieroglyphics, showing that while technology may have advanced enough to put people on the moon, humans remained creatures of habit. Eli drank his beer while eavesdropping on the patrons around him, talking about how the bar was the real Sloppy Joe's where Hemingway drank and how Jimmy Buffett first played here when he moved to Key West with Jerry Jeff Walker. He tried listening to the musician singing about taking a pony on a boat, but the words were drowned out by the guy next to him telling his wife how the lyrics to "Last Mango in Paris" were scribbled on the wall above the urinal in the men's bathroom.

Eli finished his beer and left cash on the bar, not quite the quiet drinking spot he needed. He loved the bar, the old man, the bartenders, the history, but the tourists made it unbearable on some nights. Not that they were unbearable for any particular reason. He loved tourists in general. They were his livelihood and most people's livelihood on the island. But when not working, they could sometimes annoy him. For what? Because they were enjoying things that he and the other locals often took for granted? On his way out, a couple stopped him and asked if he performed the escape acts at Mallory Square.

"Yes, mam," Eli said.

She said that she didn't think his racial jokes were very funny.

"If I couldn't joke about racism, I'd probably be in jail for killing a white lady." He regretted saying it as soon as it left his mouth.

Her husband said, "I think you are funnier than hell." After a short pause, he added, "For a black dude." He laughed loudly and slapped Eli on the arm too hard.

Eli didn't know what to make of either one. "I appreciate you watching the show," he said. And then added, "But it'd probably be best staying away from racial jokes, my friend. They don't work for everyone," and continued out the door. In his head, when the man made the joke all he heard was, "Dance, boy, dance." He also imagined splitting the guy's nose. Even more so when he heard the guy yell out, "Fuck you. Just because you're black, you think you can make racist jokes?" Eli walked on.

He grabbed two beers from the convenience store near the pier and walked down around the docks, trying to take in the surroundings as a tourist, not to lose sight of why he moved there and not to become another jaded asshole in paradise. He sat on a bench, opened the first beer, and enjoyed the couples in love and sunburnt and walking on an air of carefree jubilance that usually accompanied a vacation, something he was not familiar with, having never gone one. In the distance, the sound of a steel-drum band.

"Hey, if it ain't the magic man." He heard a voice say and knew who said it before looking over at him.

"Get out of here, Scotty. I'm just trying to have a nice quiet evening."

Scotty walked a bike and stopped in front of Eli.

"Whose bike did you steal?' Eli asked.

"Let me get that extra beer," Scotty said, pointing to the beer sitting on the bench beside Eli. Scotty's unbuttoned Hawaiian shirt showed his tanned, hairy chest. His face, freshly shaven, left a well-trimmed and luxurious mustache. He had no shoes but his jeans looked laundered and pressed. His left hand looked like a flipper, only his ring and pinky finger were left.

A group of citizens from Vernon, Florida, or, as some folks called it long ago, Nub City, ran an elaborate self-mutilation insurance scam. One guy took a shotgun and blew his foot off. Scotty attempted his scam about fifteen years after the craze wore off, taking a table saw to his hand while on a construction job site. Nearly cost him his life with the amount of blood he lost, but he recovered, bought a boat with the settlement money, moved to Key West, and lived off the little bit of disability he received every month.

"Tell me whose bike you stole first."

"I ain't steal no bike. Red owes me twenty dollars, and I'm just holding it for him until I get my money."

"Or he kicks your ass. Whichever happens first, right?"

"Fucking Red is too drunk to kick anyone's ass."

"A drunk calling a drunk a drunk."

"I'll whoop Red's ass, and you know it." Scotty let the bike drop to the ground, and a few people walking by sidestepped it. Scotty sat next to Eli, picked up the paper bag with the beer in it, and popped the top.

"You don't mind, do you?" he asked.

"Go right ahead," Eli said.

"Look, man, you got a couple of dollars I can hold? I spent my last bit of money until the end of the month, and Red damn near drank it all up in one day. Said he was going to give me twenty dollars for it, but he's been avoiding me since..."

Eli stood up, cutting Scotty off, and said, "I'm going to keep moving. Enjoy that beer."

"So you ain't going to lend me any money?"

"No, Scotty. I'm not. I'll see you around."

"Well, what about just..."

"Scotty, I done told you no. You ask me again, and you're likely to piss me off."

As Eli walked off, he heard Scotty say to some passersby, "Hey, is your wife single?"

Eli shook his head. No matter how many times Scotty got his ass kicked, he was still going to be Scotty. On his walk, Eli stopped to take a photo for a couple about to step on a dinner cruise. He said hello to familiar faces sitting on the dock with their feet dangling over the edge. He dropped fifty cents into a guitar case of a street performer. A blue heron flew off a piling. He waved to a group drinking cocktails in the cockpit of a sailboat. Music from neighboring bars seamlessly blended with the chatter and laughter of those on an evening stroll, either going or coming from dinner or off to drink more beer and cocktails, trying to visit as many bars and restaurants as possible on their weeklong escape from reality. But for some, like Eli, he strolled along on his lifelong escape from reality, an endless search for something more, something that if even for a fleeting second would cause him to stop and think: If this isn't nice, I don't know what nice is.

When he finished his last sip of beer, he threw the can in the garbage, reached into his pocket, and felt a wad of cash. He knew that he had a place to sleep and food in the refrigerator, lived in paradise, and made a living pursuing his childhood dream of being an escape artist. That was the definition of nice. He lived a nice life, which was more than most people could say.

He sat at the bar of a wharfside restaurant, ate a dozen char-grilled oysters, and drank a couple beers. Restless, he peeled the labels from the bottles with his thumbnail. Usually, he would go to Hogsbreath or the Chartroom and sometimes to what they called Margaritahell to listen to Stacy play some songs, but Stacy was driving back from Miami, having picked up a friend. So, instead, he killed time until the drag show started at Randall's bar. He swept the peeled labels into his hand, leaving no trace that he had been there, and then worked them through the bottle's opening. He thought of his final act and felt that if he carried it out he was abandoning Stacy and Randall, but what he planned was best for everyone.

Outside the restaurant, crowds wandered the docks that were once for the working class instead of the wealthy. Where yachts and high-end fishing charters were now docked used to be shrimpers and turtle fishermen. He continued on through the night.

Down Duval Street and still three bars away, he heard the thumping sound of the music coming from Randall's bar. Energy and excitement pulsated into the night and the few beers he drank were just enough for him to face the ear-ringing music.

The doorman waived him in with no cover or ID check—the perks of being a regular. The strobe lights flashed, the fog machines pumped out clouds of smoke, and young, sweaty, hard bodies filled the dance floor. It was still early, but little by little, it would get more crowded until bodies unintentionally and intentionally rubbed on one another, and the fine line between bad decisions and good decisions blurred.

Randall, or Raven as he was known while bartending, stood on the bar pouring a waterfall stream from a vodka bottle down the throat of a male patron, laying his head backward on the bar. Raven no longer looked like a charter boat captain but was transformed into a beautiful woman.

The man stood up and wiped his mouth. His buddy cheered. The woman with him laughed. The man then said to Raven, "Sweetie, I'm bringing you home with us when this night is over."

Raven said, "I don't think that's going to happen and then lifted his skirt to show that he was still, indeed, a man below that elegant facade. The male patron's eyes nearly jumped out of his face when he looked at Raven's member bulging from a thong. His female companion screeched a laugh, and his bald buddy yelled out, "Awe hell naw," and said to the woman, "I knew you was bringing us to a homo bar." The woman continued to laugh and stumbled out after the two men as other patrons jeered at the no-longer welcomed guests. One person from the darkened corner threw a nearly empty plastic cup their way but missed, and the ice scattered across the floor.

"You're such a whore," Eli said as he sat across from Raven. Raven laughed.

"I knew those two were as homophobic as they come. Didn't want them sticking around when things started heating up."

"How in the hell anyone can walk into this place and not know what to expect is beyond me. Did they not see the giant ruby slipper on the front or the balcony lined with rainbow flags? I mean, for fuck's sake, what is wrong with people?"

"Lighten up, bud. We can't save them all."

Raven set a High Life down in front of Eli. "Remember when this town wasn't overrun with racists and gay bashers?" Eli said.

"No. I don't," Raven said.

Eli laughed. "Me either. I guess they were just a bit more hidden at one time."

"Maybe it was us that was a bit more hidden."

14

S ullivan High's cheerleading squad practiced their tumbling in preparation for the week's homecoming events. The cheer captain, Stacy Ringling, shouted commands, ensuring the base and spotter worked effortlessly with the flyer. The sounds of the football practice floated across the field. The welcomed cool autumn air started settling in late October, arriving around the time of the fair setting up down in Pensacola. The Sullivan kids would pile up in their pickup trucks and rusty sports cars and make the forty-five-minute drive into town for the midnight madness after the football game. Homecoming and the fair in the same week created a buzz at the school that built a beautiful crescendo, especially when the team could win. And that energy would carry over as they arrived at the neighboring city and walked the midway as they owned it. When encountering rival schools, the arguments that began on the football fields continued on the grounds of the midway and usually ended as fist fights in the parking lot. These were country kids not feeling welcomed in the city and the country kids showing the city kids they would go anywhere they damn well pleased.

Two county police cars drove up the long dirt road to the football field, and the odd sight caused both the cheerleaders and football players to stop in curiosity. Everyone knew Stacy's dad worked at the jail, and while there were plenty of other police officers and correctional officers in town, she was the only one at school whose parent was an officer, and not just any officer but a major.

For some inexplicable reason, as she watched the dust rise behind those flashing lights, she knew those cars were for her, and she knew that all the kids and coaches that day who stopped to watch the cars drive down that road also knew that they were for her. Although she knew it, she never, for the rest of her life, ever voiced that idea for the fear of sounding crazy. When that memory would pop into her mind at some seemingly random time, in living time or dream time, she knew without a shadow of a doubt that those cars were coming for her and that no good news ever came from a police car showing up unannounced.

Reflecting on that day, she would pay particular attention to how time stopped. She even remembered seeing a bird freeze mid-flight. The only movement in the world was the two cars making their way closer and closer. She felt her heart flutter, her stomach flip, her breathing labored, and tears well in her eyes. She saw the officers step from their vehicles and slowly walk toward her, and she and everyone else knew something terrible was about to transpire. Probably about her father. What she didn't know and the others didn't know was that something horrible also happened to her mother.

On his day off, her father, Correctional Officer Major Tom Ringling, took his wife of twenty-two years out to lunch. Upon returning, a car driving in the opposite direction on a two-lane highway swerved into the oncoming traffic lane and hit Officer Major Tom Ringling's car head-on. The driver who swerved, along with the two occupants in the car he hit, died instantly at the scene.

Stacy heard this news as if told to her from the end of a distant tube, and the sound came from miles away. When it reached her, it was barely audible. Her ears rang loud enough to drown out all other sounds surrounding her. She looked at the crying faces of her friends on the cheer squad and the deep sadness and regret of the men who told her the news. She felt the arms of her coach surround her but didn't remember much more. She didn't know how she got home, how she packed her clothes to stay the night at her cheer coach's house, or what happened the next few days. She remembered people showing up with lots of flowers and covered dishes.

Her memory only seemed to return fully, and not in fractured moments, when she stood on the field before the Friday night homecoming game after not having returned to school since the news and seeing the crowd on their feet chanting her name in unison while the principal crowned her the homecoming queen, that same dream-like feeling of not being present in her body. Not until that moment did she understand that what she experienced when the police officers arrived was that she watched these things happen to her body from a different vantage point. Now, seeing the crowning moment happen from that same vantage point, she realized why the emotion wasn't what she would expect from a moment so intense. She saw it happen as if watching a movie and not truly experiencing it.

She didn't cheer that night. However, she watched from the bench, and her friends asked more times than she would've liked if she needed anything. Sullivan High won, and she rode with some of the girls to the Pensacola Interstate Fair. Inside the House of Mirrors, she saw an image of herself from three different angles, and that caused her to cry, not just because of the death of her parents, but also because she didn't know where she would live or how she would survive. She was suddenly an adult and far from prepared to handle such a sudden responsibility. Her only relative was her mom's sister in Texas, and she did not want to move to Houston during the last half of her senior year. The judge granted her emancipation because she was in her final months of high school. At seventeen years old, she lived alone and had one-hundred fifty-thousand dollars in insurance money her father left her.

Her aunt from Houston arrived to organize an estate sale and help Stacy sell her parents' home. Her aunt determined it would be better for Stacy to find a one-bedroom apartment rather than try to maintain that house on her own. She never saw any money from the estate sale or the house.

15

The morning after the football victory and the keg party at the power lines, Randall walked into his kitchen, and both his parents were gone from the house. A note on the table said they drove to Palm Beach for a day of shopping. Randall checked the coffee pot on the counter, noticed a bit left, grabbed a cup from the sink, rinsed it out, and poured the lukewarm remains into the clean-enough cup. He opened a kitchen drawer filled with condiments from Whataburger, took out a packet of sugar, and poured it into his coffee. From the fridge, he opened the carton of milk, smelled it, smelled it a second time, and then added a splash to the coffee. He turned and leaned on the counter, swirling the coffee in the cup before taking a sip. He hated that he left Jared there alone and didn't look forward to hearing the stories of that night in the locker room on Monday morning. He hated Jared for trying so hard to fit in with those guys. Hell, he hated that he tried so hard. He knew why he did it but didn't like to admit it to himself, so he stopped thinking about it.

Every time his mind started to think about it, he took another sip of his coffee or looked out the window and watched the mockingbirds and cardinals fight for a spot at the bird feeder. He finished his coffee and returned to his room, stopping in the hallway to see the family photos his mom proudly displayed. He looked longer than he realized at the picture of his older brother standing proudly in his football uniform. Senior year. Randall only twelve years old when it happened. Aaron, his brother, eighteen. Signing day to play college ball at the University of Florida on a full scholarship. All-time leading passer at the high school and now the reason Randall played quarterback, to fulfill his brother's unrealized dreams. Not Randall's dreams. And now colleges offered him scholarships for something he didn't want to continue doing.

Aaron celebrated the signing with his friends with a bottle of rum at the powerlines. After they finished the bottle, they jumped the train for fun. Tribal rights. That night was not fun. The tradition of seniors jumping on to passing by trains ended that night as well. It ended with newspaper headlines about the local quarterback who signed his letter of intent to play ball at the University of Florida and the first in his family to attend college, dead at the age of eighteen because of a stupid right of passage of jumping on a train as it sped by. As agile as he was on the field, hopping the train while drunk at two in the morning proved too dangerous of an opponent. Randall sometimes thought jumping from a train made more sense than putting up a facade for another four years.

He showered and drove his truck to Jared's. He wound down past the overgrown, abandoned lots around Lake Okeechobee and past a line of green trailers. A black man in a wheelchair who waved to him as he wheeled his way in the streets since there were no sidewalks. He drove by the old baseball field where he played little league ball, and a group of black men sat in the dugouts and drank from paper bags. In another lot, a black boy and a shirtless, skinny white boy banged on a dead oak trunk with a stick. In the yard of the shotgun house next to that lot sat an old white woman under an umbrella in a lawn chair behind a table of household wares of pots, pans, clothing, and other trinkets. A hand-painted sign said, "Yard Sale."

He turned at the former service station with its collapsed rooftop and sidewall, the bricks having long been salvaged. As long as he could remember, that building stood in disrepair. Such a familiar part of the landscape that he usually didn't pay it any mind. But that day, it seemed to hold some significance. Sharing the lot, a tan-colored row of one-story apartment units that he once remembered as a motel. Next to the apartments, a purple building with the sign that said, "Grocery and Beauty Supplies," and in the empty lot next to that sat a van with a for sale sign on the windshield. The van on cinder blocks, missing the passenger door and all four tires, sat so long it must've been forgotten. He turned into the Royal Estates neighborhood of manufactured homes. Jared's, the second to the last house. A mutt sat chained underneath a water oak, barely enough energy to lift his head, let alone bark.

Jared's stepfather met him at the door and said through the screen, "He ain't been home. I hadn't seen him since the game." He wore a Coors Banquet ball cap and drank from a canned Schlitz. His T-shirt said, "I Pee in Pools." Faded green tattoos covered his forearms.

"I haven't seen him since we left the party at the power lines," Randall said.

Jared's stepfather shrugged his shoulders.

"I guess I'll see if he stayed with any of the guys."

Jared's stepfather nodded and said, "You do that," and turned around.

He went to three more houses, but no one knew what happened to Jared after the party. He learned that Jared was visibly drunk, throwing up on himself, falling over, and acting like a fool.

Randall sped out to the power lines. Well past the historical marker that mentioned the "organized resistance" of Seminoles and Miccosukee against the United States. An organized resistance to a country that took control of the Florida territory fourteen years prior. A territory that Andrew Jackson thought of as a threat to the institution of slavery. An unnoticed territory of mosquito-infested swampland until fugitive slaves started joining forces with the Seminoles, an alliance that General Andrew Jackson couldn't allow to continue. Instead, he marched into Spanish Florida and made his point by killing nearly three hundred Free-People-of-Color living at what they called Negro Fort. And years later, during the Second Seminole War, Colonel Zachary Taylor picked up where Jackson left off by driving the Natives further south, continuing the genocidal onslaught that all but erased names like Sam Jones, Coacoochee, and Billy Bowlegs from future American history textbooks. The only remembrance, a sign that people rarely read.

In the 1950s, the city of Ft. Walton Beach in the Florida Panhandle, hundreds of miles from the historical marker that commemorated the event, would start a Mardi Gras-like pirate-themed festival named Billy Bowlegs, but made no mention of the brave Seminole. Instead, the city created a false history to celebrate a soldier from the American Revolution named William Augustus Bowles, who had no connection to the town and no record of being called Billy Bowlegs. Tourists would drink and party under the Florida Panhandle sun. Similarly, tourists who visited the Everglades could see the last remaining tribal members of Sam Jones wrestle alligators, sell wares, and take airboat rides.

Randall turned onto a dirt road between two sugar cane fields, but before reaching the turn-off to the wooded area behind the fields where the party took place, he slid to a stop, and a dust storm following him billowed around his truck. A barricade of flashing lights of police cars, an ambulance, and a firetruck blocked the road. Randall knew without needing confirmation why the first responders were there, but the scene was much worse than he imagined.

16

J anet walked the three steps of her trailer and opened the screen door to see her mom sleeping on the recliner with daytime talk shows humming in the background and a pile of cigarettes in an ashtray beside her. Next to the ashtray, a sweating ice tea glass sat on the ash-covered TV tray that doubled as a coffee table. The melted ice created a division in the glass of water and tea. Next to the glass sat a pill bottle of barbiturates.

Janet's art teacher allowed her to check out a camera to begin developing film in the school's darkroom. Previously, the teacher reserved the activity for seniors, but no seniors showed interest in photography for the past six years.

"Mom," Janet said quietly. She looked at her mom, sat her bookbag on the floor, took out the Canon F-1 camera, aimed it at her sleeping mother, and snapped a picture. She saw her living conditions with a new perspective. Through the lens, her life didn't seem as embarrassing. It didn't seem like her life at all. She felt somehow detached from it. There was something beautifully sad about her doped-up mom, living in an unkept trailer. She looked at the trash can and wondered how long it would stay over-flowed like that if she didn't take it out. TV dinner cartons tumbled off the top and sat on the floor. Would her mom finally clean up? She took a picture of it, kneeling and getting in an extremely tight shot.

She looked at the dishes piling up and wondered how long that half-eaten frozen pizza slice would sit on the plate on the counter. She then tried to think back to how long she had been cleaning up after her mother. It always seemed normal to her, but through the lens, she became aware that children were not meant to care for their parents in such a way. At least when her father was alive, the house stayed somewhat clean. She vaguely remembered her father. She remembered the sadness when he would leave and threaten never to return. She remembered the excitement when he would come home. Only eight years old when he died, but some of her memories were oddly vivid. The older she got, the stories her mom told about him grew worse. She didn't know when, but at some point, she stopped asking about him. She often wondered, though, if her mother sank deeper into drugs because of how her father treated her or if her father treated her mother that way because of her drug use.

She stepped out on the front steps of the trailer and looked around. She watched the kids in the trailer beside her run through the dusty streets. Amy, the barefoot, dirty-mouthed six-year-old chasing after her brother with a stick and the the intent to hit him if she caught him. Her brother, Ryan, nine years old, barefoot and shirtless and wearing ripped jeans. The kid never thought twice about calling any of the neighbors "a bitch." And the neighbors all laughed because there was something funny about kids cussing.

She lifted the camera, took a picture of them, and continued taking photos as they ran around the car that sat on jacks in the front yard for the last six months. Little Amy smacked the car's hood and said, "You just wait 'til I catch you."

Ryan yelled back, "You can't catch me, you bitch."

Overcome with sadness, Janet lowered the camera. Ryan saw her. "Hey, you bitch. Why are you taking pictures of us?"

Little Amy stopped and looked at Janet as well. Then she added, "Yeah, you bitch."

Janet continued to watch, almost as if seeing those kids for the first time.

"Are you stupid or something?" Ryan said to her. "Are you stupid?" Amy added. Janet couldn't tell if Amy mocked her brother or participated in his heckling. Were they now a team? She took another picture as Ryan filled an empty soda can with dirt in preparation to throw her way. She went back inside and, a few seconds later, heard the can hit her porch.

17

Snakes Alive Bingo Parlor just over the county line outside Sullivan, Florida, offered $1 games on Thursday nights. A few years back, when Arthur Dresden, a developer from Pensacola, proposed opening a bingo parlor, many people voiced concern about him choosing a town filled with citizens mainly living on fixed incomes, either social security or welfare, but come Thursday nights, the crowd at Snakes Alive proved that everyone forgot about the sins of gambling.

Preachers preached against it, the sheriff said he expected crime would get worse, and people said kids would go hungry because parents would spend their paychecks at a chance to get rich quickly. None of them were wrong. But the bingo games started, and they kept going. People said that the building that Mr. Ruddly once owned no longer sat empty. Some people won money, most didn't, and the winnings were never actually a life-changing amount. Some of those life-changing winnings would come a decade later when the Poarch Creek opened up a real casino in Atmore, Alabama, not too far of a drive from Sullivan. By that time, people would still preach about the sins of gambling, but that didn't mean they didn't gamble. And the jobs. Nobody could deny that the casino created jobs, and jobs were what everyone wanted. Especially so close to a town where the largest employer was a correctional facility.

The smell of corn dogs, cheese fries, and cigarette smoke wafted around as people slugged down pitchers of Coca-Cola. Sherrie Durango placed three golden cat figurines waiving their paw above her twelve cards laid out in front of her. Her daubers lined up precisely to her left as if they held some supernatural power. She lined them in the same color order when she first played a game six years ago. Changing the order would disrupt the good luck they possessed. The bingo caller sounded as if he ran the slowest auction ever heard, and he called out names like "Droopy Drawers" in place for number forty-four or "Heinz Varieties" instead of fifty-seven. No one looked like they were having fun. They were there to win, not attend a social event.

Andy Maxwell lifted his card and hollered a bingo on the third game of the night, a "Top and Bottom" game. Before verification ended, though, two masked men walked in, one holding a handgun. Both wore camo jackets, pants, and gloves. "Son of a bitch," Andy said and sat back down.

"Y'all know the rules," the one with the gun said, a pillowcase in his other hand. "Wallets and purses on the table." He walked toward Sarah Philips first. She handled the cash drawer and the cards. "Empty it," he said.

About twenty feet away, Sherman Kennedy set his cigarette on an ashtray, smoothed his mustache, stroked his beard, leaned into his wife, and said, "I know that voice." His wife listened.

The rest of the bingo hall sat silent. The other masked man stood by the exit door and peered through the glass door. "We good?" he hollered to his partner.

Sherman looked at his wife and said, out of the side of his mouth, "That's the Drexler boy and his buddy Lucas, ain't it?" His wife nodded to him.

Sarah Philips emptied the cash box into the pillowcase. Stacks of twenties and tens fell out, but not more than six hundred dollars.

"Bobby Drexler," Sherman shouted out. "You don't think we know that's you?"

Bobby whipped around. "Who said that?" Nobody spoke. "Who the hell was that?" Bobby shouted. "I'll make an example out of you."

Then another voice spoke out, "That damn sure is Bobby Drexler."

Bobby turned again. "I ain't either," the gunman said.

"Yeah, you is," another voice said. "I recognize that voice, too."

"Y'all shut up," Bobby said. "Before one of y'all get hurt." He tried to grab a purse from the table with the hand holding the pillow case and fumbled with it before it fell back to the table. "Open up your damn purse," he said. The woman, worn down from living hard and living out her retirement years in mundane boredness, opened her purse and emptied the contents onto the table. A pack of Salem Lights, two lighters, lipstick, a pack of tissues, some chewing gum, some hard candy, and her little snap wallet tumbled out. "In here," the gunman said.

"I know times are hard, Bobby," she said. "But you ain't gotta do this. Jesus still loves you."

"Shut your mouth," the gunman said. "I done told you, I ain't Bobby."

"I don't appreciate you talking to me that way," she said.

The gunman smacked her across the mouth with the hand that held the gun. She fell backward, and the crowd erupted in pandemonium.

"Ah, hell, Bobby," Lucas yelled. "You said you weren't going to hurt nobody."

The voices, almost in unison, erupted at the confirmation that the gunman was Bobby.

"Quiet down," Bobby shouted. Then he told the man who bent to help the lady, "Leave her be." Nobody listened. Bobby lost control of the crowd. Lucas sensed that, too, and he ran out the front door. Bobby attempted to flee, but Sherman blocked the exit. The noise of the crowd intensified into a unifying, tumultuous uproar.

"Out of my way," Bobby yelled at Sherman.

"You ain't got no bullets in there. Do you, son?" Sherman said.

"I do, and I'm going to give you a chance to move out of the way, Mr. Sherman, before I show you."

Sherman, as old and as big as he was, pulled his buck knife from his hip holster and slashed Bobby Drexler across the cheek. Bobby lifted his arm to block it, and his forearm protected him mostly, but the blade still made contact, cutting through the mask and drawing a crimson line from under the left eye straight down to his jaw. His gun dropped, and Sherman wrestled him to the ground and sat on him.

Somebody called an ambulance for the lady Bobby hit, and before the police or the ambulance arrived, the game was back in session. The lady with the busted lip held an ice pack from her cooler to her face until EMTs hauled her out on a stretcher. Sherman removed Bobby's mask and sat him against the wall until the police arrived and cuffed him. Sherman then rejoined his wife and said, "Always knew that Drexler kid was a stupid motherfucker."

18

Stacy knocked quietly and whispered, "Hey Janet, I'm sorry. I shouldn't have brought you here. I just assumed. I know I shouldn't assume anything. I just thought it would be like the way we were. I didn't think, and that's a big problem of mine. I don't think. We can go if you want."

Janet opened the door. Her eyes were red and puffed. "No, it wasn't you," she squeaked out.

Stacy hugged her in the bedraggled bathroom. "I'm here for you. I still love you. I've missed you and missed us being together. I just …" but she stopped talking. Janet hugged her back and cried again, pouring her salty troubles on Stacy's shoulder. Stacy held her like only a woman could when things were bad. Janet pulled back after a minute.

"Let's do it," Janet said.

"What?"

"Cut my hair."

"Okay," Stacy said. "I'll call my girl when we get home."

"No. Now."

Stacy paused. She smiled. "Okay. wait right here."

Stacy ran to the bar, "Momma, I need some scissors."

Momma looked around the bar by the register and handed Stacy a rusted pair. "What are y'all planning in there?"

"Thank you," Stacy said and rushed back to the bathroom.

Janet stood in front of the mirror crying, running her fingers through her long stringy hair.

"Are you sure?' Stacy asked.

Janet nodded through the tears. Stacy used two hair ties from around her wrists to make two ponytails and then began working the scissors through them. She must've cut off at least eight inches. When both ponytails were cut, Janet's hair hung just below her shoulders. It was a mess, but the weight lifted was worth it. She cried still but she smiled too.

"I'll clean it up when we get home. I have some better scissors, and I'll give it some shape. But you look so amazing."

Janet wiped her tears. "I feel pretty amazing."

Momma looked at the new haircut as they returned. "Girl," she said to Stacy, "You are crazy. But where the hell did you put all that hair?'

Stacy laughed. "We cleaned up the best we could."

Momma shook her head.

Janet sat at the bar, drank her water, and picked at the chewy, hush puppy-like fritter. Stacy gobbled it down with splashes of hot sauce and gulps of beer. Once finished, they continued down US 1. Janet sat low to the ground, the strands of hair no longer falling from the helmet and blowing in her face. The overwhelming fear that she did something stupid arose.

For some unknown reason, a memory began playing in her mind's eye. The constant hum of the motorcycle and the hypnotic motion of the broken lines passing by on the road unlocked memories she tried to forget. She no longer rode in Stacy's sidecar but felt transported back to relive a moment she kept pushed away for years. Yet, there it was again, her entering the grocery store back in Sullivan, a newlywed and three months shy of her nineteenth birthday. Bobby moved into her mother's

81

trailer. Janet and Bobby took over the master bedroom and moved her debilitated mother into Janet's old room. Bobby said it made sense to move into a place where her mother paid the rent with her social security instead of having them get a place independently. At least until Bobby found a job. He was recently fired, yet again—this time from a lawn care company. Moving in and out of her mother's house seemed to be a regular occurrence once she married Bobby.

She entered the Piggly Wiggly, looking at the discounts to decide what to cook for dinner. She picked up a pack of chicken drumsticks and a sack of potatoes. She also got a six-pack of beer for Bobby. Although the law raised the drinking age to 21 years ago, many clerks didn't check IDs. Walking by the pharmacy, she stopped and looked at different lipstick shades. Thought it could help spice things up in the bedroom since they stopped having sex nearly two months ago. Not that she particularly wanted to have sex, at least not the kind of sex they typically had. She hoped for something more tender.

When she got home, she realized lipstick wasn't the problem.

"Hey honey," she said, stepping from her car carrying the grocery bags up the porch steps. Bobby sat out on the porch smoking cigarettes. She leaned down to kiss Bobby, but he turned his face to receive the kiss on the cheek. He blew out a plume of smoke. Holding the cigarette in one hand, he got the beer from her, set it between his feet on the porch, popped a can from the plastic ring, and set the can between his thighs to pop the top. Janet tried to walk by, but he grabbed her by the wrist to get her to stay put, and she did. He then lifted the can and took a long pull from it. Janet stood waiting.

"What are you cooking for dinner?" he said.

"I found some chicken on sale," she said, "and some potatoes. I was going to make some potato salad."

"Let me see the bag," Bobby said.

"Now, Bobby, what in God's name for?" she said.

Putting the beer back between his thighs, he took the grocery bag from her. He peeked in, saw the chicken and potatoes, then looked up and said, "Where's the receipt?"

"What now, Bobby?" she said.

"I know you heard me," he said. "I ain't in no goddamn mood to be repeating myself. Where's the receipt?"

"Well, I must've left it in the car."

"Is that right?"

"I reckon," she said. "If it ain't in the bag."

"You reckon? You reckon? I reckon you go find that receipt."

Janet hesitated, but Bobby didn't take his eyes off her, so she slowly turned and walked back down the steps to the car. The driver's door creaked louder than usual. She bent down to act like she was searching for the receipt but stuck her hand down her blouse and pulled the receipt from her bra.

She then shut the door of the car and held the receipt up. "I found it," she said.

"I knew you would," Bobby said. He lifted the beer and took another long drink from it. A dribble spilled down his shirt, and he set the can between his thighs. He wiped his mouth with the back of his hand and took a deep drag from the cigarette as Janet walked back up the porch steps.

"Let me see it," he said.

She handed it to him. He looked it over.

"Where's the lipstick?"

"In my purse."

"Didn't want me to know, huh?"

"I..."

Bobby finished his beer and slowly stood. "You what?"

"I wanted to surprise you," she said. "Thought I could dress up for you tonight after dinner."

Bobby grabbed her hard on her upper arm with one hand, held the grocery bag with the other, and led her into the trailer.

Once inside, he said, "Put it on. Let me see it."

Her hand trembled as she reached into her purse and retrieved the tube.

"Let me see what it looks like on you," Bobby said again.

She removed the cap, applied the lipstick, lowered her hand, and looked at Bobby.

"You look like a whore," Bobby said. "Is that what you were going for? You thought I wanted my wife to look like a whore?"

Janet didn't say anything. She lowered her eyes.

Bobby hit her with a backhand, and she stumbled back. "If that's what you want, I'll treat you like a whore." He grabbed a handful of her hair and dragged her to the bedroom. He shut the mother's door as they walked past down the hallway. The mother slept anyway, unaware of the fighting.

He threw Janet on the bed and what he did to her didn't last long. Janet didn't resist either because she learned if she didn't fight back it ended quicker and left her with less bruising. When she left the bedroom, Bobby already stood on the porch drinking beer and smoking cigarettes. She opened the windows and fried the chicken. While doing so, she imagined the grease spilling over onto the stove and a great fire engulfing the trailer.

19

The walls of the Green Parrot were alive, shaking from the sweaty tourists and locals packed on the dance floor. The overflow crowd spilled onto the sidewalks and street. A band from New Orleans performed on stage, the lead singer shoeless and dreadlocked, singing about life on the road. Eli's height allowed him to be visible just a few inches above the crowd, and Cheryl, the bartender, spotted him, opened a Miller High Life for him, and passed it above those waiting closer to the bar. The fellow in front of him handed Eli the beer, took a couple of dollars from him, and passed it to the bartender.

"Must be nice knowing the bartender in a place like this," the man said to Eli.

"It's nice knowing the bartender anywhere," Eli said.

"I hear that," the man said.

Eli found a spot to lean against a post and watch the band. After two songs, restlessness returned and he didn't want to deal with the crowd to get another beer. He used to be able to spend hours at a bar. Sometimes, five or six hours would whirl by, but as of late, after a drink or two, he was annoyed. He never thought it possible, but he grew tired of life on the island.

He walked through the crowd on the sidewalk to a shack down the street selling Cuban burgers and coffee. He ordered one of each. Lucy, the grandmotherly lady who ran the place, knew him well. When she set his order on his table, she could see the sadness that he carried. She stood by the table, wiping her hands with a hand towel.

"Everything okay, Eli?"

He drank from his Cuban coffee and said, "Sure. It's okay, but that's it, you know? Just okay."

"Okay, is good, no?"

"It's better than the alternative."

"Girl problems?"

Eli laughed. "That could be some of it."

"I didn't want to say anything, but I wondered why I haven't seen you and Stacy around together much."

"She's busy," he said after finishing his coffee. A group of tourists rode by on bicycles, laughing and talking loudly. Their joy annoyed him. He lifted the burger and took a big bite. "I think we want different things out of life," he said chewing. He swallowed and continued, "She's got big dreams."

"Sometimes that is how it happens," Lucy said.

"I think my time in Key West has ended."

"What will you do?"

"I've got a plan. Somewhere new."

"Will you keep doing your magic tricks at this new place?"

"Not like I do now. This is my final disappearing act. It will be a good one, though."

"We will miss you here."

"I'll miss some of you, but this dancing for tourists thing is hard. And I don't think I have it in me anymore. It's not how I imagined I'd end up when I decided to be a magician. I envisioned Vegas with sold-out arenas. I don't know what I imagined, really. But not this."

"I understand." A couple approached the window, and Lucy touched Eli's shoulder. He nodded, acknowledging her goodwill, as she went to tend to the other customers. When he finished his burger, Lucy stopped by again and gave him a cigar.

"Thank you," he said.

"*Como*, thank you? *De nada*." They hugged, and Eli walked off into the overly loud night of Duval Street. Drunken revelers stumbled by. Heat lightning flashed behind some clouds. Strident sounds of loud talkers and loud laughers, music from the venues he passed, and the occasional motorcycle revving up at the stop signs. He paid one dollar to hear a dirty joke by a joke teller who looked like a wizard with a white beard, long white hair, and a wizard cap.

"Hey bud," Eli said. "Let's hear your worst one."

The wizard said, "This man walks into his bedroom with a goat under his arm, and his wife is lying in bed. He says, 'See this pig I have to fuck every time you say that you have a headache?' His wife says, 'Hunny, that's a goat.' He says, 'Bitch, ain't no one talking to you.'"

Eli laughed. "You a bad man."

Wizard said, "I'll give you a freebie. Two blondes are walking together, and one says, 'Look at that puppy with just one eye.' The other covers up one eye and says, 'Where?'"

Eli laughed again and said, "You motherfucker. I should take my dollar back."

Wizard smiled. "That's why it was a freebie."

"Be good, Ronnie," Eli said and continued walking.

He turned off Duval and walked down Whitehead. A little quieter there. He passed by a tree with a bronze plate on it that said, "Hemingway peed here."

"Fucking Hemingway," Eli said. Damn near as bad as Jimmy Buffett in this fucking town, he thought. The way Key West capitalized off both Hemingway and Buffett was enough to make his fans annoyed at the mention of their names.

He walked to the docks, sat on a bench, and lit the cigar. He contemplated how to break the news about the sale of the house to Randall and Stacy. Housing costs were so expensive in Key West that he could profit well and enjoy a quiet life in Mexico. Fish until his good eye was no longer good. Eventually, he'd become a blind man sitting in a Mexican cantina. That's how he pictured it, anyway. That's about the best he hoped for.

20

The refurbished white-painted school bus with the words Juvenile Corrections stenciled on the side bumped and rattled down the narrow dirt road way out in the Florida Panhandle. Sixteen-year-old Bobby Drexler sat handcuffed and looked out the window at the kudzu-covered pine forest. He was the only inmate on the bus, the driver in front of him behind a plexiglass enclosure. A correctional officer sat behind him, chewing on the end of a soggy cigar. As opposed to being charged as an adult in the bingo parlor robbery, the judge sentenced him to a reform facility until he turned eighteen and then, depending on his behavior, to be released or moved to an adult facility.

The reform facility was described to the incoming kids as a boys camp. The campus resembled one. A large brick building used as a mess hall and indoor basketball court surrounded by smaller brick buildings used as dorms. A small white cinder block building sat off on its own barely visible through the pines.

When off the bus, an officer led Bobby to that cinder block building into a moldy-smelling, isolated, white-walled room with a single bench. What looked like blood streaked across one wall and possibly bloody hand prints. A metal bar about twelve inches in length was attached to the bloodied wall, and hanging next to it, a leather strop. The stagnant air and stifling heat added to the uncomfortableness that made his ears ring from the silence. The bench looked as if someone shit on it.

"Have a seat," the officer said. "The warden will be in shortly to have a talk with you." The heavy door clanked shut.

Bobby chose to stand. He told himself that he wouldn't hesitate to bust the head of the first person who disrespected him, whether a guard or inmate. He would let everyone there know that they couldn't fuck with him.

In walked a sheriff's deputy. His campaign cover pulled down low over his eyes. Gray stubble grew from his broad chin. He said, "How come you ain't sitting?"

Bobby said, "Don't want to. That's how come."

"That right?"

"Wouldn't have said it otherwise."

"All right then. I'll rephrase that. Sit your ass down."

Bobby eyed the man briefly, but the deputy didn't waiver. And Bobby wasn't used to having a deep-voiced man talk to him so directly, so he listened. "Not sure what or if you've heard anything about this place, but when you leave here, you will be a respectable member of society. We turn turds into diamonds here."

Bobby nodded.

"That's when you respond, 'Yes, sir.'"

Bobby never called anyone sir. And he wasn't about to start.

"I heard you," Bobby said.

"I ain't asked if you heard me."

They sat silently for only a second, but it seemed much longer. The deputy raised his head a bit and, with the knuckle of his pointer finger, lifted the brim of his hat just enough so Bobby could see his eyes, and briefly, those eyes looked as if they belonged in the head of a great white shark. Without hesitation, the back of the deputy's hand struck across his cheek, opposite side of the scabbing slash of the buck knife.

Bobby fell backward off the bench, refocused his eyes, and looked at the man. He stood and said, "I know damn well that ain't allowed." He rubbed his cheek and steadied himself on the wall. "Ain't no way a law enforcement officer can hit a kid like that."

The man smirked. "Are you going to call the cops on me?" he said. "I don't think you understand where you are, boy. Rules are a bit different around here. We make y'all boys listen by any means necessary. We've been doing it this way for over eighty years."

Bobby never feared another person, and he didn't know what emotion sped up his heart rate and made his throat feel as if it were closing up. He felt the blood pulsing in his ears.

"We heard about you. We were ready. I didn't believe you could be this dumb. But here I am, seeing it for myself. I'm going to tell you to sit your ass down one more time, and if you hesitate, I promise you that you won't be able to sit for some time."

Bobby didn't move.

The man smirked. He pulled a can of chewing tobacco from his back pocket and thumped the can a few times. Bobby clenched his fists, and that did not bother the man. Very slowly and deliberately, he opened the lid, pinched the tobacco, and put it in his lip. He adjusted the tobacco with his tongue, positioning it just right. He then made a slight gesture, an offer of a dip to Bobby.

Bobby didn't trust the officer's sincerity and declined. The man smiled and spit on the floor before putting the lid back on and replacing the can in his pocket.

"You ready?" the man asked.

Bobby didn't respond. That emotion he fought back welled in his eyes, and the sides of his mouth trembled from holding back tears. The man loved the visible fear of a kid who, just minutes ago, seemed unbreakable. The poor kid didn't know what tough meant, but he was about to find out.

The man unhooked the handcuffs from his hip. "Place your hand on that bar over there," he said.

Bobby quickly glanced at the bar, then to the strop, and back to the man. He shook his head so slightly, almost unnoticeable, but the man noticed.

The man took a deep breath, returned the handcuffs with one hand, and unhooked his truncheon with his other. All very slowly, smiling at Bobby. He spat again, a long string of brown liquid. He wiped his chin with the back of his hand, and before his hand was away from his mouth, the truncheon crashed into Bobby's knee and brought him to the ground. The man then brought the baton down across Bobby's ribs and entirely collapsed the kid onto the floor. The man brought the truncheon down again on the back of Bobby's head for good measure. The last hit put Bobby to sleep, and the man dragged Bobby over to the wall and lifted his limp body enough to handcuff him to the bar attached to the bloodied wall.

21

Randall couldn't get close enough to see what took place on that dirt road before the turn-off to the power lines, but his gut told him that it had to do with Jared Baker. He headed back to the house, and it didn't take long for word to get moving around town.

A farmer found Jared Baker stripped naked and tied down on the barbed-wire fence and left to die. He didn't die. He welcomed death, and eventually, Jared would find it, but on his terms, before testifying against the migrant worker accused of raping him and leaving him on the fence. The jury would find him guilty anyway. But until then, Jared struggled through living hell, a turmoil not known possible until experienced. A fear so tangible that death became the only peace.

The story in the newspaper said that Jared wandered off drunk during the party. The last party-goers left unaware that Jared remained behind. No one remembered when anyone last saw him. Randall told the police about when he left and offered Jared a ride home. Jared refused and stayed at the party. Nobody knew when he left. He must've walked into the woods and passed out, some said. At some point, he came to and started walking back when the migrant worker found him, raped him, and left him for dead. At first, Jared didn't remember anything, but after hours of interrogation, he corroborated the story. Police questioned a migrant worker living nearby in a tent in the woods. He couldn't speak English well enough to give an alibi.

None of this sat well with Randall.

Monday at school, the story grew in the halls. In the locker room before practice, #63 and the other boys seemed too jovial about such a tragedy.

"Jared's faggot ass probably liked it," #63 said.

Randall charged into #63 and pushed him against the lockers. "You had something to do with it, didn't you?" Randall said, spit flying. "What the fuck happened out there?"

#63 smiled. His mossy teeth and acne chin exaggerated like a caricature. Randall looked at him and knew. But he also knew that unless Jared spoke out, no one would ever uncover the truth, and that poor migrant would take the fall.

Randall let go of #63 and turned to the rest of the team. "One of you motherfuckers know. Somebody was out there."

The teammates remained quiet. The coach shouted over the hushed crowd.

"Cut this shit out," Coach yelled. "Stadiums. Now!" The team dispersed and headed to the field. "You," Coach yelled at Randall. "My office. Now."

"No need," Randall said. He quit. Gave up scholarship offers and all.

Three weeks after the news broke about Jared, he didn't return to school. Gossip calmed down, and for most people, the incident was nearly forgotten. For Randall, the thoughts wouldn't leave. He shouldn't have left him there. He knew nothing good could come from it, yet he didn't do anything.

He knocked on Jared's door. Jared's stepdad answered. "Fuck out of here," he said.

"I just want to make sure Jared is okay."

"Okay? Hell no, he isn't okay. None of us are okay. Don't come around here asking stupid shit like that. Even if that spic hangs, we won't be okay."

Jared stood behind his stepfather. "I want to talk to him," Jared said. A large cloud sped across the sky, offering a slight reprieve from the sun.

"Something doesn't sit right with you two," the stepfather said, leaving them to talk.

Jared walked out and shut the door behind him. They walked over to the picnic table under the large water oak. The mutt approached them for a pet but couldn't get close enough before the chain tightened. Jared sat on top of the table with his feet on the bench. Randall knelt beside the mangy dog and rubbed behind his ears.

"How are you doing?" Randall asked.

"About how you think I'd be doing," Jared said.

"That man they arrested didn't do it, did he?"

Jared didn't speak. He looked away, jumped from the table, and paced around, kicking a rock into an empty soda can. He returned and sat at the table, putting his head in his hands. He then looked up. Tears flooded in his eyes. "It's worse than you could ever imagine."

"You aren't going to tell what happened, are you?"

Jared shook his head.

"But it wasn't that man, was it?"

Jared looked at Randall, and his looked confirmed Randall's suspicions. He didn't have to say anymore, and he wouldn't—ever again. Randall said, "I know it's going to take some time, but I wish you the best."

When Randall left, Jared walked back to his bedroom, strapped a belt around his neck, and hung himself in his closet. No one questioned Randall about being the last to speak to

Jared. Either glad to have a stronger case against the migrant or didn't care enough about Jared to investigate any further.

At the trial, the jury found the migrant worker guilty. He died within the first few months at the state prison. Suicide. Some inmates would say differently if asked, but no one ever asked.

22

She spent the summer after graduation down in Pensacola. Didn't bother with walking across the stage to receive her diploma. She was eighteen with enough money to try and make it for a few years as a musician. Rented a room in a small furnished place near downtown known as the Blount Compound, a house that provided rooms to poets and musicians. Shelves overflowing with books in every room. People who believed they were the new generation of The Subterraneans.

She busked on Palafox Street at the entrance of the Saenger Theater on the days there weren't shows. When performances were scheduled at the theater, she would set up on the corner of Palafox and Government on the edge of Plaza Ferdinand, a park that once held lynchings as entertainment during the Jim Crow Laws. She picked up a Monday night gig at Trader Jon's, the rowdy Navy bar down by the water. Some nights, she would come away with fifty or a hundred dollars. No one wanted to listen to original music there, though. They wanted rock and roll bands, not a lonely girl singing songs about her literary influences or the trailer parks of Sullivan, Florida. The only song they seemed to like was about childbirth, which she stole from a Joseph McElroy novel. After she would sing, "What does it look like down there?' the young pilots would shout, "A saddle of well-worked mutton." She hoped that maybe by talking about the song beforehand and telling people about the book, some would accidentally read it one day, but that was highly unlikely.

She got a couple of Thursday night slots over at the Flora-Bama, where the crowd better appreciated country music, but they wanted her to sing Reba or Dolly songs. Occasionally, she would throw in her originals, but those seemed to fall on deaf ears there, too. Her best gigs were in the dive bars on the Westside of Pensacola - Woodsy's Hill Top, The KC Flash, or the Angler. Those didn't pay. Tips only and free beer. But the patrons liked her stuff. Some even started singing along to some of her originals. Tips were meager. Sometimes, a joint or a small baggie of cocaine instead of dollar bills. She tried lying to herself that she didn't do it for the money but that's the lie all artists told themselves.

She would take her parent's insurance money and give herself five years. Five years of writing songs and playing anywhere she could. Streets, bars, didn't matter. She would become a master of shameless self-promotion, she told herself. She was prepared to put everything into it. She read Bukowski's poem about going all the way. She had some money in the bank, so she wouldn't have to go three or four nights without eating. She wouldn't have to sleep on park benches. Maybe once the money ran out and she still wasn't successful, she would have to face those things, but at that moment, she didn't have to stress over it. She just had to keep singing her songs, as Kris Kristofferson said, even if no one listened. Many didn't listen, but she would drink the devil's beer for nothing and steal his song.

She looked at it similar to Ray Bradbury telling authors that if they collected their rejection slips and pasted them to the wall, someone would say yes before they filled up all four walls.

Someone would say yes before she burned through that insurance money.

Playing through the smoky haze in the corner of KC Flash, a biker bar on the edge of a working-class neighborhood with fifty-cent pool tables and dollar beers, she noticed one man listening to her. At least, looking at her in a way that suggested he listened. She smiled at him and he walked up wearing a leather vest, pearl snap shirt, jeans, cowboy boots, ponytail, and scruffy beard. "This guy knows how to dress like a biker," she said into the microphone after she finished a song, and he placed five dollars in the tip jar.

She got a few chuckles from the crowd, and he stood directly before her, smiling.

"I mean, look at this guy," she said. "No doubt this guy rides bikes and fucks."

The crowd laughed louder. Some cheered, while some hooted and hollered.

"Ain't no doubt about it, baby," he said.

"I mean, he wanted to make sure y'all knew he was the real deal when he walked up in this motherfucker." She never talked like that in front of a crowd. Usually, she just played her songs, but the cockiness of that guy made her want to put him in his place. He ate it up instead, and so did the crowd. She began to find her voice. She thought two things simultaneously: people like the barroom banter as much as the songs, and I'm going to fuck this guy tonight. He looked younger than most of the men in the bar but older than the boys she typically slept with.

She said, "It'll cost you more than that five-dollar bill to take me home tonight." She tried out her knew persona and it worked again. The women empowered her.

"Hell yeah, sister," one woman shouted out.

"Someone buy that girl a shot," another said. Someone did. Set a shot glass by her feet. The pony-tailed man pulled out a wallet attached to a chain, opened it up, took out a twenty, and held it up for the others to see his generosity. The crowd cheered.

She smiled and winked as he placed it in her tip jar. She reached over to get the shot glass and downed it. Whiskey.

She played Neil Young's "Unknown Legend." More people tipped her. The ponytailed man stood center stage and watched her intently.

By the night's end, her tip jar held a little over two hundred dollars. With a good buzz from free booze, she left on the back of Ponytail's Fat Boy. He said he was going to New Orleans in the morning and asked her to ride along. She said yes. They went to her room at the Blount Compound. A bonfire out back where the house residents read poems to each other. The long-haired owner of the compound, Mike, performed a poetry reading with James Brown theatrics, and wearing an airbrushed Van Halen t-shirt, a harmonica-playing hobo named Kent accompanied him.

Stacy and Ponytail went upstairs to her room and took him to bed. Her roommates told her to keep it down.

They didn't.

23

S he knew it would be tough on her own, but she finally convinced herself that it was better that way. Since Bobby left, her thoughts fluctuated—one minute, glad she didn't have to deal with him anymore, and the next, scared of being alone.

She moved back in with her mother. While married to Bobby, she saw less and less of her mother. Each time, her mom looked a bit more withered away. She was on oxygen, yet still smoked. The trailer slumped in disrepair. The first day there, she tidied up. Emptied overfilled ashtrays and wiped ash from the tables. At least five ashtrays spread around the house. She did her best to scrub the black ring from around the toilet bowl. Tried to scrub the grime from the shower walls. She wasn't sure about the last time her mother bathed. She smelled of urine and cigarette smoke.

After the third night, Janet brought a TV dinner of hamburger steak and mashed potatoes and peach cobbler to her mother who sat on the recliner.

"So you just moving back in then?" her mother said during the first commercial break of Wheel of Fortune.

"Well, yes, momma. I ain't got nowhere else to go."

"For free?"

"Momma, no. I'll help you pay the bills. I still got my job at The Corner Store."

"You should've never married that boy," she said. She took a deep breath, and her machine made a hissing sound.

"Too late for should've now, ain't it?"

"I reckon so. He wasn't ever right to begin with, but ever since that boy came back from that boy's camp he went off to after robbing that place, he seemed more touched in the head than anyone I ever met."

"Momma, we don't need to keep talking about him."

"Child, if you think this is the last you've seen of him, I assure you, it ain't. People like him don't let others leave his life so easily."

Her mom would know. Daddy seemed to always be in and out of their life. Sometimes for months at a time, but never for good. They never did divorce. Her father never laid a hand on Janet nor belittled her. He would bring her treats whenever he was gone for extended periods of time. Reese's Peanut Butter Cups. They would each get one. As a young child, she believed there was something special with sharing a peanut butter cup with her father. He would pick up toys at garage sales. Dolls, stuffed animals, a rocking horse. She knew they were used and worn, but she cherished those gifts, as rare as they were, because they came at random times. She couldn't recall him ever giving her a gift on her birthday or Christmas.

While it seemed he treated his daughter decently enough, the same couldn't be said for how he treated his wife. It wasn't until after his suspiciously accidental drowning in the bathtub that Janet's mother found some semblance of peace in the form of opiates—but the years of abuse already did the damage. She no longer had to endure the abuse from another person.

Her father's death had a different effect on Janet, and she ended up convincing herself that her fear of Bobby could be a form of love.

She looked up at Stacy who sat next to her on the rumbling motorcycle. Stacy smiled and pointed to the expansive view of the deep blue ocean as they crossed a bridge. Stacy slowed down to point out an iguana sunbathing on a sidewalk. Janet nodded and smiled, but in her mind, she continued running through memories of Bobby.

They stopped at Robbie's Marina in Islamorada. "Thought this might be a fun place to rest," Stacy said.

Janet nodded.

"You ever see tarpon before?" Stacy asked.

Janet shook her head.

"They're huge fish, three or four feet long. You'll see. You can feed them here."

They walked through the oyster shell parking lot, past the stands that sold coconuts painted to look like pirates or monkeys, necklaces and other handmade jewelry, hand-stitched dresses and handbags, and homemade honey.

"We can look at this stuff on the way out. Maybe get you some Florida clothes. Get you out of that Stepford wives get-up."

Janet's lower lip quivered.

"And then we gotta break your habit—crying every time you get embarrassed. And then we're going to stop you from getting embarrassed. But baby steps, baby steps."

Janet swallowed hard. Tears welled up, blurring her vision.

"Want something to drink?"

Janet nodded. "A Coca-Cola," she said, her voice trembling. Bobby only let her drink half at a time and only on special occasions.

The sugar would make her fat, he would say. He was only looking out for her health.

She followed Stacy into the bait shop. Stacy reached into a tub of ice and pulled out a can of beer and a can of Coke. "And a bucket of bait," she said as she paid. "Wait'll you see these things." The big man behind the counter took her money and pointed to a ledge with ten or so buckets of bait lined on it.

Stacy grabbed the bait and led Janet to the dock where people fed dozens of tarpon that frequented the waters. Kids screamed in excitement, and seagulls flapped around trying to steal the bait from the buckets or mid-toss before it hit the water. Twenty or so pelicans floated nearby and sneaked up below the docks to snatch a dangling cigar minnow from an unsuspecting feeder's hand. Janet stood on the pier's edge and stared into the clear water at the large fish swimming below. She popped the top of her soda, put the cold, fizzy, sugary caramel water to her lips, and swallowed. Her eyes closed, not remembering a Coke ever tasting as good. She took another swallow and then another until she drank almost half the can. She lowered it and let out a deep belch that burned her nose and made her smile in surprise. Janet looked over and saw Stacy watching in fascination. Janet smiled, and Stacy thought she witnessed the emergence of the girl she used to know.

"This place is pretty great," Janet said. Janet seemed to slowly shed her past the further south they traveled.

They stood at the edge of the dock. "Here." Stacy held the bucket up with one hand and sipped her beer from the other. "Take a fish."

Janet declined.

"Come on. They won't hurt. They don't have teeth."

"I'm fine. Really," Janet said.

"Hold the bucket." Janet grabbed the bucket from Stacy, and Stacy reached in a grabbed a slimy firm fish. She lied down, belly to the dock, and hung a hand close to the water's edge. A few men stopped watching their kids feed the tarpon and watched Stacy instead. With the right angle, one could get a glimpse under her skirt and make out the lower portion of her butt cheeks peeking out from her thong. She dangled the minnows, sometimes dipping them in the water, teasing the tarpon, daring them to strike. A few kids and older men who fed the tarpon would jump back and drop the minnows in the gaping mouths, scared of the quick striking fish. But Stacy held firm, not even so much as a flinch. Her arm stayed straight as the first tarpon struck and took the minnow and Stacy's arm to the elbow before sliding off and entering the water again. The kids hollered in fascination, and the men clapped in admiration.

"Try it," she said. "It's okay. They don't have teeth. It's more like sandpaper." She showed her arm. White streaks covered her tanned forearm, but no blood. After several more displays of bravery, she finally convinced Janet to hold a minnow by the tail. Janet held it out from her as if it were a soiled diaper. She knelt and held the fish over the water.

"Now, just wait for them to jump. It's scary the first couple of times, but remember, they don't have teeth."

One of the workers walked the dock with a rake to scare off the pelicans. A man next to Janet held a fish just at the surface but jumped back when the fish lurched at them.

The next moment, a tarpon shot out of the water, and Janet snatched her arm back, dropping the minnow into the wide mouth. An unmistakable smile broke on her lips. Stacy put a hand on her shoulder.

"Give me another," Janet said. "That was amazing." Janet never got her hand into the mouth but came close several times.

Stacy did it a few more times to the amazement of the crowd but stopped when the skin finally broke, and drops of blood trickled down her arm.

The sun began to lower as they crossed the Seven-Mile Bridge. Stacy pointed out Fred the Tree. They exited off US 1 as they entered Big Pine Key, turning onto Wilder Road following signs to a bar with no name.

"You've gotta see this," Stacy shouted through the wind.

"I'm just getting really tired," Janet said back.

"But wait until you see this. It's cool. Tiny little deer."

"Stacy, do you ever stop?" Janet shook her head in amazement at her friend's unending enthusiasm.

They didn't see any deer before making it to the bar that didn't have a name.

"It's still a bit early. We'll get a beer and some smoked tuna dip. At dusk, when we head out, we'll see some. I promise."

They walked into the yellow and green building. Thousands of dingy dollars hung on the walls and ceiling. Few folks sat at tables. Two bearded men sat at the bar. The girls took the corner seats. The bartender, Coconut Tam, joked with the men.

"How goes it, fellas?" Stacy said.

"Better now," the one with a bandana said.

Coconut Tam hobbled over wearing a boot from a recent injury.

"Girl," Stacy said. "What in the world did you do to that leg?"

Coconut Tam told her about her scooter accident. "The asshole didn't have any brake lights and I ran right into the back of him. Wait until you see Scuba," she said. "Poor dog."

"He was with you?' Stacy asked.

"He was, but he's fine. Just walks a little funny."

Stacy ordered a beer and the smoked tuna dip, while Janet ordered an unsweetened tea. Janet squeezed the lemon before taking a drink from the straw. Stacy watched her. She picked up her cold bottle of beer and took two big swallows.

"You always drink your beer like that?" one of the bikers said.

Stacy rolled her eyes. "Not always," she said. "Sometimes I drink it like this." She put the neck of the bottle in her mouth and simulated oral sex. The men laughed. Janet looked the other way.

"You are trouble," one of the men said.

"Yes, I am," she said. She noticed Janet looking away. "I'm just joking around with them," she said.

"I get that, but do they know that?" Janet said. She slowly looked back at Stacy. "Don't you think you should be a bit more careful?"

"Ah hell, these guys are harmless," she said.

"Do you know them?"

"Not yet." Then, to the men, "Hey, I'm Stacy Ringling, and this is Janet Schroeder."

"Drexler," Janet said quietly. Stacy looked at her and then looked back at the men.

"I'm Scoot," the bandana man said.

"I'm Harrison," the other said. "It's a pleasure."

"Coconut Tam," Scoot said to the bartender. "Pour these ladies a whiskey, will you?"

"Very nice of you," Stacy said.

As Coconut Tam poured the shots, a family of four walked in and sat at a table. The father stayed on his feet and looked at the pictures and the dollars hanging on the wall. Coconut Tam then went to tend to the new customers.

Stacy lifted her glass to the men. They lifted their glass and took the shot. Stacy still held hers and looked at Janet, waiting to take the shot together. Janet shook her head no.

"You know I don't drink," she said.

"No. I don't know that, Janet Schroeder."

"My name is Janet Drexler. I haven't been Janet Schroeder in a long time."

"Well, drink that shit up, Schroeder. Maybe Janet Drexler doesn't drink, but Schroeder sure as hell does."

Janet sat there. The men watched. Stacy looked straight ahead, shot the whiskey, and sipped the beer. Out of her peripheral, she saw Janet smell the whiskey and then take a sip, just enough to wet her lips. She saw Stacy watching her. Janet smiled, pinched her nose, and then drank about half. Stacy cheered. The men clapped. Janet shivered and scrunched up her face and pushed the shot glass further from her.

Stacy finished it for her.

Leaving, dusk washed the world in a hue of sepia. A three-legged Dalmatian walked up for a pet. "This is Scuba," Stacy said, rubbing the dog behind the ears.

Two small deer approached them from the shrubbery. Janet stood in awe of their beauty.

24

The summer after 10th grade, Bobby Drexler showed up at Janet's trailer on his dirt bike while she sat out on the porch reading *Little Women*.

"Hey now, girl. What do you say we go for a ride?"

She shook her head and walked inside. He spun his tires and left. She hadn't seen him in two years since he was sent to that boys' camp. She didn't know he had been released, and her fear of him came rushing back, like reliving the first night after the dance when he pushed her over the four-wheeler and the year after when she became his girlfriend and felt coerced into doing things with him out of fear.

After Bobby's arrest from the bingo parlor robbery, she felt free. That freedom was now taken from her just as he took her virginity.

A couple of weeks later, the phone rang. People didn't call often and that startled her. Stacy asked her if she wanted to go to the beach in Pensacola with her.

"I'll come by and pick you up," Stacy said.

"I don't think it will be a good idea," Janet said, afraid to leave her house now that she knew Bobby was back. "I don't have a bathing suit," she said as an excuse. It was true, though. While only a forty-minute drive, Pensacola sounded like a big city.

"That's nonsense. We are on the way."

She didn't know what the "we" meant. Were her parents taking them?

"Momma," Janet said. Her momma turned and looked at her. Half-smoked cigarette in her mouth. "Stacy is going to come pick me up and go to the beach."

"Okay," Momma said. She turned back to the soap opera on the television.

"In Pensacola, momma."

"What?"

"We are going to Pensacola."

"Okay."

"I might be gone for a few hours."

"Yes. You might. Do you need some money?"

"That ain't why I asked, momma. But I should probably take some money. Are you okay with me being gone so long?"

"Yeah. Better than you sitting around here all summer reading them books."

Momma reached into her small change purse and pulled a crumpled five-dollar bill.

"Thank you, momma." She bent and kissed her on the head. She wondered how long it had been since she washed her hair, which was frail, stringy, balding, and smelt of sweat and smoke.

Janet waited on the porch, not wanting Stacy to knock on the door and get a glimpse inside. She hid the book under her chair when she saw a truck pulling into the trailer park.

Bobby Drexler drove. Stacy sat in the middle. Lucas on the passenger side.

"Come on," Stacy yelled out of Bobby's open window. "Look who's back."

His left arm hung out the side. His sleeveless shirt showed the rippling muscles of an eighteen-year-old, toned from two years working out in the woods and recently hauling sheetrock and doing lawn maintenance. A kid who would always know the challenges of manual labor yet never earn enough to help support a family. A kid who learned how scarce work could be yet never learned fiscal responsibility. He spent his first paycheck on beer, cigarettes, and gas to drive to Pensacola.

Janet froze. The boys weren't much older than she was, but they seemed like grown men, and she still felt like a child.

Bobby wore gas station aviator glasses that already had a slight bend to them and lowered them on the bridge of his nose. He winked at Janet and smiled—another tooth missing from the side of his mouth.

"Janet, come on, girl," Stacy said again. Janet didn't move. She took a deep breath and looked away. The driver's door opened, and Janet looked back. Stacy crawled over Bobby's lap. He laughed and smacked her butt as she climbed out. Bobby and Lucas laughed again. Bobby stepped out of the truck, walked around to the back, and peed a stream that sounded like a waterfall behind the truck. Stacy walked up the steps to the porch.

"Everything okay?" Stacy asked. She leaned on the railing across from Janet.

"Look," Janet said. She pointed at the opposite end of the porch where a hummingbird feeder hung. The August heat stifling, and she didn't expect to see a hummingbird. It was the first time she had ever seen one in the wild. The tiny little thing flapped its wings as fast as it could while hovering at the bird feeder and then zipped off just as quickly.

"That was beautiful," Janet said.

"It was," Stacy said. "You ready?"

"I don't have a bathing suit. I didn't know we were going with Bobby either."

"He's the only person I know with a car. Don't worry about him. Y'all ain't together anymore. And I've got an extra suit in my bag. Come on. Have you ever been to Pensacola?"

Janet had only a vague memory of going with her parents on one of the occasions when they were getting along. It was as if she were watching a film instead of reliving the memory, like the camera pulled back and she saw her family returning to Sullivan after a day at the beach and about halfway home the parents were no longer getting along. The dad pulled off the side of Highway 29 and forced mother and child from the car. They walked for what felt like hours. The child, maybe four, maybe six. She couldn't remember exactly. She remembered complaining and the mom trying to carry her at times, and then the mom said that she couldn't carry her anymore, and the mother cried. They stopped, and the mom stuck out her thumb, and cars zipped by honking but none stopped, and they continued walking until, finally, the mother spotted the car in the gravel parking lot of a bar on the side of the road. The mom put the child on her hip and entered the bar. Dark and smoky, and there the dad stood over at the pool table and the bartender saying, "you can't bring a child in here", and the mom yelling, "fuck off," loud enough for the dad to stop aiming the cue ball and look up and see the mother and child he abandoned just a few hours before.

"Well, I'll be damned," the father said. He picked up the beer bottle from the edge of the pool table, took a long drink, and set it back down.

The mother, still standing there with the child on her hip, didn't say a word but stared at him, murdered him in her mind. She imagined having a gun and shooting him dead where he stood. And he returned the stare but with a smile, as if he could see what she imagined but knew she would never have the guts to do it. The father said, "The car's open. Y'all wait in there. I'll be out when I finish this game."

Mother and child slept in the backseat, and maybe two hours later, the child woke up because of the mother's snoring and looked out the car window. There were less cars than before in the parking lot. The father walked out some time later, stumbling and laughing with two women. He walked the women to another car before coming to his car and tried to open the locked driver-side door. He saw the awake child, and he made a silly face. Little Janet giggled and made a silly face back. The father then ducked down and disappeared before popping up at a different window, making the child laugh even louder, loud enough to wake the mother and to see father and child playing as if nothing had taken place, as if all were forgotten. The mother unlocked the car doors, and the father got in the driver's seat. Little Janet slept on the drive home, and when she woke up, her father was gone, and her mother told her he was going to live in another house.

25

4 AM, last call. 5 AM and Randall scrubbed the makeup from his face and changed into jeans and a t-shirt. It was one thing to ride into work dressed up as Raven. It was another to ride home like that. Also, closing in high heels and a dress made the job more difficult. He cleaned and locked beer tabs, took the floor mats to the back dock, emptied trash cans, melted the ice, restocked the beer coolers, swept and mopped the floors, and counted his tips. $439. Almost as much as he made out on the water.

He opened the door quietly, knowing that Eli would already be asleep, although he would wake up in another hour or sooner. Stacy would be back home with her friend whom she picked up in Miami. Her childhood friend was coming to stay for a while and trying to escape a bad relationship. Just what they fucking needed, he thought. Rescue a stray when they all needed rescuing themselves.

He grabbed the bottle of vodka and a beer bottle, sat back on the porch, and lit a cigarette. He took a swig of the vodka, a sip of the beer, and then a long drag from the cigarette. Blew out a plume of smoke. Tried shaking the image of the bodies he saw earlier in the day. No use. He knew he had to call it in. He reached into his pocket and pulled out the receipt with the coordinates. Stared at it as he drank his beer. Sighed, took another drag, and set out for a pay phone. One hand held the half-finished beer, the other, the scribbled-on receipt.

Two couples, still going from the night out, walked by in a state of perpetual glee. One of the males wore a pink boa and twirled every few steps. The other male walked with an odd gait, almost as if he tip-toed, like a cartoon villain creeping up on his victim. The two women held hands, swung their arms far out, and howled into the night. Parading around the late-night streets like Merry Pranksters.

"Someone had fun tonight," Randall said.

"It's what happens when you take acid too late in the night," one of the girls said.

The others laughed.

Randall stopped taking psychedelics because it became increasingly more difficult to keep his demons at bay. He wasn't prepared to face them and fight through it. Instead, he attempted to numb them out with alcohol and tobacco, but clearly, that wasn't working either.

He stood at the payphone. He looked around to make sure no one watched him. He finished his beer and then set it on top of the phone. He dialed the police station. When dispatch answered, he held his shirt over his mouth and spoke.

"Write the coordinates down," he said. "Just trust me." He read out the coordinates.

"There are bodies out there," he said. "Weeks, maybe. They are bloated and beginning to be eaten." He listened and then said, "No. I have no idea who they are or how they got there. No. I'm not giving my name, and no, I won't meet with anyone." He listened. "How do you think I saw them? Look. I've said all I need to say. My conscience is clear. On this one, at least." He hung up.

He went back home. Eli sat on the porch. Pajama pants and no shirt. Coffee in one hand and cigarette in the other.

"Are you good?" he said as Randall walked up the steps, sat in the chair next to him, pulled out a cigarette from the pack, and searched his pockets for a lighter.

"What're you doing up?' Randall asked. Eli handed Randall his lit cigarette, and Randall used the cherry to light his. He handed the cigarette back to Eli.

"I should ask you the same. I already heard you come home once," Eli said.

"Couldn't sleep. Just went for a walk."

"Bullshit."

Randall blew out his nose, which could have mistaken for a laugh.

"What about you?" Randall said.

"Shit. You know I don't sleep more than a couple hours at a time."

"Stacy's friend here?"

"Yeah, she's here."

"You talk to her?"

"I met her. She's in your room."

"She's what?"

"Stacy said that you said that she can use your room."

"Are you fucking kidding me? For how long?"

"I don't know, man. A couple of weeks."

"Goddamn it."

"Look, man," Eli said. "I think I'm going to bail on this place. I think I'm finished here. I can't keep doing this, you know? Fifteen

years of making black jokes for white people and letting them fulfill a fantasy of chaining up a brother."

"I hear you. Crazy what we do for money, isn't it?"

"Downright degrading at times."

"What about Stacy?"

"Come on, man. I love the girl, you know that. But she's young. She has her whole life to find someone better than me."

"Not sure she's even looking."

"You're probably right."

"Mexico?"

"I think so."

"Any idea when?"

"Soon. I have someone who wants to buy the rental home. Let me rephrase that. We are closing on it tomorrow."

"Hot damn. You made a killing, didn't you?

"Pretty good."

"What about this one?"

"I ain't kicking y'all out if that's what you are asking."

Randall laughed. "I appreciate that."

"I have something set up for it, too."

They sat silently and watched a helix of insects swirl about the yellow street lamp. A cat marched by, owning the road, proud and full of self-assurance until something spooked it, and it paused and crouched low, unmoving in an attempt to go unnoticed before it darted across the street under the bougainvillea.

"It's really happening, huh?"

"I already have a plane ticket."

"Goddamn, man. Like soon?"

"Yeah, and now Stacy bringing this girl in kind of threw me off, but everything is already set in motion. Can't turn back now."

"Damn, man. Stacy doesn't know anything about this?"

Eli shook his head.

Randall didn't know what to say. He sat in silence.

"No charter today?" Eli asked.

"Shit. Don't have one scheduled until next week."

"I bet *Victory* ain't got that problem."

Randall looked over at Eli, and they both laughed.

"I'm sure they don't," Randall said. "I'm going to try and get some sleep." He stubbed out his cigarette and left the half on the ashtray for when he awoke.

"Good luck."

26

A guard dragged Bobby from a bed stained with urine, blood, and shit. He never felt pain like that, a burning fire as if someone held a flame to his anus. Three different men took turns on him as he went in and out of consciousness. Powerless for the first time in his life. Instead of crying, anger welled up inside more than he ever experienced, so much so that he briefly thought he would die. Mortality never crossed his mind until that moment. Fear. Helplessness. All these were things he could suppress previously but never again.

Once the last of the men finished with him, he slept until another guard dragged him from the bed, undressed him, and shoved him into a cinder block shower. He squatted in the corner, arms around his legs, shivering. The guard stepped in, turned on the water, and stepped out. Stood watching over him. The cold shower water blended with the remaining streaks of shit and blood that dried on his ass and legs and swirled down the drain. The fire in his ass was nearly unbearable. The guard tossed him a bar of lye. It slid across the mildewed tile and rested against his feet.

"Scrub down," the guard said.

Bobby lifted his eyes and saw the man standing over him, not averting his eyes but with a look of indignation. The guard didn't enjoy this treatment as the others did, but he wasn't doing anything to stop it. Bobby pulled the soap to him, slowly scrubbed his arms, armpits, and chest into what little lather he could, and ran his hands through his greasy hair. He shivered now nearly uncontrollably, his lips turning light blue. He rubbed the soap on his balls and his legs and then grimaced as he washed between his crack.

"That's enough now," the guard said, handing him a towel. Rough and frayed.

Bobby stepped from the shower and the guard handed him a white T-shirt, blue pants, woolen socks, and boots.

"Tuck your shirt in, boy," the guard said.

Bobby did. He led Bobby out of the cinder block building and down a pine straw driveway to another building. Bobby walked in front, and the guard followed closely behind. Another guard waited for them, the same guard from when he first arrived, the first man to have beat him.

"I got him from here," the man said.

"I'm sorry," the other guard said quietly, leaning close into Bobby's ear. He turned Bobby loose and turned away.

The guard smiled and said, "How're you feeling?"

Bobby didn't answer. He stood still against a terror that he never felt before, afraid to step any closer. He didn't know what hid behind the doors. His chest heaved with every breath. He struggled to slow his breathing.

"Maybe you didn't hear me," the guard said.

"I heard you," Bobby said.

The countenance on the man's face changed.

Bobby noticed quickly and added, "Sir. I heard you, sir. I'm okay."

The man smiled. "You beat a dog enough, and he'll learn. Let me show you where you'll be sleeping." He opened the door to the large bunkhouse—a military-style dorm. Enough beds stacked on each other for forty kids to sleep. The kids were all black.

Bobby stood looking around. About half of the kids sat up on their beds. A few sitting at the card table stopped their game of spades to look at the new kid. The rest of them didn't bother showing any change at all. It was just another day, and it didn't matter if the new kid was black, white, or orange.

"He'll only be here for a night until we get him a bed in the other dorm. Y'all don't be hard on him now." He patted Bobby on the back a little extra hard and whispered, "Ain't no way I'd close my eyes in here tonight. Not surrounded by this many niggers," and then he walked out.

A squirrely-looking boy stood and said, "Why would they throw a white boy in here?"

Bobby stood still, carefully avoiding eye contact with anyone. He focused his eyes on the water-stained ceiling tiles in the back of the long room.

Another larger kid stood, not wearing a shirt and looking well over twenty years old with a nearly full beard and said, "What kind of welcome are we giving him?" in a baritone voice. He started a slow walk toward the front. He smiled.

Bobby lowered his eyes to see who approached him. "I don't need no goddamn welcome," Bobby said. "Just show me to my bunk."

The room erupted in laughter. More kids stood. "Ah, shit," someone shouted. "Let's get ready to rumble," another said. Someone else hollered out, "White boy's crazy." The shirtless boy got within a few feet of Bobby and said, "You like to fight?"

"I like it all right," Bobby said.

Before the fight started, another boy, light-skinned with reddish hair and freckles, wearing glasses, lying on the first bed closest to Bobby, and reading a collection of poems from Etheridge Knight said, "Ain't a damn one of you fighting in here." The room quieted. "You all are some stupid motherfuckers. That's what they want. They put him in here in hopes that one of us beats his ass. Then whoever beats his ass will be dragged out to the White House and beat too. They get you to do their dirty work and get one of us as a bonus."

The big boy stopped and said, "Damn. Reggie is always speaking the truth, ain't he?"

Reggie said, "Just show him to his bed."

Big Boy did as Reggie said. "Come on. It's in the back."

Bobby looked down at Reggie. When he looked up, no one seemed to pay him any mind. He limped forward. Every step caused pain. Reggie shook his head.

"Hey, white boy," Reggie called out. Bobby stopped and turned back. "They fucked you up, didn't they?"

Bobby nodded. Very slightly. Reggie shook his head again. "Fucking monsters," he said. Bobby nodded again in agreement and shuffled on.

The bed, a flimsy twin-sized mattress on the last row next to the toilets. The only one not a bunk as if it were just dragged in. There were no blankets or pillows—just a thin, lumpy, stained mattress.

"They didn't give you anything?" Big Boy asked. "No toothbrush, shower shoes, nothing?"

Bobby shook his head. Looked down at the bed.

"Don't talk much, huh?"

Bobby shook his head no but didn't bother looking up.

"Damn shame."

Bobby lowered himself to the bed, adjusting his weight on one buttcheek so as not to put pressure on the pain. It hurt to lean over to take off his shoes. He used his toes to press on the heel to remove them. They wouldn't come off. He gave up and lifted his feet to the bed, but it hurt to lay on his back. He rolled onto his left side and lay there quietly while the rest of the bunkhouse continued as if before. Some played cards, some read, some played dominos, and a couple folded a piece of paper into a triangle and flicked it between hands held up like goalposts.

The end-of-the-day routine began about an hour before lights out to ensure everyone could use the bathroom and brush their teeth. A row of cubby holes in the back held their toiletries. The toilets were behind a half wall with no doors. Three stainless steel toilets next to each other with no partition. Four sinks hung on the opposite wall. The showers were in the same room. Five shower heads along the far back wall. Beige, peeling paint covered mildewed cinder blocks.

Bobby watched the boys work in perfect, synchronized order. As some finished up, the next went in. When they all finished, Bobby still lay there. Big Boy approached him with a toothbrush still in plastic and a small travel-sized toothpaste.

"Here ya go," Big Boy said. He tossed them both onto the bed.

Bobby didn't say anything in return. Didn't move.

"Hey," Big Boy said a bit louder.

Bobby looked up but still didn't move.

"Get your ass up and brush your nasty-ass teeth."

Bobby shifted his gaze away, but Big Boy didn't move. Slowly, Bobby stood from the bed and went to the bathroom. When he came back to the darkened room, a yellow glow shined from an outside light through one of the small windows. A sheet and pillow were on his bed.

27

E li acquired the two-bedroom, two-bath cottage built in 1943 nearly fifteen years ago. When he first arrived in Key West, he met an older widow, a white woman, who gave him a room to rent. He kept her company in her old age, and she grew to love him. He loved her, too. People around town thought that sex was part of the arrangement, but no one knew for certain, and Eli didn't care enough to discuss it. Her husband and only child, a nineteen year old son, died in a tugboat accident off the Cayman Island shores. They typically spent months out on commercial jobs and would return home for an extended stay. Her son only worked with the father for two months when the tragedy happened. She never got the full story. All she knew was that there was an explosion, and both her husband and son were killed. She received a very large insurance settlement, but millions of dollars didn't replace the loneliness she felt.

Eli and her relationship didn't make sense to many people, and Eli comforted her by saying most things didn't make sense. When she died at the age of seventy-eight of an aneurysm while tending her flowers, she left Eli the house. She left him another one-bedroom rental house a few blocks away, too. He knew she didn't have family left but never expected her to leave him anything. She donated her money to the arts. But with the real estate boom, he sat on plenty of money.

When Stacy moved to Key West, Eli heard her play some songs. In between her humorous songs of sex and violence, she sang some very tender ones that made him want to cry. Stacy lived in a van. Eli offered her a room. Not long after, she shared his bed. Later, they rented the extra room to a charter boat captain. Stacy made enough money playing guitar and singing songs to pay her portion of the utilities and buy enough food to survive. She didn't have to work besides continuing to work on her craft.

Just after dark, Stacy and Janet pulled into Old Town, Key West. A shadowed figure sat on the front porch drinking a beer when they arrived at the house. A big man, maybe six-five. Janet never really knew a black person before. The few at her school kept to themselves, so she interacted little with them. A few customers came in at the convenience store where she worked, and she once realized that every time a black person entered, she got nervous and wondered if they would rob her. She was robbed twice before. Both times by white men. One she knew. She was aware of her unfounded fear of black people, but it was there regardless.

Janet wondered how Bobby would feel about Stacy pulling up to her house and ... a black person waited on the porch. Bobby would've used the other word, and that was the word she stopped herself from saying in her head. She felt horrible for even thinking it and was surprised that was the first word that she thought. Bobby was very open about how he felt toward black people. Although she was used to racism, and she was aware of her unintentional racism, the way Bobby displayed it always made her feel a bit uncomfortable. She remembered their first Christmas together when Bobby came over to her mother's and brought a bag of mixed nuts as a gift for Janet's mom. And when Janet's mom opened it, Bobby started rattling off their names, "Walnuts, pee-cans—hell, I don't know what these are. Some other kinds. I think there might even be a few nigger toes in there, too." And he said it not as a joke and with no hesitation. Just as matter-of-factly as he named the other nuts—as if the company used that name on the packaging. Janet said he shouldn't say things like that, and he yelled at her when they got back in the car, telling her never to correct him in public again and purposefully humiliate him. "Hell, that's what everyone calls them," he said.

"They are called Brazilian nuts, Bobby," she said.

He lifted a hand so fast that it took her a minute to realize he smacked her in the mouth. Her lip scabbed over by the time they arrived for dinner at his uncle's house.

Rooster, that's what they called his mother's brother, stepped up as the male figure in Bobby's life after his daddy ran off. Bobby saw Rooster off and on growing up because he was regularly in and out of jail. But he would take him around when he wasn't in jail. Took him to some dog fights, the clay pits to shoot guns, and bought him a whore when he turned thirteen.

Janet was jolted back into the present when she saw Stacy run up, put her arms around the big man, and kiss him. Janet had never seen a white woman kiss a black man—and not just any black man—a very large, one-eyed black man.

"Janet, this is Eli. Eli the Great," Stacy said.

"Your boyfriend?" Janet asked. She quickly became aware of the tone of her question and wondered if the whisky made her talk that way. Then, she wondered how long since she last drank alcohol. With Bobby's drinking, she became a firm believer in the evils of it. Stacy made her forget that for a brief moment. She questioned if maybe the devil tested her back there at the bar and she failed. What if she were to stay and be by Bobby's side when he finally realized his mistakes? What if she were placed on this earth to be Bobby's savior? And yet, she abandoned her purpose, her calling, and jaunted off to Key West to drink and consort with a woman like Stacy.

"Something like that, but Stacy wouldn't ever call me that," Eli said. Stacy gave him a sideways glance. "It's a pleasure to meet you, Janet." He extended his hand.

Janet was taken aback by his slow, deep, theatrical voice. She took his hand, large and soft.

"You have no idea how excited Stacy's been since you agreed to visit."

She only nodded in response. When he let go of her hand, hers lingered and slowly lowered to her side.

"Guess what he does for a living?" Stacy said. She reached into a cooler by the porch chairs and pulled out a bottled beer. She stuck the bottle under her shirt and twisted off the cap, letting the cap fall to the porch.

"I don't know," Janet replied, afraid to find out.

"Oh, come on and guess."

"Baby, why don't y'all come inside first?" Eli said.

"In a minute. Come on. One guess." Stacy bounced from foot to foot, childlike. She took a long pull from her beer and wiped her mouth with the back of her hand.

"I don't know," Janet said. She feared that if she said what she thought, it would offend him. "I don't know."

"He's a...you'll never believe it...a magician."

"Oh," Janet said. "I would not have guessed that."

"I know," Stacy said. "How cool is that?"

"An escape artist," Eli said.

"But you do magic tricks, too. You get hired to put on other kinds of shows besides escapes. He just did a kid's birthday party."

"That's just to pay the bills. I'm an escape artist, though."

"Yes, honey. You're an escape artist—the best I've seen, too. It's fascinating, Janet."

Eli said, "You go on inside. I'll get your things." He stepped from the porch to retrieve the bags from the motorcycle.

It was dark and hot inside. The windows were open, and when Stacy turned on a lamp without a lampshade, a few insects hovered over the exposed light bulb. A skink scurried across the far wall.

"You're in the tropics, honey. You'll get used to the insects and other creepy crawlers. And the heat." It was mid-September, muggy and hot—not too unlike Sullivan. However, when Janet left Sullivan, she felt the first hints of an early fall: lower humidity and cool mornings. The difference in climate between North Florida and South Florida was noticeable in the winter.

"We don't have central air. Can you believe that? In this day and age, a house without AC. All we got is tiny window units in the bedrooms."

It seemed Stacy forgot what Sullivan was like, as if she were explaining Florida to a Northerner.

"You hungry?" Stacy asked.

"A little," Janet said. "I could eat, but I don't want to be any trouble."

"I could fry up a few eggs?"

"Whatever you want to do," Janet said.

"Hey, babe," Eli said, coming inside with the bag and the squished dozen roses. "Where would you like these? Is Randall letting her use his room?"

"Yeah, yeah. Just throw it in there. I think he said it's cool."

"No, that's all right," Janet said. "I'm okay on the couch." She didn't know another man lived there, too.

Stacy scrambled eggs with diced tomatoes served over Cuban bread, and Janet stood by the counter while she cooked. Eli grabbed two beers from the fridge. "Would you like one?" he asked Janet. She shook her head. He popped the tops and gave one to Stacy. Stacy took a drink and sat it beside the stove, next to her other one, a swallow left at the bottom.

"Would you like anything to drink?" he asked.

"Just a water, thank you."

He took a plastic cup from the cupboard, a Sloppy Joe's souvenir cup, and filled it from the faucet. "Sorry, we are out of ice."

"I'm okay without any ice," she said.

Stacy served the eggs, tomatoes, and a slice of toasted bread, and they ate.

28

Twelve-year-old Eli lay in his mother's bed with a patch over his eye. When the doctor first said he would never see out of it again, Eli didn't believe him. Four years later, he started to think that it was true. He would never see his father again either, his mother told him. He was in trouble, and to protect them, he would have to stay away forever. And now, his mother was in no shape to care for him and sent him off to live with her sister in Miami.

He left and that was the last he saw of his mother.

Because he was a big kid, his mother bought him a Greyhound bus ticket down the coast to Naples and across the Tamiami Trail. She told Eli that if anyone asked, he was to say he was fifteen. No one asked. He sat near the front and did his best not to cry. A woman smelling of mothballs sat next to him. She snored. The sky burned orange behind them as they began the crossing of Alligator Alley. Eli had never been out of Tampa, and this was the first time seeing the Everglades. He knew this was where the Seminoles lived. His father, although black, used to tell him he was part Indian, that his ancestors were Black Seminoles. He didn't know what that meant. But looking out at the vast prairie land, he imagined the ghosts of his past family living out there.

He carried a book with him that he forgot to return to the school library but knowing he was never returning to that school, packed it with him. *The Unmasking of Robert-Houdin* by Harry Houdini. He found it tucked in the biography section and, having heard of Harry Houdini, thought it would be a book on performing magic tricks.

Being a one-eyed kid in elementary school and as big as he was made him an outcast. Kids feared him, and he thought they would like him if he could entertain them with card tricks or juggling. The book revealed nothing about performing magic tricks. Houdini wrote the book to debunk another magician that came before him, Jean-Eugène Robert-Houdin. He didn't know the definition or how to pronounce many of the words, but it fascinated him that the most famous magician, Harry Houdini, wrote a book calling another famous magician a fraud. And so he kept reading.

On the little card in the back of the book that he signed to check it out, he saw that nobody checked it out before. The pages were yellowed, and when he held it, it felt like he held a book of spells. He decided that even if he didn't understand everything he read, if he would still read it, somehow, the spirit of Houdini and the spirit of magic would possess him. Something told him that reading that book was necessary for him to learn magic. And so he trudged on. When he finished reading chapter eight, "The Suspension Trick," he reread it. He was rereading this chapter on the bus and realized that he had performed his first escape trick. The other students in his class would think he just disappeared. He imagined his dad as an escape artist and performed an escape so extraordinary no one could ever locate him. If anyone ever asked about his dad, that was the story he would tell.

The urge to pee brought him out of his head and brought him back to the sensory world. Afraid to wake the sleeping lady, he held it until it hurt. Finally, he chose between waking the snoring lady or pissing himself. He nudged her shoulder.

"Excuse me, mam," Eli said. She didn't move. "Mam," Eli said louder, shaking her shoulder harder. She awoke with a start.

"Don't touch me," she said too loudly.

Eli panicked. "I'm sorry," he said. "I need to go to the bath-room."

"What?" she said too loudly again. Passengers started peering over their seats at the commotion. Eli saw the driver's eyes watching through the rearview mirror.

"I really need to go to the bathroom," he said.

"Excuse me, son," the driver said, looking through the rearview mirror, "Is there a problem?"

"I don't know what he needs," the woman said. More heads perked up from the seats behind them. Excited about a possible confrontation.

"I just need to go to the bathroom," he said a bit louder.

"Then why didn't you say that?" the driver said.

"I did," Eli said. He felt tears welling in his eyes. He felt his breathing get faster. His bladder hurt. The woman didn't move. "Mam," Eli said louder, "I'm about to piss my pants."

The bus driver looked through the rearview again and said to no one in particular, "This is why kids shouldn't be riding alone." He then continued, "Kid. You are causing a nuisance. I need you to sit down."

"I have to pee," Eli said through the tears. And then he peed. He felt a warmth of shame and relief.

The woman screamed and stood in the aisle. The bus driver pulled off the side of the road. Everyone stepped off the bus while the driver cleaned the puddle with disinfectant. Passengers smoked cigarettes. Eli stood off by himself with his head hung in embarrassment. People complained about the heat. Not everyone could squeeze into the little bit of shade the bus provided. A white lady of about thirty traveling with two younger kids approached him.

"I'm sorry that happened to you," she said.

Eli looked up.

"How old are you?' she asked.

Eli wiped the snot from his nose with the back of his hand. "I'm fifteen," he said.

The woman looked at him. He knew she didn't believe him.

"I'm twelve," he said.

She shook her head. "Do you have luggage with you? A change of pants?"

Eli pointed to the belly of the bus. "It's in there."

The lady stepped onto the bus and spoke with the driver. The driver agreed to find his luggage. People moaned as he removed suitcases and duffle bags until he found Eli's. The lady unzipped the tattered suitcase and found him a pair of jeans. He went into the bathroom on the bus and changed clothes. When he came out, people boarded again and were ready to continue to Miami. The bus driver made him leave his wet pants on the side of the road.

The old lady moved to a seat in the back of the bus, and Eli sat by himself in the front. He closed his eyes and pretended to sleep until he did fall asleep. He dreamed that it was not on a bus full of strangers and that he would not live with a lady he didn't know. He dreamed he belonged to a family that didn't abandon him. He dreamed of standing in front of a crowd, strapped in a straight jacket and chains, and performing escape acts that amazed strangers and made him a household name—the Evil Knieval of escape artists.

29

Spending the night in the black boys' dorm didn't result in the beating the guards hoped, so early the following day, Bobby Drexler was transferred to the white boy's side. No time to get dressed or put on shoes. The guards yelled at him to grab his belongings, which weren't much, and start walking.

He carried his issued uniform, shoes, and toiletries bunched up in his arms and, forgetting to slip his feet into the dorm slippers, limped over barefoot on the dewy pine straw path. During the walk, two guards yelled for him to move faster. One kicked him in his ass, and the pain and humiliation shot through him. His head swam in confusion, still half-sleeping. It seemed like a boot camp that he didn't sign up for. The guards escorted him to the dorm, and the door shut behind him. No introduction. He stood there dumbfounded, staring at the white boys who started their day—making beds, doing pushups, brushing teeth, taking shits.

He heard someone say, "Nigger lover arrived." Some boys laughed. Another said, "That's why he's walking funny. They took his booty last night." More boys laughed.

An acne-faced boy with eyes too close together and ridges on his forehead that gave his face a permanent scrunched-up scowl walked toward Bobby. When Acne got within reach, Bobby dropped his belongings and threw a quick punch that landed directly on the kid's nose. Blood splattered. The kid folded to the ground. Bobby lifted a leg high and stomped down on the wrinkled forehead. The place grew quiet for a second before other boys swarmed him. He threw wild punches. Connected a few. But ultimately, he ended up curled on the ground with hands over his head as kicks bruised his ribs. Two guards pulled him out of there, and he spent the next week in the hole.

Isolation. A small slit of a window allowed little light to see during the day and just enough air circulation to not suffocate. A wooden cot. A bucket for a toilet that didn't get emptied every day. Toasted white bread and an apple in the morning with a cup of water. A cup of water in the afternoon. Beans, bread, a hunk of brown meat in the evening. He didn't eat the first night. The guards didn't serve him until he ate the previous meal. By the third day, the toilet bucket needed emptying, and the smell was unbearable. A guard wearing a mask and gloves entered to empty it and returned it, not washed out but emptied. The guard never spoke to him, and Bobby didn't say anything either. He cried more than he ever cried. He wished for death but couldn't devise a way to kill himself in there. He thought about starving himself but didn't know how long that would take. Without realizing it, he prayed. He didn't know to what or to whom. Having never been to church or raised in a family that spoke of God, he wasn't sure how he learned of the concept of God, but there it was. His voice rusty and unfamiliar, as if someone else prayed for him.

"What do I do?" he said, dropping to his knees. "Like this?" He clasped his hands together. "Do I just speak? Like, ask for what I want?" He remembered one time in elementary school when the kids wrote out Christmas lists to Santa Claus, and the teacher mailed the letters to the North Pole. Of course, he didn't get anything he asked for, and when he asked his uncle, his uncle told him that Santa wasn't real. He always thought of prayer like that, people making stupid wishes to an imaginary being, some goofy genie. But at that moment, he wondered, what did it hurt?

"Can you kill me, Lord? Just let me die."

And just like Santa, his wish didn't come true.

"Let's go, you nasty little shit-stained rat," a guard said one morning instead of giving him his breakfast, and that solidified it. No magic fairy could save him. To survive the cruel and lonely world, he would become more ruthless than anyone he knew or met.

Bobby followed him, weak-legged, to the same building as when he first arrived, the same showers. The guard hosed him off again, told him to wash up, and led him to an open hall cafeteria. White and black boys ate together. Maybe one hundred of them. They watched as Bobby entered the line to get his tray. Powdered eggs, toast, hockey puck sausage patty, a carton of milk. He sat down at the closest table. The boys talked in a low murmur.

"We had bets to see if you'd die in there," a skinny black boy said.

"We ain't ever seen someone go to the hole on their first day," a white kid said. He whistled through two chipped front teeth, one in a late stage of decay.

"Wasn't too bad," Bobby said. "They could've left me there. I'd've been fine."

Another white kid said, "Just so you know, fighting isn't allowed in here. We are only allowed to fight when they have boxing matches. After they saw what you did to Malcolm, I bet we see some boxing matches soon."

Bobby ate everything on his plate and then vomited it back up onto the tray when he finished.

A guard walked by and laughed, "Goddamn Bobby. Don't you know you must ease back into the real world after a week in the hole? You don't have to act tough no more. We see you, young buck. Ain't no one here going to mess with you anymore. I mean, none of these kids will. And we won't either as long as you obey. You hear me?"

Bobby looked up and nodded.

"What did you say?" the guard said. "I ain't quite hear you."

"I said, yes, sir."

"Good, now clean your mess up."

30

Janet stared at the ceiling in the strange bedroom in the morning, not wanting to be awake before anyone else, so she lay there and listened for any sign of movement. The walls were bare. A dresser with a makeup vanity setting on it and a nightstand. No door to the closet. A few men's button-up shirts, but mostly women's gowns. She knew the bedroom belonged to a male, and she thought the clothing was curious. She felt odd sleeping in another man's bed and hoped Stacy washed the sheets before she got there. If all men were like Bobby, the sheets may have never been washed. She didn't think too hard about it when she went to sleep the night before, exhausted from traveling, but now she moved her legs around to feel for sand. She didn't feel any and that gave her some slight relief.

She thought she heard some movement. She listened more intently. Did a door shut? And then the noise happened again and became rhythmic. She heard Stacy moaning. She tried to cover her ears with the pillow but surprisingly felt the urge to listen. She felt disgusted with herself but also turned on. But then she thought of Bobby and became disgusted again. Bobby was the only person she ever slept with and never enjoyed it, unlike Stacy, who sounded like she enjoyed herself very much. Janet hated it. She loved it when Bobby would get too drunk and fall asleep on the couch or the porch or, better yet, not even come home—only a slight tinge of guilt for hoping that he would die in a car accident. Sex with Bobby was always violent, but the noises in the room next to her were not. It sounded like what she imagined it would sound like before she met Bobby. She learned to fake the sounds because it would end quicker when she did. Stacy sounded genuine, though.

She cried. Not sure if she cried because she was finally free or because she wasted so many years allowing Bobby to control her. Although still frightened of him, she slowly gained strength with him gone. Stacy caught her at one of her most decisive moments when she agreed to fly down and visit, and that strength continued once on the plane and led to this moment. She knew if she waited for Bobby's release from prison, and if he came back home, which she knew he would, all that strength would've drained away from her almost immediately. Bobby possessed that kind of power over her. And she hated herself for it. With his release soon approaching, she found the courage to flee. It still felt surreal and frightening, but she couldn't change anything that happened. All she could do was endure what came next.

The noise in the next room stopped. A shower started, and movement sounded in the kitchen. A cabinet shut, some pots and pans banged around. She wiped her eyes and waited a couple more minutes, hoping the redness subsided and that it wasn't too obvious that she cried.

In the kitchen, Eli stood in plaid pajama pants and a tank-top undershirt, making a pot of coffee.

"Good morning," he said.

"Good morning," she said, still not used to such a deep voice. "Stacy up yet?"

"Shower. How do you take your coffee?"

Randall lifted his head over the couch and said, "Black."

"I know you like it black. I asked the lady. I apologize about him."

"I'm Janet," she said. "Thank you for the room."

"Ain't no problem," Randall said. "Nice to meet you."

"Cream and sugar?" Eli asked.

Janet nodded her head and sat at the round dining table. Randall walked around from the couch wearing a "Where is Bum Farto?" t-shirt and frayed jeans cut above the knees. He shook her hand, and sat at the table. Janet looked at him a bit longer, trying to discern the remnants of makeup on his face.

Eli brought them each a cup, got him one, and sat down.

"Did you sleep well?' Randall asked.

"I did," Janet said. "I'm so sorry about using your room. I didn't know you would end up on the couch."

"It's no big deal."

"I'll take the couch. You take your room back."

"No, seriously. I've got a boat I can crash on."

Eli looked at him. He knew Randall's boat didn't have a cabin. Randall gave him a look back, presumably saying, I'm a grown man and can figure out what I will do.

Stacy then walked from the bedroom, wearing shorts, a tank top, and a towel on her head.

"How'd you sleep?" Stacy asked. She tilted her head and looked at Janet with such sympathy Janet nearly cried again.

Janet nodded her head in response.

"We are so glad you are here," Stacy said. Eli looked back down and nodded in agreement. Stacy reached across the table and took hold of both of Janet's hands. "You are amazing, and we are here for you."

Janet lowered her head. Tears fell. "It's okay," Stacy said.

Janet looked at Eli and Randall and said, "Y'all must think I'm crazy."

"I've told them why you are here. They know about Bobby," Stacy said.

"And if that motherfucker tries to contact you," Randall said, "He'll have to answer to all of us."

Eli set Stacy's coffee on the table and sat back.

"All right," Stacy said. "You'll have plenty of time to cry. But right now, I want to show you your welcoming gift." Stacy stood. You could still see her cheerleading ways. Eli smiled. That was one of the things that he loved about her and knew he'd miss the most about her. Her joyfulness, her optimism, it was all contagious. And he didn't know if he still had it in him anymore. He wasn't sad. He didn't feel hopeless either. Maybe ambivalence. But he didn't think that was the right word. He felt content with the acceptance of everything. Good, bad, evil, miraculous. True acceptance, he thought, and he didn't ever want to see Stacy reach that level in life. She still spoke of hopes, dreams, and ambitions. He no longer did, and he knew that meant they should part ways. Now his decision centered on when the right time would be to tell her. Housing in Key West was nearly impossible for working-class people. Maybe he could write out an agreement that left her the house, but as long as he still lived, they would send him rent money, and he could use that to live in Mexico. That seemed reasonable to him.

Stacy saw him looking at her contemplatively, and she scrunched up her eyebrows in a questioning look. He smiled at her. She smiled back—a truly radiant smile—a smile that wasn't for anyone in particular but for the world.

"Janet," Stacy said, "I told Eli and Randall what a brilliant artist you were in school. It was unbelievable the things she

141

painted. She won first place in the Pensacola fair when we were in middle school. Remember that?"

Janet nodded. Her lips trembled as if she might cry again.

Stacy left the kitchen and came back from her room with a tripod easel. She set it up in the living room, and she set a digital camera, a Casio QV-10, and a map of Old Town on the table.

"What is that?" Janet asked.

"What do you mean, 'what is that?' You know damn well what it is."

"I know what it is. What I meant is, why are you bringing it out here? I don't paint anymore."

"I tried to tell you..." Eli began to say, but Stacy cut him off with a look. But he said it anyway, just a bit quieter. "Don't be forcing shit on to this girl."

Randall looked at him and smiled.

"Look," Stacy continued in her bubbly manner as if she were clueless to Janet's reaction, but she wasn't. She was never clueless to people's reactions. She believed that if she maintained an upbeat, optimistic attitude, those around her would eventually take on that same sentiment, and oftentimes that proved right. "I got you a couple of different sizes of canvases. Didn't know which you prefer. And I got oil paints, isn't that what you use? Hold on." She returned with her arms full and laid them on the table. Eli moved her coffee out of the way.

"I told you that I don't..." Janet started to say.

"Look, and here is a pallet. Everything you need. Wait, look, even an apron."

"What have you done? Do you know how long it's been? I can't paint for nothing now. I appreciate it, though. I do, but..."

"But nothing. Remember, I would be a musician, and you would be an artist. I haven't given up."

"Well, I did." Janet cut her off this time. And it stopped Stacy briefly.

Eli raised his eyebrows. Randall smirked. In a way, they knew that Stacy worked her magic by hearing Janet speak assertively.

"I'm going to head down to the boat," Randall said.

"I'm going to join you," Eli said.

And as they left, still no one spoke.

"Not yet," Stacy said. "Not while you're here with me. You asked for my help, and I'm going to help you. You're going to start back up. A natural's a natural. You haven't lost any talent. You'll be back in no time. I have to go to work here in a bit, but take a walk around—plenty of things to paint. Take my camera, too. Just enjoy it. Enjoy being alone and being able to do whatever you want. Absolute freedom. I know. It's hard. But you've already taken the biggest step. I love you."

"I don't know how to use a camera like that." It was the first time Janet had seen a digital camera.

Stacy showed her. Janet couldn't contain a smile when she saw that the photos were instantly displayed on a screen on the back of the camera.

"I want at least one small canvas done before I get home from the lunch shift. Then, you can come with me to watch Eli perform before I return to work. Got a gig tonight at the Hog's Breath. You'll love it. It's a good time."

"I don't know," Janet said again.

"If you get hungry, stop by where I'm working—the Blue Heaven. Just ask around if you get lost. Someone will point you in the right direction. Eli checked the tires on a bicycle and said he'd leave it locked out front in case you'd rather not walk. Biking in Key West is the way to go."

"Thank you," Janet said.

"But first, let me fix your hair."

31

Eli's Aunt Liza lived alone in Carol City and cleaned condos in Surfside. A few days after Eli arrived, she told him matter-of-factly that his mother died as he ate a bowl of Cheerios before school.

"What happened to her?" he said, unsure why he didn't cry.

"Drugs," Aunt Liza said.

Drugs. Such a vague word that didn't mean anything to him. It contained nothing solid for his brain to imagine.

"What kind of drugs?" he asked.

"What?" Aunt Liza said. She made a ham and cheese sandwich on white bread to take to work.

"What kind of drugs killed her?"

"Heroin." Aunt Liza looked over at him.

"Okay," he said, looking back down into his bowl of cereal and eating a spoonful. When he swallowed, he said, "What is that?"

"You inject it. With a needle."

Eli nodded. "Yeah, she was doing that."

"I know," Aunt Liza said. "I'm sorry, sweetie." She put the sandwich in her purse, slung it over her shoulder, and squeezed his shoulder as she walked by him. "I'm working late tonight, okay? There is a pizza in the freezer."

"Okay," Eli said. "Did you sign my permission slip? We are going to the fair today."

She stopped and looked at him. "It's on the table."

Aunt Liza left for work, and Eli washed his bowl, set it on the drying rack, brushed his teeth, grabbed his book bag, and headed out the door to catch the city bus to school. Sixth grade. New city, new school, new home, no parents, and one eye.

Three male teachers took thirty one students on a school bus to spend the day at the Miami Youth Fair. The three teachers taught their classes in portable classrooms and operated outside the norms of the rest of the school. The students passed freely from class to class throughout the day, and the administration allowed these teachers to follow their own rules. Wasn't easy to find male middle school teachers, or teachers in general, so certain things were overlooked. Eli felt lucky to be in their classes, and when Mr. C discovered he knew magic, he would often ask Eli to perform the latest tricks he learned, such as simple card tricks, sleight of hand, and juggling. The kids were intrigued, and Mr. C cheered loudly, making Eli feel like a true performer. Instead of being known as the one-eyed freak, he felt like he belonged, even though he didn't have friends. He felt that the teachers were friends enough. The other kids still thought him weird, but at least they didn't make fun of him. Mr. C made sure of it.

The bus parked. Mr. C quieted the kids down, and they listened. The other two teachers already stepped off the bus. Eli sat up front and looked up at Mr. C as he spoke.

"All right. Here is the plan," Mr. C said, "You have three hours to do what you want. Check out some of the student exhibits. Don't spend all your time riding the rides. Or do. It's your field trip. It's 9:30 am, so be back on this bus by 12:30 pm. Stick with a friend. Don't do anything stupid. Don't be late. If

I have to look for you, you'll be sorry. Don't ruin this, and don't get me in trouble. I'm going out on a limb so you guys can have fun. Now go have some fun and be smart."

The kids cheered, and Mr. C walked off the bus.

The other teachers at the school couldn't understand how Mr. C got middle schoolers to listen so well, but they did, and because of that, the principal didn't bother him. The other two teachers followed his lead. Mr. Humbert had been teaching for a while and was initially skeptical of Mr. C's teaching style but warmed up to him and played along. The other teacher, Mr. Schultz, a first-year teacher with a ponytail and earrings, the week before school started, Mr. C pulled him aside and said, "Stick with me and you'll be alright. The key is to never write a referral. Handle all the discipline yourself. Just like when you were a student, your goal is to stay out of the principal's office." Mr. C was able to get Mr. Schultz placed in one of the empty portables next to him. Mr. Schultz appreciated the mentorship.

Eli didn't go with the other students. Instead, he followed the three teachers out of the fairgrounds. They crossed the street to a convenience store, and Eli watched from afar. When the next crosswalk signal flashed white, and the teachers were inside the store, he crossed the street. He stood next to the gas tanks as the three teachers exited the store with bottles hidden in paper bags, walked to the side of the store, and sat at a picnic bench under a palm tree. Mr. C handed Mr. Schultz a cigarillo and lit one for himself before handing over the lighter. Mr. Schultz lit one and gave the lighter to Mr. Humbert, who finished unwrapping the cellophane for a cigarette pack and smacked the package against his palm a few times before pulling one out and lighting it. They then opened their drinks, cheered, and took swigs. Eli watched from a distance. He never saw teachers behave this way. The three teachers spoke loudly and laughed loudly. Then, Mr. C stopped and pointed in Eli's direction. The laughing stopped, and they looked his way.

"Hey kid," Mr. C said, "Eli. Get over here."

Eli turned and looked behind him.

"I ain't talking to anyone but you, bud," Mr. C said. The other two teachers laughed.

Eli sheepishly joined them.

"My man," Mr. C said, "Are you trying to get us fired? If you get hit crossing that street, we're toast."

"I'm sorry," Eli said.

"Look, we aren't the friends you are looking for. Why aren't you over there instead?"

Eli shrugged.

"How old are you?"

"Twelve."

"Goddamn, you're a big twelve-year-old." Although Mr. Schultz and Mr. Humbert weren't paying too much attention to the conversation between Mr. C and Eli, they laughed at that. All three teachers continued smoking and taking sips out of their paper bags.

Eli stood there looking stupid.

"You do magic, right?" Mr. Schultz said. "Show us a trick."

Eli smiled. "Okay. Can I see your cigarette?" he asked Mr. Humbert.

Mr. C laughed. "This kid is wild."

"I'm not giving you a cigarette. You crazy, kid?"

"I'm not going to smoke it, but it has to be lit."

Mr. C said, "Just give him a cigarette. He already sees us smoking and drinking beer. What's one more thing?"

Mr. Humbert handed Eli his half-smoked cigarette. Eli took it and quickly made it look like he stuck it up his nose and showed his hands. It was gone. The three teachers loved it, and then Eli opened his mouth. The lit cigarette flipped around on his tongue, and he held it between his lips.

"Shut the fuck up," Mr. Schultz said. "Did you see that?"

Eli loved the attention. He then took the lit butt from his mouth, showed it clearly in one hand, and within an instant, the butt disappeared.

Mr. Humbert said, "All right, show us how you did that?"

Mr. C stepped in. "Don't. Never show anyone how you did. You've got a gift, kid. Do you know any more?"

"Do you have a dollar?"

"One of you give him a dollar," Mr. C said.

Mr. Schultz gave him a dollar. Eli folded it, appeared to rip it, and restored it. And then, while the three teachers were still excited, he made it disappear.

"Kid, you can make money from this," Mr. C said. "But look here, the only magic trick I want to see now is you cross back over the street and not get hit by a car."

"And don't tell the other kids what you saw us doing," Mr. Humbert said.

"That goes without saying," Mr. C said.

Eli walked off with a smile.

"Hey, my dollar," Mr. Schultz said.

"You can forget it," Mr. C said. "We just changed that kid's life."

32

After seven months, Bobby was free. The girl he left Janet for moved during his incarceration, and he didn't know where she lived. New tenants occupied the house where she previously lived.

"Well, where the hell did she go?" he asked the black woman who answered the door. A man walked up behind her.

"My man," the man said. "We don't know who you are looking for, but I can promise you this: You don't want to come knocking on this door anymore."

Bobby smiled. His tongue poked from that missing side tooth. "I hear you," he said, "but if you see her, let her know Bobby's back."

The man shut the door. Bobby walked two hours to the house from the correctional facility and still carried the thirty-five dollars of gate money. His only option was to go back to Janet. She was still his wife. After a mile of walking with his thumb out, a driver in a pick-up truck pulled over on HWY 29.

"How far you going?" the man said through the rolled-down passenger window.

"You know where Sally's Cricket Shack's at?" Bobby asked and started to climb into the bed.

"Ah hell, brother. You don't have to ride in the back. Climb up here in the cab."

Bobby did.

"Sally's, huh?" The man looked at his watch. "Ten-thirty in the am. They open?"

"We'll find out, won't we?" Bobby said.

"Hell, maybe I'll go in and get a drink with you."

Bobby smiled.

They drove down the road with windows down and Marty Robbins on the stereo.

"Where are you walking from?" the man said.

"Prison," Bobby told him. "Seven months in that shithole."

"Shit, man. I'd want a beer, too."

"Beer and pussy is all I thought about for the last seven months."

"You got the pussy lined up?"

"Hoping I'll find some at Sally's."

The warm wind blew through the windows, but the low humidity said fall was coming. Marty Robbins sang about the Mexican maiden Felina, and Bobby thought he never felt better.

"What you go to prison for?" the man asked.

Bobby turned and looked at him.

"This ol' girl I shacked up with claimed I beat her and threatened to kill her."

"Did you?"

"Goddamn right, I did. Lucky for her, she moved while I was locked up. Nearly killed the people living there now just out of principle."

"Shit," the driver said. "You don't fuck around, do you?"

"Nope."

"So where you going after Sally's?"

"I reckon back to my wife."

The driver smirked. "Hope I ain't overstepping here, but does she know you're out?"

"I don't know," Bobby said.

The man reached into the console and pulled out a pack of Camels. He offered one to Bobby. Bobby accepted, and the driver pushed in the cigarette lighter. When it popped, Bobby beat him to it. He held that red coil to the end of the cigarette and took in that familiar comfort of carcinogens.

Sally's sat near the creek that led out to the river and emptied into the bay. Three motorcycles were out front. The oyster shell parking lot shined bright. The driver parked.

"You know, I've never been inside here. Is it true that you get a free beer if you eat a cricket?"

"Come in and find out," Bobby said.

"I would," the driver said, "but I got to keep moving on."

"I didn't frighten you, did I?"

The man wouldn't look at Bobby. "Maybe a little."

Bobby smiled. "Give me twenty bucks and a couple more cigarettes, and I'll let you be on your way."

The man reached into his pockets and pulled out some wadded bills.

"I only have eighteen."

"That'll work. Appreciate the ride." He took the entire pack of smokes, too.

33

With the house to herself, Janet showered, and nearly instantaneously when the warm water poured over her, she dropped to the shower floor and wept. She let out a cry that she couldn't remember ever crying before. Her face scrunched up, and snot hung off her lip. She wailed and hugged herself and rocked back and forth. She tried to end any other cry as quickly as possible, to hide it, if even from herself, but she couldn't contain it now so she embraced it.

When it ended, she felt like she could breathe easier. She never noticed how constrained her breathing was until she expelled that cry that she carried for so long.

She stepped from the shower, wiped a small area in the condensation of the mirror, and looked at her reflection, squeezing her soft stomach. Bobby used to tell her if she gained weight, she would be out on the street on her fat ass. "Fuck you, Bobby," she said and smiled at herself. She liked how that sounded. "Fuck you," she said again. "I'll get fat if I damn well feel like it." She laughed. Felt silly for doing so, and then, like with the crying, let it go. She laughed audibly. Couldn't remember the last time she laughed like that—a genuine from-the-gut laugh. And that laugher continued as she ran her fingers through her shortened hair.

She regained her composure and looked at her naked body again, lifting her breasts and then letting them drop. She turned and looked at the beginnings of cellulite. She stared at herself a bit more and wondered what she would look like with lipstick. Maybe a bit of eyeliner. She shook the thoughts from her head and put on a dress that was pretty similar to the one she wore the day before. For the first time in a long time she realized she didn't have much variety in clothing.

She pulled the plastic from the three small canvases wrapped together, set two on the floor, placed the other on the easel, and stared at it for a minute, trying to remember what she used to paint. Besides winning first place in middle school, in high school, a painting she did of an old woman sitting on her porch peeling potatoes won her third place in the county fair. She ripped the picture from a National Geographic running a series on rural America. After that, she started taking photos and did a series of "trailer park" paintings from the photos, mostly her neighbor's two barefoot kids who ran loose and terrorized stray cats.

She picked up the digital camera and the map. The bike, a red Schwinn with an oversized basket hanging from the handlebars, leaned locked to the railing on the front porch. She placed the camera and map inside the basket and undid the lock using the combination Stacy told her before leaving. She walked the bike to the street and scanned to see if anyone was outside to watch her, self-conscious of her riding abilities. Hiking up her dress enough to lift her leg over the step-through bar, she put one foot on the pedal and rested her other foot on the ground before tucking her dress between her crotch and pushed off, wobbling down the street, not much different than the drunk tourists leaving the Duval Street bars on rented bikes.

The late morning air felt good against her face, and the freedom radiated from within, and she couldn't help but smile. It nearly made her cry again.

She rode down the shaded streets lined with conch-style homes. Decorative hues. Pinks. Blues. Yellows. Shutters. Tropical floral. It all seemed movie-like. A chorus of birds chirped. Was that a parakeet? Why are there roosters roaming around? An Iguana? Everywhere she looked felt unreal. The heat radiated down on her, and the cerulean sky above transplanted her to another life, a life she never knew existed outside of fantasy. She didn't know what she wanted to photograph and wasn't sure if she wanted to take any pictures at all, afraid looking through a lens might detract from the experience.

Margaret Street dead-ended at a cemetery, and she stepped off, locked her bike to the fence, and walked in. Tombstones and above-ground graves among a scattering of palm trees. A historical marker told her the cemetery was established in 1847 after a hurricane destroyed the previous cemetery at present-day Higgs Beach. Seventy-five thousand people were buried there. She thought it the most beautiful burial ground she ever saw, unlike the one in Sullivan which was overgrown with kudzu, broken markers, and half-opened graves from teenage drunks looking for jewelry. Live Oaks with Spanish moss blocked out the sun, and when the Magnolia trees bloomed, the fragrance from the large white flowers seemed out of place.

She read the names Austin and Tina Griffin and noticed they shared a death date. The next tombstone she saw read James and Baxter Parsons, also with identical death dates. The hair on the back of her neck stood on end. Her arms goose pimpled. The sounds of birds quieted. She walked by the USS Maine Memorial where the bodies of a dozen or more sailors killed in the explosion off the coast of Cuba were transported and buried. "Remember the Maine." A sense of nostalgia washed over her for those days she would spend on her mother's porch and read, and the books transported her to a different world. That same feeling came back and immersed her in the past, and the spirits surrounding her were palpable. She never felt like she belonged in Sullivan, but in Key West, it was as if she found a home for herself.

She strolled along a bit more, passing a tombstone that read, "I told you I was sick." She knelt and took a picture. She took a few more from different angles. She used to take hundreds of photos only to end up with one or two that she would turn into a painting. It must have been at least five years since she last painted something. Bobby seemed jealous when she displayed her work at the Pensacola fair her junior year of high school and refused to drive her down to see it. He told her the rest of the paintings must've looked like shit when the judges awarded her the third-place ribbon. After they were married, her mother's friend, Doris, suggested she set up a booth at the flea market and sell paintings. She told Janet that people liked paintings of seagulls, crabs, dunes, sea oats, and piers. She painted a few, and she set up a booth for twenty-five dollars and sold four paintings at thirty dollars each. She was so excited when she got home and put the one-hundred twenty dollars on the table to show Bobby.

"You only made ninety-five dollars all day? What a waste of fucking time. Get a real job."

She wanted to tell him it was more than he made in the last week—he recently lost his roofing job—but she knew better than to say that to him. He took the money from the table, left her a twenty to buy some groceries, and walked out the door. He didn't return for two days, and when he did, he took her painting supplies, threw them in the back of his truck, and hauled them off to the landfill.

34

He didn't find a woman to take him home at Sally's Cricket Shack, Sally wouldn't run him a tab to keep drinking when he ran out of cash, and Skeet told him to get out of there before things got messy. With some strange moment of clarity, Bobby listened and walked out into the gloam. The sun sank quickly, and if Bobby didn't get another drink soon, he'd be sinking just as quickly, if not quicker. He stood out on that oyster shell parking lot and swayed, bile rising as he belched. He steadied himself on the blue dumpster and pissed, splashing on his shoes and dribbling some down the front of his jeans.

He considered wandering down to the creek to sit but thought better of it and instead walked out to HWY 29 to try and make his way to Janet's mom's house and see what kind of welcome his wife would give him. Over a year since he'd seen her. Seven months in prison, and six months before then when he moved out. *That can't be right. Seemed like I left high school in less time than that. How old am I? Twenty-seven? Twenty-eight? Goddamn, time moved fast. Did it always move that fast?*

A car approached from behind him. A champagne-colored Corolla, front bumper rattling down the dusty road, back bumper held on with wire coat hanger and duct tape. Spider web crack across the windshield. He recognized the man driving and the woman in the passenger seat. They were shooting pool at Sally's. The car stopped next to him, and the lady in the passenger seat rolled down the window.

"Need a ride?" she asked.

Bobby stopped and focused his eyes. The woman wore a too-bright shade of red lipstick and the remnants of a bruise under her left eye. The man looked like he kicked many of asses in his younger years. He barely looked at Bobby, kept his eyes mostly forward, but side-glanced at him several times. Bobby spotted a styrofoam cooler on the back floorboard.

"I really would appreciate it," he said.

Bobby pulled on the backdoor, and it opened with a rusted screech.

"Crissy's going to climb back there with you, partner. She's looking to have a little fun," the man said, still not looking at Bobby.

"I ain't got no money," Bobby said.

"I ain't ask you if you got any money." Bobby slid behind the man so Crissy could get in next to him. "Nu-uh," the man said. "You stay right there." The man then turned and smiled a nearly toothless grin. Bobby understood the man intended to watch.

The woman got behind the driver's side in the backseat and shut the door. The car smelled of motor oil and cigarettes, and there were burn holes not only on the seats but also on the ceiling.

"You got any beer in here?" Bobby asked as he began opening the cooler on the floor hump between the two seats.

"Getcha one," the man said. "And me one, too."

Bobby got out two beers from the icy water and looked at the woman as he handed a beer to the driver. The woman unbuttoned her blouse, and her massive breasts hung exposed. The car lurched forward.

"Them pretty, ain't they?" the man said.

Bobby agreed, opened the beer, and took a long drink. Having not seen a woman naked in seven months, he thought for sure he would have an instant erection, but he felt no tightening in his jeans.

"Where am I dropping you off?" the man asked.

Bobby gave him directions. The woman leaned over, unzipped Bobby's jeans, and pulled out his flaccid member.

The man looked back over his shoulder as he turned the car onto the main road. "Having trouble back there?" he said.

The woman put the soft penis in her mouth and then lifted her head and looked at the driver and said, "Maybe he's queer." The man laughed.

"I ain't no damn queer," Bobby said.

"Well then, get that pecker working."

Bobby tried, but to no use.

"He's fucking queer," the woman said.

Bobby said, "Say that one more time, and I'll knock those last four teeth out of your goddamn mouth."

The driver slowed and turned around to look at Bobby and said, "You ain't gonna touch her, and if you talk to her like that again, I'll pull this car over and fuck you myself, and when I'm finished, I'll bash your goddamn head."

The car drifted onto the shoulder's rumble strips, and the lady leaned forward, put a hand on the driver's shoulder, and said, "Pay attention to the road, baby."

The man turned back onto the road and said, "I'll run this motherfucker right into a tree and kill us all. Try me, motherfucker. Tell me how to get to where we're going."

Bobby told him.

He grabbed the beer between his legs and finished it. Bobby did the same.

"Reach in that cooler and get the peach schnapps, will you, baby?" He handed her the empty can, and she placed it in the cooler and took out the pint of schnapps.

"Want some?" she asked Bobby. Bobby said he did. She unscrewed the top and handed it to him. He took a long pull and then handed it to the driver. The driver did the same and handed it back to the lady. She put it back in the cooler and massaged the driver's shoulders until they got to Janet's mother's trailer. They drove the remainder of the way in silence.

35

J anet continued on her bike ride and passed a little barefoot girl wearing overalls riding a bike, still on training wheels, and the little blond girl with her hair blowing back out of her face lifted her arms and pedaled like that for a good ten yards. Janet turned the bike around and saw a lady she guessed was the girl's mother sitting on the tailgate of a pick-up truck in a front yard.

"Excuse me," Janet said. "I don't mean to be a bother, and I hope this isn't a strange request, but is that your daughter?"

The lady said it was.

"Would you mind if I took a picture of her? I'm an artist and would like to paint a picture similar to her."

The lady said she could.

"Do you mind asking her to lift her arms again?" Janet asked.

The lady called out to her daughter, who turned around and rode back towards them, her arms spread wide and her smile wider. Janet snapped the picture and, without looking at it on the LCD screen to check the composition, asked the woman on the truck if she could take her picture, too. The woman said yes and smiled and posed, turning her shoulder a bit out, crossing her legs, and putting her hands on her knees.

"Thank you," Janet said.

"Where can I see your work?" the lady asked.

"I just got to town," Janet told her. "But hopefully soon."

Riding down Windsor Lane, weaving through the residential area, turning on Amelia and William until it dead-ended at Seminole Street and the historic Casa Marina.

The famed hotel was the brainchild of Henry Flagler. He died in 1913, the year after he completed the railroad to Key West. Five years after his death, the hotel's construction began as a final monument for the man who built Florida. Of course, a grand hotel for the luxurious travelers would never mention how he treated his workers. Instead, his legacy would be untarnished, and events like the burning down of the black community, the Styx, in Palm Beach County would be all but forgotten and, if remembered by a select few, be cast off as urban legend since no proof existed that it ever happened. People like Janet would never stay in a place like Casa Marina, and people like Janet would be too intimidated even to step foot in a place like that, assuming wealthier guests would not welcome someone like her. The six and a half acres, including twelve hundred feet of beach, were purchased for $1,000. Cheaper than buying a trailer in Sullivan, let alone Key West, even when adjusted for inflation.

When the military left in the early 70s, the place nearly became a ghost town. And people like Jimmy Buffett moved down. He commercialized the lifestyle, and people have searched for that lifestyle ever since. The myth existed, and people like Stacy, Eli, and Randall looked for it. Eli got lucky when he met a wealthy widower. But he became jaded. Like his acts, it was all smoke and mirrors. The magic wasn't real. Randall got lucky that he met Eli. He tried escaping the ghost of Jarod. That ghost followed him, but if he were to live the rest of his life running from a ghost, Key West was the best place for it—plenty of distractions. Stacy lucked out meeting Eli as well. She would've burned through her inheritance and maybe would've given up on her dream. But as it stood, she didn't have to consider the what-ifs. Things were working out at the moment. And now Janet got lucky. She didn't know anyone outside of Sullivan except Stacy, and because of Stacy, she could escape Bobby. Seemed luck often had as much to do with success as anything else. Maybe the only thing that made the difference. Hard work could only take someone so far. Maybe endurance, too. One had to survive long enough for the luck and hard work to pay off.

She locked the bike to the post and sat on a bench, and her mind wandered back to Bobby. Everyone back home knew how Bobby treated her, and nobody tried to help. People didn't mind gossiping about people's business, but they didn't want to actually get involved. Especially with someone like Bobby. That split second memory of Bobby, just a flash thought, flooded her with dread again. Life had seemed good for a brief moment. But maybe that was part of the process. Perhaps the memories would pop up at longer intervals—minutes, hours, days, weeks, and then months. Maybe one day she would remember him, and years would have gone by without a thought of him. Perhaps she could never entirely forget him, but she could have stretches of reprieve. That bike ride seemed like the first. So, instead of fighting the memories of Bobby, she would let them happen and then eventually learn to let them go.

Bobby once brought her to The Beulah Sausage Fest, a day trip south of Sullivan. An actual date, Janet thought. They weren't married yet, and two months prior, Janet graduated high school. They were to be married soon enough, though. No proposal. It just happened. One day, Bobby woke up and said get in the car. She did, and they drove to the courthouse, and when they walked down those courthouse steps, they were married. Looking back, none of it made any sense. At the Sausage Fest, they watched a young country music act, and Bobby went to buy himself another beer and told her to stay put. She saw a lady nearby selling hand-made purses and blouses and went to look at them. No more than a couple of minutes passed, but Bobby couldn't find her. When he spotted her at the booth, she was talking with an older man. Bobby walked up behind her and didn't say anything, just listened. The man asked if she heard the band earlier. Janet said she did. The man said his son was the guitarist and that he thought they could potentially make it big. He told her the name and said, "Keep an ear out for them." She said she would, and the man walked away. Bobby whispered into her ear, "You trying to fuck that man?"

That caught Janet by surprise. She never thought of cheating on Bobby. She never really thought of sex at all. Janet thought maybe she misheard him and tried to think what else he may have said.

"No answer? I told you to stay put. You had me walking all over this goddamn place looking for you."

That was the first time Bobby accused her of wanting to sleep with other men, but it would soon become a common habit anytime they were in public. So much so that she started going out in public less and less. One time, the cook at the Waffle House turned just as they entered the restaurant and said, "Good evening," as they sat down, and she smiled and said, "Hello." When the waitress came and asked what they wanted to drink, Bobby said he wasn't hungry anymore. "I think we are just going to leave." Bobby stood up and walked out the door before Janet could protest, and when they sat in the car, Bobby said that he saw the way she looked at the cook and the flirty way she said hello. Janet cried the entire drive home and went to bed without eating. Bobby left the house and didn't get home until two in the morning and woke her up by drunkenly having sex with her while she silently cried and allowed it to happen.

She thought she could smell Bobby's beer and onion breath over her shoulder and shivered with disgust. She took the map from the basket and looked at it. Higgs Beach was just a few blocks away. She left the bike locked and walked. A truck drove by, covered in barnacles. A squished iguana lay in the middle of the street. Flies swarmed around the entrails and dried blood smeared across the asphalt.

The beach didn't look like the beaches in the Panhandle. It didn't have that white squeaky quartz sand. Instead the sand was imported from the Caribbean and mostly made up of crushed coral and shells and other maritime organisms giving it a yellowish, sometimes brown color. Coconut palms provided shade. One man climbed the palms, collecting the coconuts, tossing them to the ground. He then climbed back down, hacked them open with a machete, and sold them with a straw. Some young men played volleyball. She looked out at the turquoise water. She remembered a couple weeks after her father died, she must've been eight, and her mother drove her down to Gulf Shores, Alabama. All his things were already removed from the house. Her mother sold his pick-up truck, and the van they drove to the beach was bought in its place. Looking back as an adult, she wondered how her mother could afford that trip, and if that was her way of taking Janet's mind off his death. But in reality, his death didn't seem to bother her very much.

They didn't rent a hotel room but slept for three nights in the van, just mother and daughter, and they never mentioned the dad. Her mother ate raw oysters for the first time at the Flora-Bama Lounge. They picked seashells in the morning, showered at the public bathrooms, and swam. Swam until she tired and lay on the beach with the drying salt tightening her skin. And she remembered how good it tasted when she licked the little drops of salt water from her upper lip. She thought how good it felt to have a slight sunburn, just enough to hurt a little when she tried to sleep that night. They built a sand castle, which wasn't much of a sand castle, but a giant hole in the ground and a pile of sand off to the side of the hole. Her mother told her the hole was the lake. She enjoyed digging, and calling it a castle and a lake gave it some purpose instead of just digging for the heck of it. It could possibly be her favorite memory. Digging and spending that undivided time with her mother and feeling the sand go from hot to cool, digging deep enough for the hole, to start to fill with water and then watching as the water slowly filled the hole eroding the sides of the hole, which helped to make it larger. When she tired of digging, she climbed down into the hole and her mother shoveled the sand over her and left nothing but her face sticking out. She never wanted to go home again.

She told Bobby about that one summer to see if he would like to take a drive down there, and he told her, "That sounds like the dumbest fucking thing you have ever said. Why in the hell would I want to dig in the goddamned sand and get sunburned? And eating raw oysters is like swallowing a loogie. For Christ's sakes, Janet."

36

Randall and Eli sat on Randall's boat at the marina in Stock Island. Randall tied lures. Eli lounged in the captain's seat with his feet on the console, drinking a beer and reading the Key West Citizen. A Shearwater skimmed the waters. Another floated nearby. Eli struggled with the words blurring. His one good eye watered and went in and out of focus.

"You hear this shit?" Eli said.

Randall looked up. "What's that?"

"Found three bodies floating out in the mangroves. Cops think it's some kids from up in the Panhandle that went missing after coming down here to buy some coke. Said they found a girl that was with them taped up in a hotel closet. Goddamn kids, man. Not even out of high school."

"Kids will do some messed up things," Randall said. "I know my high school years weren't all that pretty."

Eli rubbed underneath the patch on his eye. "Don't talk to me about pretty," Eli said.

"We're all hiding demons, ain't we?" Randall said.

"Shit, man. Some more than others. That's for damn sure. This whole goddamned island is hiding an ugly secret. Lure people down here with a vacation lifestyle, but people can't even afford to live. It's all a sham."

"Pretty sure that's what our country is built on, ain't it? A facade? The land of the free?"

"Brother, who the fuck are you talking to?"

Randall laughed. Eli, not so much.

"So you're out then? Is that it?"

"Heading to the closing in about two hours."

"When do you plan on telling me and Stacy to start looking for another place?"

Eli laughed. "I ain't your daddy."

"Maybe not mine, but I have heard her call you that once or twice."

That got Eli to laugh. Randall stopped tying a lure and looked up at him. Seeing Eli laugh wasn't a common sight, so he stopped to take it in.

"You are an alright guy, you know that?" Eli said. He took a sip of his beer, folded the newspaper, and tucked it under his leg to keep the wind from taking it.

"How much are you making?"

"I'll have enough money to live pleasantly in Mexico. But I'm only selling one house. Thought of offering Stacy the other as a rent-to-own kind of deal. Figured she'd let you stay on as a roommate. It'd give me a bit of monthly income, and y'all would still have a place to live."

Randall continued tying the lure. "That's nice of you," he said.

Eli finished his beer.

"Can I ask you a question?" Randall said. "As long as we've known each other, we don't really know much about one another, you know."

"I'm not sure I like where this is heading," Eli said. "Stop fucking around and get to the point."

"How'd you lose your eye?"

167

Eli looked at him.

"You don't have to answer if you don't want to," Randall said.

"I know I don't have to answer. I don't need you telling me that."

"Sorry. I was just curious."

"It ain't a big deal," Eli said. "I don't mind telling you. You remember when the Challenger exploded?"

"Yeah."

"Well, my class went on a field trip to see it and when that shit exploded a piece of the shrapnel fell in my eye. Ain't that some bullshit?"

Randall sat quietly before seeing a slight smirk on Eli's face.

"You motherfucker," Randall said. "Nearly had me."

Eli laughed.

"Welp," he said. "I better head into town, sell a house, and prepare to entertain some white folks. Hope someone calls you for a fishing trip soon. Rent is about due."

37

B obby didn't bother knocking when he hobbled up the porch steps to Janet's mother's trailer, leaning on the handrail for stability. It gave a bit, nearly sending him tumbling backward. He regained his footing and walked inside as if he and Janet weren't separated. A foul stench circulated throughout. Musty, smoke, urine, filth.

Janet's mother slept on a recliner with her oxygen tank next to her and a tube running into her nose. A cigarette smoldered in an over-filled ashtray. The woman looked like a sack of skin draped over bones. Her grey hair brittle and thinned. Bobby stood for a minute, waiting to see if her chest rose in breath. When he saw her breathe, he glanced around the room, looking for any sign of Janet. He thumbed through a pile of mail on the countertop and stopped at one labeled by the US Treasury. He opened it. Social Security check. He folded it and put it in his pocket. A purse hung on the back of a chair. He opened it, took out the two twenty-dollar bills, and put them in his pocket. He removed her ID card and slipped it in his pocket as well. He walked to the back of the trailer and looked inside both back rooms. No sign of Janet. He looked in the bathroom. Nothing. He walked back to Janet's mother.

"Ms. Schroeder," Bobby said. He placed his hand on her frail shoulder. He picked up the pack of cigarettes from her lap and looked inside. Five or six left. He put the pack in his pocket. "Ms. Schroeder," he said again, shaking her harder. She opened her eyes briefly and then fell back asleep. A pill bottle sat next to the ashtray. He picked it up,

rattled it, and then read the label. Oxycodone. He put the bottle in his pocket.

"Ms. Schroeder," Bobby said again, a bit louder. He shook her once again. "Do you know when Janet will be back?"

He shook her again. She opened her eyes and stared at or through him until her eyes focused.

"Bobby?" she said. Her voice rough.

"Yeah, momma. It's Bobby. I'm back."

She reached a hand to him, and he held it.

"Bobby?" she said again. "Janet ain't here."

"I know that. Do you know when she will be back?"

She looked at him, confused about why he was in the house.

At that time, the sound of feet walking up the porch steps came from outside, followed by the sound of the door opening.

Bobby stood and watched for the person who came through. A young Hispanic girl entered carrying a cooler and a bag and wore scrubs.

"Oh, hi," the girl said. "I didn't know there would be a visitor today."

"I'm Bobby. Her son."

"Bobby? Janet's husband, Bobby?" the girl asked.

"That's right."

Her demeanor changed. Bobby could tell that Janet spoke of him.

"I'm Myra," she said. "Ms. Schroeder's in-home nurse. Ms. Schroeder?" Myra asked. "How is everything today?"

Ms. Schroeder didn't respond. She looked at Myra with a countenance of confusion and fear of her confusion, almost like she suffered from Alzheimer's, which the nurse previously noticed that she began showing the early signs.

"Mr. Bobby, would you mind stepping out for a minute while I bathe Ms. Schroeder?" Myra set the cooler on the kitchen counter and the bag on the floor before turning to the living room where Ms. Schroeder still sat in her recliner, and Bobby stood looking over her.

Bobby smiled. "Yeah, I mind. I ain't going anywhere. Not until Janet gets back."

Myra looked at Ms. Schroeder, and Bobby didn't like that look.

"What is it y'all ain't telling me?"

Neither lady spoke.

"Oh, y'all ain't talking to me now. Is that it?"

"Mr. Bobby," Myra said. "I'm just here to bathe Ms. Schroeder, drop off medicine, help clean up a little, and put her dinners in the refrigerator. I don't know anything else."

"Why don't you come over here and have a seat?" Bobby motioned to the loveseat. He still stood in the middle of the living room.

Myra stood.

"Look here, Myra, is it? Sit down."

Myra walked slowly and sat on the loveseat.

"When is Janet coming back?" Bobby asked.

Neither lady spoke.

"Goddamn it, listen here." His voice rose, but he lowered it again. "I ain't leaving until she comes back or you tell me what the fuck is going on. And Myra, you ain't leaving either."

"I thought y'all divorced," Ms. Schroeder said.

"Divorced? What makes you say something like that?" He took a deep breath, controlling his anger again.

"Mr. Bobby," Myra said. "Sometimes Ms. Schroeder says things she doesn't mean. She gets confused."

"No. No," Ms. Schroeder said. "Isn't that why you've been gone for so long? You were living with another gal."

"Is that what she told you?" Bobby said.

"Mr. Bobby," Myra said.

Bobby snapped his head around and looked at Myra. "Don't you say another goddamn word."

Bobby stepped closer to Ms. Schroeder, bent down at eye level with her, and placed both hands on her shoulders. "Where is Janet?"

"She isn't coming back," Myra shouted. "I'm sorry, Ms. Schroeder."

Bobby let go of Ms. Schroeder's shoulders and turned to face Myra.

"Sweet Myra," he said. "I'm going to hate what I'm about to do to you. But either tell me what you know, or I will do it whether I like it or not."

"Key West," Myra said, her voice trembling.

"Key West? Janet ain't ever left Sullivan."

Nobody spoke.

"Who does she know in Key West?" Bobby stood thinking. "Stacy?" he asked. "That fucking slut from high school?"

Still, neither lady spoke. He turned back to Ms. Schroeder. "I remember a few years back when that bitch called here and told Janet she was making music in Nashville and was moving down there. We didn't hear from her since high school, and she calls out of the blue to brag about her success and shit. I told Janet not to talk to her anymore. You telling me that's who she went to see?"

Silence.

"All right," Bobby said. "All right. Y'all don't have to say shit else." He took the social security check from his pocket. His hands trembled. "I'm going to need you to sign this."

Ms. Schroeder didn't move.

"I don't think you understand," he said. "Or maybe I wasn't clear. Sign the goddamned check."

Ms. Schroeder looked at him. She understood.

38

S he walked along Atlantic Boulevard and passed where archeologists would discover the African cemetery in the future. Janet had no way of knowing that underneath where she walked lay the bodies of three hundred enslaved people who died in Key West in 1860 when the US Navy intercepted three ships off the coast of Cuba carrying 1,500 slaves. The slaves were brought to Key West and nursed back to health. The ones that died were buried along the shores of Higgs Beach. The survivors were sent to Liberia.

Next came the newly constructed AIDS Memorial—seven hundred and fifty names inscribed on the wall and dedicated on December 1st, 1997. Seven-hundred and fifty Key West citizens died of AIDS in a town of only twenty-five thousand. The number of names on the walls would grow every December 1st as new names continued to be added. Janet never knew anyone with AIDS and rarely thought about it. Even during the 80s, in small-town Sullivan, it was seldom mentioned. It was an illness of gay nightclubs in New York City or San Francisco, not a tropical island like Key West. Little did she know about the city she visited.

She then walked onto the White Street Pier, or as some called it, the unfinished road to Cuba, where anglers and dog-walkers shared the path, and she snapped a few more pictures. There was nothing particularly picturesque about the pier, a quarter-mile slab of concrete jutting out into the Atlantic, and there was no historical significance to it either. However, that was what Janet found appealing.

Standing at the pier's edge, she shed tears again but didn't know why. She stood with her hands on the rail, staring out into the green waters, and allowed herself to cry. She didn't think about Bobby or her father and didn't miss home, although she was concerned about her mother being alone. She hoped her mother understood why she couldn't be there when Bobby was released from prison. Maybe, she thought, she cried because she didn't miss home or Bobby or her father. She cried from happiness. She wouldn't miss being married, although technically, they still were. She would worry about that another time. She cried because of a memory that she thought she forgot. The baby she lost in her third month of pregnancy. She didn't cry when she miscarried. It came as a relief. And now that relief emerged as grief. She cried an uncontrollable and inconsolable cry because she remembered being happy when she looked down at the toilet and saw the lime-sized clump of bloody tissue, happy because the child would've bound her to Bobby forever. Yet, she still struggled to find the courage to leave. She cried because she wasted her early years of adulthood. She cried because she remembered how much she enjoyed photography and painting and how she abandoned those passions to please Bobby. She cried because life sped by in the last six years, and she didn't notice until now. She cried because, for the first time in the past six years, she wasn't waiting to die. Life once seemed long, and now she yearned for longevity, no longer hoping that something terrible would happen to her. Death once seemed her only chance of freedom, countless days contemplating taking her mother's prescription pills or hanging herself in a closet. Her day wasn't preoccupied with hoping something terrible would happen to Bobby either. And she wasn't contemplating killing him with bleach in his coffee or smothering him with a pillow in his drunken, bed-pissing sleep.

Instead, life showed signs of excitement, and she welcomed the future. Around her, others also seemed to be enjoying life unlike in Sullivan, where dread hung over everyone. Outside, alone, with no worries about "getting caught," alleviated from an irrational fear of getting caught doing something she didn't know she wasn't allowed to do. She cried because it had been so long since she really cried and not just fought back the tears that welled up inside her at every little word. She cried because she felt something. She went so long trying not to feel anything. And now she felt again. She felt the air, the warmth of the sun, the pain, the love. The birds singing and the water lapping against the pier's pilings evoked emotions she didn't know how to describe. She felt what it was like to feel again. She cried because she knew that unless someone had been as low as she had been, no one could ever understand what it felt like to rise again, even briefly. Happiness was fleeting, and she decided to recognize it when it emerged, appreciate it, and tell herself that if she were capable of feeling it now, she would be capable again.

"Mam, you okay?" A voice asked from behind her.

She turned to look at an old man with more wrinkles than she ever saw on anyone. He wore a captain's hat and blue work coveralls and carried a cane fishing pole and five-gallon bucket in one hand and tackle box and rod and reel in the other.

"Yes," she said, barely audible, trying to quiet her crying. She wiped her nose with the back of her hand.

"Those don't look like tears of joy," he said. He handed her a handkerchief.

"Some of them are," she said, taking the handkerchief and wiping her nose. She then laughed a little, which caused her to cry again. Then, seeing what she looked like to others standing nearby, she laughed harder, which in turn forced her to cry more.

The man set down the tackle box, rod and reel, and cane pole. He then lowered the bucket into the water by a rope and brought it back up about half full before casting out with the cane pole.

When she finally regained control of her emotions, she said, "I'm sorry." The man paid her no mind. A small child, a girl of about three or so, stood staring at her. The child's parents, or who she assumed to be her parents, walked hand in hand a few feet behind the child, sipping canned beers. "I'm just really screwed up right now." She didn't know if she spoke to the child or the old man. A brown pelican skimmed the waters before landing near the old man and waited to be fed, knowing that the old man had thrown bait fish to him before. After a while, he spoke.

"Well, that's all right, sweetie. Sometimes, we need a good cry to get us back in the saddle. I know Hemingway might disagree with me. But fuck him. Maybe if he cried more, he wouldn't have blown his brains out," the old man said. "You don't mind if I fish here, do you? Fish are attracted to weeping women, you know."

"I'm sorry," she said.

"Don't be," he said. Take all the time you need." He pulled in a small bait fish with the cane pole and put it in the bucket. Before he cast out again, he looked at Janet. "Are you better now?"

She nodded.

"That's good. I do hate to see such a pretty girl cry like that." He then threw out the line but looked back at her when she started again, but not so severely and for a short while. She couldn't remember the last time someone called her pretty.

"Do you mind if I take your picture?" she asked, through some sniffling.

"No, mam. You go right ahead."

She took out the camera, zoomed in close, and focused on the weathered face—a beautiful portrait, she thought. She then took another of his whole body so she could get him holding the pole, the tackle box next to him, and the endless water behind him.

"Thank you," she said. "Good luck with the fish."

"Honey, when you get as old as me, you realize that luck plays a much bigger role than you ever imagined. You have to be ready, though, either way—if luck shows up or not. If luck does show up and you aren't ready, then luck is useless. But if you are ready, if you prepare for the moment that luck presents itself, well then, you might succeed."

She smiled at him and gave a wave goodbye.

"Come back and see me if you'd like. I'm here every day. If I'm lucky."

39

The Greyhound bus stopped in Orlando nearly twelve hours after leaving the Pensacola station. The driver shook Bobby's shoulder.

"Hey, my man," the driver said.

The rest of the passengers exited, and Bobby lay with his head sunk into his chest, snoring, drooling. A pocket full of stolen social-security cash and a half-empty bottle of pain pills with the label peeled off. He dumped the emptied pint of vodka he finished off around Tallahassee in the bus toilet to hide the evidence.

Bobby opened his glassed-over eyes and focused on the black man's face standing before him.

"That you that's been drinking on this bus?" the driver said. "Ain't no drinking on the bus."

"Ain't drank nothing," Bobby said.

"If I find out you've been drinking, I've got to kick you off the bus, and you don't get a refund. You understand what I'm saying?"

"I hear you," Bobby said. "I ain't been drinking."

"We have a sixty-minute break here. I'm going to ask you to step off, and we will then reboard."

Bobby lifted his head and looked around. He tried to speak slowly to hide his slurring, "Where are we at?" He could not hide his slurring.

The driver told him where they were. "Go in there and get you some coffee, bub."

"How much further to Key West?"

"Shit boy. You've got about seven more hours until Miami for a transfer and then another five hours to Key West."

"Shit."

"It's a haul."

Bobby stood, steadied himself, and then walked down the aisle, holding on to every seat he passed. He stepped off the bus into the balmy evening, the sun setting into a mix of purples and oranges.

He stumbled into the Love's truck stop. His mouth felt like hair grew on his tongue. The murmur of the crowd rang in his ears. He focused his eyes and ignored the looks of the other passengers and patrons in the store as he walked to the bathroom. His piss looked the color of sweet tea. He felt like there was a rock in his mouth. The tooth he spit out rattled in the porcelain urinal and swam in the bubbles he didn't flush. He moved his tongue along the gums of the known missing tooth and felt a much bigger hole. He didn't wash his hands, mainly because he didn't want to have to look at his disheveled self. He scratched his neck and felt the stubble. He wiped the snot from his nose by pinching his thumb and pointer knuckle on his columella and then wiped his hand on his jeans.

He bought a can of Mountain Dew, swallowed down two more pain pills, and smoked a cigarette before boarding the bus again and falling back asleep.

There was an hour layover in Miami to transfer onto the bus to Key West. In that time, he made his plan. The long ride didn't change his mind so it must be what he had to do. It was beyond his control. It was not a crime of passion. It would not be done in the heat of the moment. When he found her, he would walk up to her, no matter where she was or who was around, and put his hands around her neck and strangle the life out of her. Nothing worse could be done to him in jail than hadn't been done before. Sentenced to death? That would be the gift. But one thing was certain. Janet would not leave him, and he would not sign divorce papers. Until death do they part. So death it would be. He was prepared to carry out the ultimate vow. He never killed anyone and never really thought of it, at least not seriously. Sure the thought entered his head occasionally. Like with the wardens at Boys Camp, or the woman that made fun of his flaccid cock. Those only seemed like brief visions. Unlike now, where he stood ready to show the world the only love he knew.

The ride through the Keys was uneventful. He stared out the window, and whenever memories emerged, he played them out differently, becoming the victim at any event spontaneously playing in his mind's eye. His cellmate of seven months read him passages from the bible. If God existed, the world was forsaken. There was no way for a god to allow a life like Bobby's, defeated from birth, and he played his role in what seemed like a sinister fairytale. Janet entered his orbit so that he could commit the ultimate crime. His entire life prepared him for that moment, hardened him to make it happen. No guilt, no remorse. Predestined from the beginning of time. As if read from some atavistic storybook. The universe planned it out. It was always to be. His parents met by chance for him to exist. And their parents the same. And her parents. Infinitely backward to the beginning. To Adam and Eve and Cain and Abel. When his cellmate read to him about the two descendants of good and evil, it became clear from which lineage he belonged. He swelled in the knowledge of his purpose.

At the Islamorada Burger King, he ate a burger and smoked a cigarette. Neither satisfied his hunger.

40

She rode by the Southernmost Point and saw people waiting in line to get their picture next to the buoy marking the point that stood on the water's edge only ninety miles away from Cuba . She knew if she wanted to sell paintings, paintings like that would sell the most. So she snapped a picture of it. But she also took a picture of the people standing in line and left just enough of the brightly painted buoy at the edge of the frame so viewers would know why the people were standing in line. She continued on and after a few turns ended up on Duval Street.

In the morning heat, she passed by loving couples walking hand in hand, stopping at windows to read funny shirts like "I got Duval-faced on Shit Street" or "Tell your eyes to stop staring at my boobs." She passed by drunken college-aged kids having a frozen alcoholic drink for breakfast and other folks zipping by on motor scooters with shoulders burnt so bad that they already peeled. She passed by older folks with white hair and Hawaiian shirts enjoying the six-hour land excursions before having to return to the cruise ships for the early bird dinner special. And she passed the occasional regular folks who truly loved Key West, people who wandered the streets knowing that in the past, Key West was nothing like the present but still loved it for what it once was. The piratical outpost. To wander the streets of history. The history that Hemingway helped solidify and helped become an outlandish tourist attraction, an adult-themed Epcot Center. The mythical-like place Jimmy Buffett heard about and ran away to with Jerry Jeff Walker and Thomas McGuane and created a new brand of music that became much like Key West itself: filled with stories of debauchery, run by outlaws and corporations that catered to the tourists who were bored with their lives but not bored enough to chuck everything away for a life of adventure. Tourists who instead lived vicariously through the stories about such characters. A fun fantasy but not a reality for most.

She stopped next to a woman walking the streets with an arm full of roses.

"Excuse me," Janet said. "Do you know where the Blue Heaven is?"

"Of course," said the lady, her blond curls blowing across her face as she turned to look down the street. "Stay on Duval until you get to Petronia and take a left. You'll pass Whitehead Street, and the next right should be Thomas. It's on the corner of Whitehead and Thomas. So take a right on Petronia, then a right on Thomas. Great food, better atmosphere."

"Thank you," Janet said.

"No problem. A rose?"

"I don't have any money," Janet said. She did have some money, just not enough to spend on a rose.

"For you, free," the woman said. She put the rose in the basket and walked on. Blue Heaven was right where the lady said it would be. She chained her bike to a fence post and walked in, holding her rose and her camera. Open-air seating, chickens scattered about, and an air of tranquility. She took a picture of the outdoor shower in front of the bar. The sign read: "Showers - $1; To watch - $2." Another possible painting.

"Hey, I told you it was easy to find," Stacy said from behind her. She held two Bloody Marys. "I see you are using the camera. Good."

"Thank you. I've had a great morning. Unbelievable, really. I forgot how much I love taking photos. I've got a handful that I'm thinking of painting."

Stacy smiled and couldn't believe the metamorphosis of Janet already taking place. In just twenty-four hours, Janet seemed to be sprouting wings.

Stacy took a long drink and held out the other for Janet. Janet looked at it and smiled.

"A bit early, isn't it?" Janet asked.

Stacy laughed. "It'll make my songs sound better."

Janet took it and then handed Stacy a rose.

"Thank you. It's beautiful. But don't make buying those roses a daily habit."

"She gave it to me," Janet said. "And now I give it to you."

Stacy spoke to the hostess to find Janet a table in the shaded courtyard surrounded by loose chickens and happy people or happy chickens and loose people. Who is to say which?

"Let me finish setting up, and I'll be back before I go on."

Janet looked at the happy chickens and happy people. She remembered wanting to one day be one of those happy people that others hated because they couldn't find happiness themselves. It didn't seem fair that some people could be happy in this life. It seemed like happiness was forbidden in Sullivan, except for Stacy. She was always happy. Happy from the first day she met her in elementary school.

Happy in middle school when girls started calling her slut for no other reason than being happy. Happy in high school when girls started calling her a slut for sleeping with guys and then breaking up with them when they couldn't satisfy her. There were rumors that she slept with the baseball coach her junior year, and she never denied the rumors. Her happy disposition didn't change when her parents died either. It was as if she chose to enjoy life no matter the obstacles. Was it inherent? Was it a conscious decision? There seemed always to be a light, a glow that followed Stacy. And then, with Bobby, the opposite—darkness and anger.

She fell prey to Bobby's influence, as if he placed her in some spell that she wasn't aware of until she finally got far enough away to break the force, and she could now see through the shadows. Was it just Bobby, though? Could it be the town? Could it be Sullivan itself, the history? Were people under some doomed curse in a town like that? Was leaving the only way to break free? The thought made her eyes wet, and she felt her lip quiver. The idea that she was blinded for so long and people like her mother would never be free. Heartbreaking. She covered her face, and as the tears fell, she tried her best not to make too much noise and control the shaking that accompanied the sobs.

"There's no crying at the Blue Heaven," Stacy said, touching her shoulder.

She took her hands from her face and looked up at Stacy with red eyes, "I'm sorry," she said.

"For what, babe?"

"Making a scene at your work," and she began to cry a bit more. Stacy bent down and hugged her.

"You're not making a scene."

Janet looked at her, and Stacy's deadpan face made her laugh. She did that weird laugh-cry thing again, and Stacy laughed with her.

"This isn't funny," Janet said. "I've been a mess all morning. I cried while watching an old man fish."

"It happens. You'd be surprised at the stupid shit I cry over. It does you good." Stacy hugged her again, this time tighter, and Janet, through her sobs, said, "People are watching."

"I'm aware," Stacy said. "So if you could wrap it up, that'd be great. I've gotta start my set."

Janet pulled away again. "That's not funny."

"It's a little funny."

Stacy stopped hugging her.

"Relax," she said. "Drink your Bloody Mary. Order you some food. I'm going to sing some songs. Just sit back and listen to some music, and you'll wish lunch could last forever. You'll be okay."

"Thank you."

"And forget about Sullivan. You're never going back." Stacy walked off before Janet could respond.

Stacy took the stage, a small wooden structure that looked like it belonged at a seaside honky-tonk instead of an up-scale tourist-filled lunch spot. But unlike some places explicitly built for tourists, the Blue Heaven rightfully earned their spot through good food, authenticity, and the all-American hallmark of hard work. A dog lay in the dirt next to the speaker, and a chicken pecked near the dog. A calico cat rested on the privacy fence. Stacy tuned her guitar and spoke sweetly into the mic, welcoming everyone to a beautiful day at the greatest place on Earth.

Janet took a sip of her peppery and acidic Bloody Mary, the tomato juice giving her instant heartburn. She ate the crisp, tangy, garlicky pickled green bean. She waved down a server and asked for a coffee and an order of banana pancakes, not knowing that those were the staple at Blue Heaven, but she would soon find out.

Stacy began her set. She played a cover tune of that once local myth-creating celebrity who owned a recording studio down on the harbor where in the 70s fisherman unloaded marijuana in the open in daylight. But she didn't play the song that sparked a Key West tourism revival and launched a business empire of restaurants, resorts, retirement villages, cruise ships, frozen shrimp, and tequila. She didn't play that song because people played it around town *ad nauseam*. Instead, she played a slightly more obscure one from him and still a crowd-pleaser to those who recognized it. A song about eating oysters, drinking beer, and filling a tin cup with cheap red wine. It got the tip jar started. A man handed a woman a twenty dollar bill, and she danced it right up to the stage and placed it in the beer pitcher tip jar.

The man in an aloha shirt clapped and hollered as his wife swayed her large hips as if that song were being sung just for her. Stacy smiled larger than Janet thought possible for someone to smile, and that infectious smile spread to every one listening.

Stacy's following songs were about the Southern Cross, Bogie and Bacall in Key Largo, and then that fictional place called Kokomo. She knew what the crowd wanted to hear, and when she got the crowd on her side, she asked if she could play one of her original songs.

"I really hope y'all don't mind," she said. "I know what y'all want to hear, and I promise I'll get back to that." The crowd clapped. Some yelled out in encouragement, the mimosas working. "I have an EP of original tunes and cassettes or CDs for sale. I'd love to sell a copy or three when I take a break. Help me pay for my lunch, you know? Nothing too crazy. Maybe just make a cool million or so." That got a chuckle from the crowd. "And if you want me to stop playing originals, there's the tip jar. I'm here for y'all." That got another laugh. A young guy with a ponytail, maybe in his early twenties, approached the stage, dancing to music only he could hear, and dropped a five in the tip jar. She winked at him. At his table sat a cute brunette girl with sunkissed cheeks enjoying her time in the tropics, and Stacy smiled at her and said into the mic, "He's cute. Good for you, girl." The brunette girl laughed, held her hands above her head, and clapped. That compliment went directly into the young man's ears, and he added an extra shimmy before sitting down.

Janet was in awe. She always knew Stacy was remarkable, but on stage she witnessed the full display, a rock star, and people recognized it. She couldn't be prouder to call her a friend. She never knew people to shine like that. The only people she knew who garnered attention were people like Bobby, who demanded it and accomplished it through fear. Stacy did it through authenticity and love.

Janet sipped her coffee—bold and smooth. The food exploded with flavors. Not only did the server bring a plate of pancakes, but Stacy ordered her a plate of luncheon tortillas, made with Jerk chicken, black beans, brown rice, melted Vermont cheddar cheese, sour cream, cilantro salsa, and avocado on top of a flour tortilla. When Janet protested that she didn't order those, the server said Stacy insisted that she try them.

Laura, the server, was a lady in her mid-fifties, maybe, but just as bubbly as if she were in her twenties. She had an attitude as if she saw the worst of humankind and lived through it only to see the beauty that was left.

After dropping off the food, she stood near Janet's table for an extra second, listened to Stacy play, and swayed with her eyes closed, her many bracelets making a slight jingle-jangle. Janet smiled and took a bite of the chicken and rice. It tasted like nothing she ever experienced in Sullivan or knew existed. She never tasted cilantro, avocado, Jerk chicken, or brown rice and was initially hesitant. She took little bites to try to figure out the taste. Spicy but sweet. Cinnamon? It didn't taste like someone drowned it in salt. It tasted fresh. It tasted real. She ate every bit of it, including the pancakes, drank the coffee, and finished the Bloody Mary. She never ate that much and typically would've been judged if she did, but she felt alive and, for a brief moment, happy even though her belly felt like it would burst. She never ate until she hated herself but could now see the joy in it. The music, the food, the roosters, the drinks, the dog, the hummingbird that fluttered by, the butterflies, all of it, the coolness of the shade, it was unexplainable, and tears filled her eyes again. Stacy was right. She never wanted this to end. She ordered a glass of white wine, and Stacy saw the server set it down and smiled, and Janet blushed.

Stacy explained that the next song was about a different Florida—the opposite end of the Florida spectrum—a place on the Florida-Alabama border. She paused and then said, "I've got my friend visiting from that Florida. Y'all give her a big Key West welcome." The patrons did. Janet blushed again. She shook her head and covered her face. Stacy sang a song of melancholy and dirt roads, bingo parlors, and kudzu.

The song transported Janet back home but from some weird outsider's perspective. She saw Sullivan for what it was. She felt oddly nostalgic but happy she wasn't there. It was as if she hovered above that place and watched as a poor girl who grew up in the trailer park struggled to find a way out. She felt sorry for that girl. She wanted to help her. She wanted to let her know that there was beauty out there. Unfortunately, sometimes, people's circumstances cloud that beauty. But if they could find some way to lift the veil, a magnificent view would open up.

When Stacy finished her set, Janet watched her stop and talk at different tables. Some bought her CD, and Stacy signed it for them. Janet felt proud to know her. People loved her. They loved her voice, her positivity, her songs, even the heartbreakingly sad ones and the ones that depicted a life a lot of people never experienced or pretended didn't exist. She sang about those characters with empathy and humor. It was a unique talent that would never make it on mainstream radio.

When Stacy sat down with Janet, Laura brought her a Rum Collins, and Stacy stood back up and hugged her. The hug lasted longer than people were accustomed to hugging, and she brought her in so tight as if the pain they both harbored acknowledged each other and said they were okay. A genuine love passed between those two ladies—comfort, acceptance, warmth. Stacy sat back down. Laura placed a motherly hand on Janet's shoulder as she walked to another table. Instinctively, Janet reached to touch Laura's hand, but it slipped away before she could reciprocate. Janet left her own hand on her own shoulder for a brief second.

"Stacy," Janet said, "I knew you were talented, but my god, that was something else."

Stacy gave her a downturned smile. And mouthed the words, "Thank you."

"Speaking of talent," Stacy said, "Have you decided what your first painting will be? I can't wait to see what you do."

"I have."

"Then get on home," Stacy said. "I'm packing up here, and I'll see you at the house. After my gig tonight, we can explore together. I can't wait for you to experience the Key West nightlife."

"Thank you," Janet said, "for everything. And for bringing me here. This place really is magical. I don't know what it is, but it just makes you feel good. Sitting here, in this courtyard. It's the most perfect place I've ever been."

"It's the ghost of Hemingway," Stacy said. "That, and a bit of alcohol."

"What? Who?"

"Hemingway? Surely, you know who that is, right?"

"I've never read him."

"He used to hang out here way before it was Blue Heaven. Refereed a boxing match here once or twice. His ghost is everywhere in Key West."

"I guess I'll have to read his work while I'm here."

"You don't have to read his work. I mean, it's fun. If you are into dudes that act overly masculine to cover up for the fact that they might be gay."

"What?"

"I'm just being stupid. Read his books. They are fine. A lot of women talk shit about him, thinking he's a misogynist. Read *The Sun Also Rises* and see how he writes about Lady Brett Ashley. She's stronger than any of the men in that story. And then when you become a fan, I'll take you to his house. Look on our bookshelf in the living room when you get home. You'll see a copy there. Eli loves him. And don't worry, I didn't know who he was either until I met Eli. But not knowing about Hemingway in Key West is borderline criminal."

"Thank you again for lunch."

"See you in a bit. Go do some painting."

41

The Greyhound bus unloaded at the Key West bus terminal. Every passenger exited except for the smelly drunk guy in the back. His head leaned back, and he snored short of swallowing his tongue. The driver was warned about him when he transferred buses in Miami. He kept an eye on him, but the man slept the entire ride and gave him no issues. He woke him, escorted him off the bus, and left him in Key West to make his way among the other bums. Every day, more made their way down. Everyone trying to capitalize on the warm weather and the tourist dollars.

Bleary-eyed, Bobby stepped into radiant sunshine, ready to find his wife. He'd give her one chance to go home with him, but otherwise, he was prepared to do what he planned.

He looked around. The airport was behind him, the Atlantic Ocean in front of him. Turquoise waters as far as he could see. He didn't know what to expect of Key West, but it wasn't the paradise before him. He saw no buildings, just Roosevelt Boulevard and cars zooming by. The American flag waved proudly. He asked someone who stood next to him, a short, browned-skinned woman, where the city was. She didn't speak English. He asked an older man with a great mustache.

"Old Town or New Town?" the old man asked.

"Fuck if I know," Bobby said. "If someone was on vacation, where would they go?"

The old man pointed in the direction of Old Town.

"Walking distance?" Bobby asked.

"Not for me," the old man said.

Bobby waved him off and started walking with his thumb out. He stayed on the west side of the road, opposite the water, to catch a ride into town. He reached into his pocket and counted what was left of his money from Janet's mother. A lady walked a dog. A couple passed by on bicycles. He walked on. Palm trees to his left, sand live oaks to the right. He shuffled along on the sandy path parallel to the highway. He took off his shirt. His mouth parched. His buzz wearing off. He worked up enough spit in his mouth to swallow another oxycodone and lit the half of a cigarette he returned to the pack at the last stop. Only three left in his pack. Thunder roared from the opposite side of the island as a storm rolled in from the Gulf. He walked for twenty or thirty minutes and still no buildings. If it weren't for the cars that whizzed by, he'd think he walked on an uninhabited island.

Finally, up ahead, a pink three-story condo. Windsurfer sails visible across the street in the Atlantic. Pavilions. A tropical city coming to life. He passed another mid-sized condo. He walked through the parking lot, checking car door handles until he found one unlocked. Tossing the lit cigarette butt into the bushes, he rummaged through the console and glove box, scoring three dollars and sixteen cents and four cigarettes. He continued through the parking lot. Four mopeds parked next to each other. Rental signs hung from the back seats. A key in the ignition of the yellow one. He laid his shirt down on the seat, sat, turned the key, and it started. Pulling onto the boulevard, he drove toward town. Life was good for a rare, brief moment.

He followed the curved road and took the first left onto Atlantic Boulevard without knowing where to go. He harbored the wild idea that perhaps he might see Janet walking the street.

He passed a nature reserve to his left, and a crowd of tourists on the sidewalks walked with beach towels on the way to the beach. Single-story homes on the right and the beach on the left. Parking lot. Still waiting for a town. He felt a bit of frustration and moments of confusion or clarity. He didn't know which. After traveling for twenty-four hours, the possibility occurred to him that she might not be in Key West. It could've been a ruse by the mother and nurse to get him out of town and further from Janet. He shook himself from thinking that way. She was there, and he would find her. He watched two women in bikinis riding bicycles on the sidewalk. He swerved into the other lane briefly, and a black man with a patch on his eye driving the truck in the oncoming lane honked in time for Bobby to swerve out of the way. The black man shouted out something about drunk tourists. Bobby raised his middle finger and continued. He rode behind a tourist trolley that slowed nearly to a stop by an old brick building, explaining the West Martello Tower to those onboard.

He stopped at the first beachside restaurant that he saw. He parked, put on his shirt, and walked in. He told the hostess that he didn't need a table.

"I'll be in and out," he said. He looked at the young girl uncomfortably long. He went to the bathroom and dribbled out an amber liquid. Then, he went to the bar where he ordered a shot of whiskey, the cheapest they offered, and a beer. He drank them both in a matter of seconds. He paid and left no tip. He smiled at the young hostess, showing his remaining yellow teeth. The oxycodone and the alcohol working nicely together.

On Reynolds Street, he became frustrated riding through neighborhoods. Cars parked on the street, palm trees in every yard, along with many other trees he never saw before: banana trees, mango trees, kapok trees, gumbo-limbo trees, banyan trees, orchid trees. A world away from the pine forests of Sullivan.

Two women on moped scooters rode by him and waved. He showed them his middle finger.

Headed south on United Street, he passed a row of conch houses. A larger two-story house flew a rainbow flag alongside an American flag. He rode on and looked at every woman he drove by. Traffic increased and he came to a stop sign at Duval Street. Packs of bicycles, pedestrians, a small motorized train with people sitting under covered yellow cars, and a red caboose that read "Conch Train." The smiling faces waved to him from the back. He scowled. The entire place seemed fake to him, like a movie set.

He turned west on Duval. Shop after shop and bar after bar on either side of the narrow street. Ornate Victorian mansions that were renovated for commercial purposes. Restaurants. Tattoo shops. Souvenir shops. T-shirt shops. Crowds of people looking way too happy. Four motorcycles revved their engines. People drank on balconies. The place was unlike anything he imagined. More rainbow flags. He saw two men walking hand in hand. He muttered, "faggots" as he stared, turning his head to look at their mustached faces. Sunburned, tank tops, short shorts, flip flops. He had never been more out of place. A leather-skinned lady wearing a bikini top rode by on a bicycle with a small dog in her front basket. A gray-haired, pony-tailed man, maybe a pirate, walked by with an iguana on his shoulder.

Traffic slowed nearly to a crawl. Further down, diners eating and drinking outside at tables under umbrellas. Lines of bicycles chained to posts or bike racks. Mopeds lined up on the curbs. Crowds waiting to cross the street. People sitting at kiosks on street corners offering tourist information and selling excursions. Thunder clapped as if it split the sky. Fat raindrops fell hard making a sound on the asphalt. Petrichor filled his nostrils. He saw an Irish bar named after Kevin, the owner, and pulled off the road, walked the moped onto the sidewalk and left it, oblivious to the people walking by and watching him abandon a vehicle.

The bar just opened its doors for the morning and was already filled with merrymakers. Tables lined with pints of Guinness and empty shot glasses. A man stood on stage, played guitar, and sang about unicorns left behind from Noah's Ark. He ordered a beer from the big-breasted barmaid wearing a low-cut t-shirt and kilt and dropped some crumbled bills on the bar. Bobby's view of the city shifted from annoyance to a realization that he might be in the greatest city in the world, full of morning drunks and beautiful women.

A woman ran in from the downpour with her t-shirt clinging to her skin. Braless and nipples showing through. No attempt to cover up. She pulled the shirt that suctioned to her skin and wrung out water from her hair. Bobby made no effort to conceal his gawking. He wouldn't have been aware that he stared if she would've confronted him anyway. He was swimming in the effects of the drugs and alcohol. Floating above himself. Waves of euphoria, of warmth, washed over him. He drank his beer and watched the torrential downpour just feet away, people scurrying to find shelter, laughter, shouting, the crowd inside singing along to a song about life being pretty plain and puddles gathering rain. Bobby never experienced this many people collectively enjoying themselves and ignoring the troubles that seemed to occupy life. Was it possible to live a life of unburdened joy? He felt a tinge of anger because moments like that so seldom happened in Sullivan. Maybe if they did, things would be different. His life would've been different. Where did these people come from? If he found Janet, would it be possible for them to live a life like this? Could they start new? Would she understand that he was a victim of his circumstances, but if removed from those circumstances, he could change?

Just as quickly as the rain started, it stopped, and Bobby floated back down into his body. His beer was empty, so he set the glass on the bar and walked out into the blinding daylight. There were two suns and the denizens looked like marionettes come alive in a fun house out of a fever dream. Steam rose from the asphalt. Bird song sounded like it arose from a thousand bird choir. The world moved slower. An osprey seemed to hang in the air with its dinner in its clutches.

He walked on, amazed at the number of people pouring in and out of Sloppy Joe's. Bicycles at every intersection, maneuvering alongside cars, golf carts, motor scooters, funny cars, and the conch train once again. Pedestrians walked in and out of shops with bags of clothing in one hand and plastic cups of alcoholic drinks in the other. Women with big hats, men with big hats. Floral shirts. Some with matching floral shorts. All of it was the oddest thing Bobby ever witnessed. One woman stepped from a motorcycle with her cutout leather pants exposing her ass cheeks. She wore a black bikini top that barely covered her giant fake breasts. The man with her was burly-chested and shirtless underneath his leather vest.

At the next intersection, tourism was even more pronounced. On one corner, the ticket booth for the conch train tours. A clock on top of the ticket booth seemed to be ticking backward. Bobby focused, but his vision blurred, and he saw two clocks. A rolling cart hawking wares: Panama Jack hats, cheap sunglasses, leather bracelets, wooden necklaces, seashell earrings, and silver rings.

On a bench, a man sat covered in rags. Bobby stopped in front of him and looked down.

"Can I help you?" the man mumbled. A gray beard hung to his chest and dread-locked gray hair down past his shoulders. A yellow, calloused toe with a curled, fungus-ridden toenail stuck out the end of a hole in his shoe.

"You ever hear of a girl, a singer, named Stacy Ringling?" Bobby asked.

The man shook his head.

"I'm new here. First day. How is the law about me finding a place to sleep on the street?'

The man made a noise that resembled somewhat of a laugh. "Ain't the cops you gotta worry about. It's the other guys. There is some rough ones out there. I just keep to myself."

"You sleep right there?"

"Until I'm asked to leave. Then I go somewhere else. Hell, they know me by now and know I ain't no trouble. Some of the other guys, though. They get harassed pretty bad."

"Is there someone in particular I should know?"

"There is a guy named Scotty. Everyone knows him. He ain't homeless. Lives on a boat anchored out near Wisteria Island. Has three fingers. You'll see him most days down by the wharf, befriending tourists until they buy him beers and whatnot. Good-looking guy with a great mustache. Trust me. You ask enough people, you'll find Scotty. He'll know anything you need to know about this town."

"Appreciate you," Bobby said. He handed him a cigarette.

The homeless rag-covered man nodded his head and accepted it. Bobby continued toward the wharf.

Along the waterfront, a cruise ship recently docked, inundating Mallory Square with even more tourists. Five twenty-somethings, four boys and a girl, as far as Bobby could tell, with long, nappy hair, sat in a circle passing a joint followed by a paper-bagged bottle. Their soles blackened from roaming barefooted, dressed in brown shabby clothes. One lazily finger-picked a Spanish gypsy song on a nylon-stringed guitar while a sleeping dog lay at his feet.

"Hey there," Bobby slurred.

The red-eyed girl with large pupils looked up at him. She was once pretty. No one else in the group acknowledged him. Was she a ghost? Was he? A scruffy-bearded young man looked over his shoulder and up at Bobby, presumably to see what the girl was looking at. When he saw the dumb look on Bobby's face, he turned back around.

"Y'all know where I can find Scotty?" Bobby said.

The one playing guitar stopped strumming and said, "Fuck Scotty, man."

The one that looked over his shoulder said, "Just look for a three-fingered bastard hustling tourists. He'll be dressed like Magnum PI."

The street kids laughed. The guitar started back up, and they sang a chorus out of sync with the words, "Fuck Scotty, that three-fingered son-of-bitch."

"Appreciate you," Bobby said and started to leave.

"Hey," the girl called out.

Bobby turned and looked at her.

"That's him there," she said and nodded to a man sitting on the ledge talking to a young couple.

42

J anet sharpened the pencils Stacy included in the art set and began sketching a plan on the small canvas, starting with the shape of the buoy, which she decided would take up most of the canvas, nearly out of the frame, with maybe a quarter inch of canvas left on the top and bottom. When she outlined the buoy, she looked at it and hated the proportions. It didn't leave enough room for any of the people waiting in line. And how bland would a painting of a buoy be, she thought. Why the hell would anyone want a painting of a buoy? She then began to play with the dimensions of the shape a bit. She never really attempted abstract art before, usually preferring realism. Still, as she sketched and erased and became frustrated with her drawings and erased some more, she began hearing Bobby standing behind her and criticizing her work. *What the hell is that? That looks so fucking stupid. It looks like a retarded kid with no arms tried to draw with his fucking toes.* Tears began to blur her vision. She kept sketching, and although she hated what it looked like, she kept on. Erasing then sketching, eventually stopping, before pushing the easel over, throwing the pencil across the room, and letting out a scream like a frustrated child.

She sat on the couch and cried with her head in her hands. After about five minutes of tears, she wiped her eyes dry, set the easel back on its legs, and picked up the canvas. She looked at it, and although it didn't look quite like the Southernmost Point, she thought it possessed a unique quality. Art existed somewhere in there, she thought. If she used the right colors and wrote the Southernmost Point somewhere on the painting, it could pass as the famous landmark. The more she looked at it, the more she liked it. She mixed some colors and painted the deformed object, making it look almost like a buoy with a few streaks off the side that could pass as people. And finally, legibly and the only thing that didn't look like a toddler just learned to finger paint, she wrote on the buoy The Southernmost Point. The precise realism she practiced in high school was nowhere in that painting, but she loved it. The forgetting of everything she learned allowed her to paint like a child, a more accurate expression of herself.

She stepped back and examined her work, proud of what she saw. She didn't care if anyone else liked it. She painted for herself, and if she liked it, chances were someone else would too.

She didn't do any more paintings that day, but she did look over her pictures and think of what she would do next. She wasn't ready for the little girl on the bike yet, so she thought, maybe a few more silly ones—perhaps the chickens at Blue Heaven or the shower.

While she waited for the water to boil in the tea kettle, she looked at the bookshelf of paperbacks. She skimmed through titles. *Ninety-Two in the Shade, To Have and Have Not,* fifteen or so books all by the same author, John D. MacDonald, and all the titles mentioned a different color. *The Unmasking of Robert-Houdin, Islands in the Stream, Old Man and the Sea, Far Tortuga,* and many more. She saw *The Sun Also Rises,* pulled it from the shelf, carried it under her arm as she poured the boiling water into a mug, and steeped a tea bag. She went to the porch with the book and mug and breathed freely. She felt good. Better than she felt in years and, for a short time, didn't think of Bobby. When she did, she stopped pretty quickly without getting upset. She thought Bobby would never just sit on a porch and drink tea. *What's the point? We ain't doing shit but sitting,* he would say. And for the first time, she began to pity him. Her face made an upside-down smile. A tear dropped. But one of the good ones. She opened the book and read about Jewish boxer Robert Cohn.

Later, she called home, and her mom told her that her voice sounded different. She wouldn't recognize her in another week or so. Maybe one day, her mom said, you'll love your broken parts. She hadn't heard her mother sound like a mother in a long time. She told her she painted. She told her about the lunch. About the bike ride. Her mother listened.

"How long are you staying?" her mother asked.

"Bobby gets out in a week. I don't want to be anywhere near Sullivan when he does."

"I'm scared, Janet," her mother said. "I'm scared of dying alone."

"Mom, the nurses are coming in and taking care of you. I won't be gone long. I promise. I just need to be gone when Bobby gets out."

"I might be dead before you get back."

"Mom, please don't do that. Please. I love you, but I can't be there right now. You know this."

"Well, I'm glad you're painting again. You always had such talent. Hope I'll be able to see them. Hope you're having fun. Don't forget about your mother."

"You'll see them, Momma. I love you."

Her mother hung up.

She took another cup of tea and sat. She sat until Stacy arrived. An hour or two later. She didn't know.

"What have you gotten into?" she asked. She parked her bike, her guitar hung on her back, and, towed behind her bike, her amp in a trailer meant for a child.

Janet smiled. "I had a good day," she said.

"You didn't get into my happy pills, did ya?"

"No, but I feel good. Better than I have in a long while."

"Enjoy every minute of it. Feeling good doesn't come around too often. And when it does, it doesn't last nearly as long as feeling bad does. Shit, give me some. I'm tired as hell, and in a couple of hours, I've got to go right back to work. Some nights, music hardly feels like work, but other nights I wonder why I'm wasting my time," Stacy said. She kissed Janet on the cheek and sat beside her on the porch. She kicked her feet up on the rail. "You know what? Let's take this moment and bask in your feel-good."

Less than ten seconds of silence went by.

"What are you drinking?" Stacy asked her.

"Tea."

"I could use a beer."

Janet lifted from her chair.

"What the hell are you doing?" Stacy asked.

"Getting you a beer," Janet told her.

"I said I could use a beer. I didn't say get me a beer. If I want one bad enough, I'll get it."

Janet put her hand on Stacy's shoulder. "Years of habit is hard to break," she said. "You forgot to add bitch after saying you could use a beer though." Janet smirked and went into the house.

Stacy raised her eyebrows, stunned at Janet's response.

"Close your eyes," Janet said to Stacy before coming back outside. She held a beer in one hand and the painting in the other. She sat the beer on the porch rail and held the painting before Stacy, who still held her eyes closed.

"Go ahead and open them," Janet said.

"What's this?"

"What's it look like?"

"Girl. Are you shitting me? One day and this is what you've done already?"

Janet couldn't hold back her smile.

"Holy shit," Stacy said. She crooked her neck to look at it from another angle.

"Well?" Janet said.

"Well, nothing. I fucking love it," Stacy said. "You sure you didn't get into my happy pills? This is unbelievable."

"You really like it?"

Stacy looked at Janet. "Stop asking me that. I done told you. I love it. She stood and hugged Janet. "You crank out more like this and you'll be selling some in no time. Hell, I might take it with me to the show tonight and see if I can sell it."

"I'm not sure I'm ready for others to see it yet."

"We'll let the public decide if it's ready. I'm proud of you."

They sat on the porch with their drinks and Eli came home before they finished. He wore the clown suit. He leaned in front of them on the rail.

"How was work, babe?" Stacy asked.

"Humiliating. I think I'm finished with kid parties. I'm serious. I can't do that shit anymore."

"Then quit," Stacy said. "Just do the escape stuff."

"I can't keep making fucking balloon animals and juggling and swallowing goldfish. I'm not a jester. And the kids throwing shit at me and the parents laughing at the idiot. I'm done."

"Good. Tonight you'll put on a show that blows people away," Stacy said. "People come night after night to see Elijah the Great. They know you're great. I know you're great." She lifted the last half of her beer for him. He downed it in a second.

"What would I do without her?" he said to Janet.

"Look what Janet painted today." Stacy lifted the painting from behind her chair where it leaned against the house.

"I'll be damned," Eli said. "We got Salvador Dalí staying with us."

Janet blushed and looked down.

"I'm not kidding. That's damn good."

"Thank you," Janet said.

"Dinner plans?" Eli said. "I got about two hours before I got to go set up."

Randall's moped puttered down the street.

"Am I in time for dinner?" he said, walking up the steps with a bottle of wine and a baguette.

"Of course. Whenever are you late?" Stacy said. "In fact, I think it's past your turn to cook anyway."

"Wine and bread. What else do you want?"

Eli changed from his work clothes and then grilled a pork loin. Stacy made black beans and rice. After dinner, Randall took a shower, emerging from the bathroom in an evening gown, wig, and makeup. Janet's eyes widened, and she looked at Stacy and then back at Randall.

Stacy laughed. Randall smiled and said, "Y'all ain't tell her?"

Eli shook his head. Stacy laughed again. "It's his night job," Stacy said. "He's a Drag Queen bartender."

"Oh," Janet said. "You like men?"

"What?" Randall said.

Eli laughed this time. "I'm going to clean the grill." He took a beer and stepped outside.

"I mean, you dress like a woman to sleep with men?" Janet asked.

Randall looked at her sideways. "No," he said. "I dress like a woman because I get paid to dress like a woman. And well, you know what? I kind of like it."

Stacy stepped in. "Randall, you know she didn't mean anything by it. She just doesn't know. I'll bring her by tonight and she can see you work."

"I'm so sorry if I offended you. I don't know why I said that. I really didn't know. I've never met anyone who does that. I just assumed..." She stopped herself. "I'm sorry."

Randall kissed Stacy on the cheek and said to Janet, "No offense taken. I'll see y'all a bit later."

Eli poked his head in the door, "I'm heading out."

Stacy said, "I hope you get all their money."

"I didn't offend Randall, did I?" Janet said.

"It takes way more than that to offend him. I promise you are good."

Stacy and Janet were going to watch Eli perform and then after sunset go back to the Hog's Breath Saloon for Stacy's three-hour show of cover songs and the occasional original.

"How'd you meet Eli?" Janet asked.

"When Nashville didn't work out, I moved down here and was living in my van. For three years, I did that. Showered at the Bight Marina, worked as a waitress, and played music on a bench on Mallory Square, selling what CDs and cassettes I had left. Didn't sell many. Some people would stop and listen though and drop a dollar or two in the guitar case and if it weren't for those people I'm not sure I would've kept going. Finally landed a regular gig at the Hog's Breath where Eli walked in one day and then the next and then the next. He listened to me so intently. Wouldn't take his eyes from me. I think I even saw him cry, but he never admitted it. Eventually, he asked me to dinner and then he took me in. I sold my van and bought a motorcycle."

43

Having learned from Scotty where Stacy Ringling regularly performed, Bobby Drexler stumbled into the Hog's Breath Saloon. He was nearly out of oxycodone, having traded most to Scotty in exchange for information. He saw the girl he remembered from Sullivan singing her songs on the outside stage. A fifty-eight foot tall Cuban mahogany grew through the tin roof. Stickers and car tags from all fifty states covered nearly every inch of the wall with sayings like "TwatLVR" or "MUFFDVR." One sticker said, "Fuck the Manatees, Save the Titties" and another sticker said, "Divers Do it Deeper." First time patrons could spend a significant amount of time reading all the messages.

Bobby snuck into an unoccupied seat at the bar. He remained hidden behind the crowd that sat at the tables in front of the stage and stood by the bar and drank his beers slowly. His body itched, but he wanted to save the pills for when he really needed them. Stacy looked just as beautiful as always. Listening to her sing, Bobby welled up with anger. He hated her strength, and here she sang away as confident as ever. And she lured Janet away. She always tried to, and this time, she almost did. But he would find her.

He watched her with such intent that he imagined it as her instead of Janet so many years ago after the middle school dance, bent over the four-wheeler. He remembered Stacy walking out into the pond. She was always openly sexual. She must've fucked six different guys while at Sullivan High. But never him.

He listened to her sing and watched people dance and drop money in her tip jar, and at one point, he thought she locked eyes on him. He thought he noticed her suck in an air of surprise as she saw that familiar face from so long ago. He half-smiled. Her eyes squinted. When she took her first set break, he slunk out.

He returned to the docks and found Scotty again sitting on a park bench, cat-calling tourists.

"That was her alright," Bobby said.

"No shit," Scotty said. "I'm going to ride out to Christmas Tree if you need a place to crash tonight."

"Where?" Bobby asked.

Scotty pointed out to the Gulf. Bobby could barely make out the shape of an island by the moon's light.

"Wisteria Island, Christmas Tree Island, whatever you want to call it. If you don't have a place to sleep, it's better than staying here and being harassed by the cops."

"Is that where you live?"

"Nah, motherfucker. Do I look homeless? I live on my boat. But you sure as hell ain't staying there with me. I don't give a shit where you stay, but I'm heading out there for a bit and if you want a ride. I'll give you a ride is all I'm saying."

"I'll take a ride," Bobby said.

In the early 1900s, the US Navy started dredging the harbor, and the sediment from the recurring project over the years eventually created an island. It remained unnamed until 1925 when a lighthouse tender ship, being used as a floating hospital, sank off the manufactured island. The ship was called *The Wisteria*. The island came to be known as Wisteria Island. Some folks called it Christmas Tree Island because of the invasive Australian pine that covered the land. Besides the underbrush, seagrape, black torch, and gumbo-limbo, native plants mixed in with the non-native plants, make-shift housing scattered about, and rusted boat parts, beer cans, discarded tarps, and migratory birds. Homeschool children ran free, living on the boats anchored offshore. At night, bonfires started. The inhabitants cooked fish over an open fire. Reefer filled the air. Bottles were passed around. Guitars were strummed. The thirty people who called that island home lived in a modern-day Gilligan's Island or Swiss Family Robinson.

A privately owned island, although some debate existed about ownership. Since the 50s or 60s, those who couldn't afford to live in Key West or those who no longer wanted to be found made Wisteria Island their home—a sophisticated homeless camp. Booby Red, the patriarch of the island, the one who lived the longest on the island, owned a generator that he would sometimes crank up to turn on the TV to watch the World Series or the news if something was worth knowing. Sometimes, he ran a blender and made daiquiris. When hurricanes whipped through, they packed up what they could, caught a bus from Key West onto the mainland, and then returned and rebuilt. It was here that Scotty dropped off Bobby for the night.

44

Mallory Square bustled with tourists when Stacy and Janet arrived. Stacy explained the tradition of the Sunset Celebration to Janet on the walk over. Music blared from different speakers, blending in with chatter and laughter and street performers and artists jostling for dollars. Birds squawked. A cruise ship bellowed. The smell of grilled oysters drifted with the breeze. A tarot card reader. A booth of Christmas ornaments. Another booth sold trinkets made from guitar strings. Touristy paintings sold every couple of minutes. A man played a guitar and harmonica at the same time while carrying a snare drum and a high-high hat on his back that he controlled with his feet by wires attached to his ankles. Mallory Square was overwhelming but beautiful in its chaos.

"So people just cheer when the sun sets?" Janet asked.

"We survived another day. What's not to celebrate?"

"Every day?"

"Every day," Stacy said.

"Doesn't it hurt your eyes to stare into the sun?"

"Squint. Or look kind of off-angle, you know. But you don't want to miss the green flash."

"Is that a real thing?"

"Who is to say?"

212

"You've never seen it?"

"Oh, I've seen it."

A crowd gathered around two barefoot boys with faces painted like the Joker. They stood side by side, juggling bowling pins and passing them back and forth mid-flip.

"How old are those kids?" Janet asked.

A cardboard box sat on the ground before them, and people filled it with change and dollar bills.

"The taller one, Ricky, is fourteen, and his brother, Jacob, is twelve," Stacy said. "Not bad for kids, huh?" They both had shaggy light-brown hair and shorts that hung below their knees. Above Ricky's lip, the slight beginnings of a peach-fuzz mustache.

They walked by the juggling kids, and Stacy bent as they walked by. She dropped a dollar in the cap, winked, and saw Jacob catch sight of her cleavage. He nearly missed a catch, but instead, he caught all three pins and started over. People clapped, as it looked like a rehearsed part of the show. Ricky played along and caught his as well.

With a brief break in the performance, Stacy said, "You boys sure are getting better."

"Thank you, Ms. Stacy, " Ricky said. Jacob couldn't erase his grin.

"Would you mind showing my friend here what you guys can do with knives?"

"You bet, Ms. Stacy," Ricky said. He pulled out six sheathed machetes from a large duffle bag on the ground behind him.

"You know we usually do this last," Jacob said, "But for you, Ms. Stacy, we'll just have to do it twice." He smirked.

"I appreciate that, Jacob." She kissed him on the cheek and then stood back with the rest of the crowd. Jacob's cheeks flushed, and his buck-toothed smile somehow got larger.

"What do you mean knives?" Janet asked. "Those are a lot larger than knives."

"You'll see," Stacy told her. "It really is pretty remarkable. These kids are going to be something someday. You watch."

"You don't think they're too young to do this stuff? Are their parents around?"

"Look at those things," Stacy said. The boys unsheathed the twelve-inch blade machetes. A bigger crowd gathered. A murmur went through the crowd with the same concerns Janet expressed. "Whoo hoo," Stacy shouted. "That's what I'm talking about." Her shouts attracted more people.

The boys performed flawlessly, and Jacob set his machetes down behind him, picked up an apple, and tossed it over his shoulder to Ricky who was bowing for the pleased crowd, acting like he didn't know his brother tossed the apple. He stood and swatted at it with the big knife, and the crowd gasped when the apple split in two as if made of paper. The noise from the crowd exploded, and the box in front of them filled with bills, not just ones but some fives and tens, and a few people dropped in twenties.

Stacy and Janet moved on as the crowd swarmed the boys, asking them the same questions they were asked after every performance.

"Can you believe those boys?" Stacy said.

"Stacy," Janet said. "Aren't they a little too young to be working? Let alone working with such dangerous objects. I don't know. Doesn't it seem a bit exploitative to you?"

"Honey, we are all exploited eventually. It's just a matter of if you want to have fun while doing it. And I think those boys are having fun."

"What about the parents?"

"They are sitting right over there. They live on a boat and homeschool the kids. Those kids are living free. Don't worry about them."

Another crowd formed at the next piece of entertainment. A small, dark man with a foreign accent. West Indies. He stood on a garbage can, calling people toward him. He got the predominantly white crowd to come closer by saying, "Hurry up folks, it will be dark soon, and then you won't be able to see me." He flailed his arms to his side in an overly animated way and smiled. "Except for these," he said, pointing to his teeth. The crowd roared.

"There's Eli," Stacy said. Eli's head could be seen just above the crowd as he watched what the crowd watched. The same routine every night, and he had the timing down perfectly. He wore the unfastened jacket so he could begin as soon as the other act ended so that his show wouldn't interfere with the sunset and the illusory green flash. Nobody could compete with Mother Nature.

The small, black man was an acrobat. He backflipped off the garbage can and landed in the splits. The crowd roared. He then said he needed to warm up and did ten one-handed push-ups with each arm. He then jumped, spread his legs, and did a toe touch.

"You like that, huh?" he said to a young man standing with his girlfriend. "You wish she could do that," the performer said. The crowd laughed. The young man blushed. "How about when I do this?" He picked up a beer can from his plastic box that held his props and set it on the ground, exaggerating, bending over slowly and flirtatiously.

"I see you looking," he said to the young man. The crowd laughed some more. The young man now became seemingly uncomfortable. The girl he was with thought it funny. The performer asked for a five-dollar bill from anyone in the crowd. People held out money. He grabbed the one closest to him. He then asked for another. He put the first one in his pocket and grabbed the next one. He asked if anyone would give him a twenty. The crowd laughed. One guy held out a twenty. The acrobat gladly accepted. He crumpled the twenty in a tight ball and placed it on the garbage can he previously stood on.

"Now," he said. He took a few steps back from the can and continued, "I will run like this." He briskly walked towards the can on the ground, using his hands as little wings. "My hands do this because I'm a fairy." The crowd laughed. They loved gay jokes. Almost as much as black jokes. "And when I get close to the can, I will...Oh, you'll see," he said, returning to his original starting point. The crowd remained silent, anticipating what the little black fairy would do. He stood, lifted his arms, and did some meditative breathing.

"People are okay with these jokes?" Janet asked Stacy.

"Honey, it's what the crowd wants to hear. Please the crowd, make some money. It's the way the world works."

"It seems kind of gross. Doesn't seem right. "

"Well, the world ain't right, now is it? Look at him."

The acrobat ran and did a no-handed cartwheel over the can, grabbing the crumbled twenty-dollar bill from atop it. The crowd wanted more. The acrobat bowed. He then snatched a ball cap from one onlooker's head and walked the circle collecting money. He walked by Stacy, and she blew him a kiss. He winked back at her.

"You know him, too?" Janet asked.

"Jamie?" She pronounced it with an H. "Of course. It's a small island, you know."

"It's not humiliating to make fun of yourself for others' enjoyment? Isn't that what Eli complained about when he got off work today?"

"The job of the jester. Life is hard, as you know. We can either laugh at it or fight against it. But guess who always wins that fight? We damn sure don't. We are part of life's grand performance. Hell, maybe it's all just one huge cosmic joke, you know?"

Janet seemed struck by Stacy's insight. "But some things that happen in life aren't so funny," Janet said.

"Not at all," Stacy said. "So people like Jamie and Eli and I hope to give people a brief respite from the horrors that exist."

Jamie, the acrobat, grabbed a young man from the audience for his next trick, and he picked the one he flirted with earlier to lie down in the center of the circle. The young man, although blushing, did as instructed. Jamie then bent down and spread the young man's legs. The young man refused at first. "It's okay," Jamie said. "Trust me. You'll like it. I'm gentle." The crowd again roared at the innuendo. The young man's girlfriend took a picture with the camera hanging from her neck.

"All I'm going to do," Jamie continued, "is stand right here." He stood as close to the young man's genitals as possible and then turned around. "And then do a backflip."

The young man jumped up. "Hell no," he said.

"Sit down," Jamie yelled at him. "Don't embarrass your girlfriend by showing the public you are a coward." He admonished the young man with a smile and over exaggerated the wagging of his finger with a hand on his hip.

The girlfriend laughed the loudest. The young man got back into position.

"Now, with your hands, cover your eyes." The young man once again did as he was told. "And on the count of three, I will do the back flip. But you mustn't move. Otherwise, you may lose something precious." The young man covered his eyes in a clear state of nervousness. The crowd shouted at the uneasiness of another. "You guys count with me," Jamie yelled over the crowd's noise. The crowd said one in unison, and Jamie did the flip. The crowd screamed with joy, and the young man jumped to his feet.

"Oops," Jamie said. "I should have warned you of my premature problem." The crowd laughed. "Give a round of applause for my assistant." The young man bowed, and Jamie did another backflip, much to the crowd's enjoyment.

Janet looked up at Eli, who watched, not with enjoyment as the spectators did, but with respect for Jamie's command of the crowd, an understanding of a street performer's way of life. While they may not be on a stage in Vegas, as Eli once imagined, they were in the next best venue.

For his last trick of the evening, the acrobat chose two more assistants: a young lady and a young man. He placed the young lady straddling a bike, but instead of sitting on the seat, she leaned just in front of it with the rest of her body bent close to the handlebars. The young man then held a hula-hoop just over the girl's back. Jamie took a few steps back.

"It is essential that you do not look up," he told the girl. "I'm serious. Stay with your head down. That's how men prefer it anyway." The crowd cheered. Gay, black, misogynistic, couldn't go wrong with those jokes. The small, black, acrobat then ran and, like a true fairy, launched through the air, over the girl, and through the hula-hoop and landed in a clean, tucked roll on the hard concrete as the crowd stood stunned. Jamie stood and bowed, and the crowd screamed with delight.

"Now," he said, "If you just enjoyed what you saw, please help us out. All of us here work hard for your entertainment. Help us make this living that we love. Thank you." He took another bow, and the crowd poured money into his cardboard box.

"How much do you think he makes a night?" Janet asked.

"Not enough," Stacy said.

Eli was next.

He made his racist jokes as another white man chained him up in his straight jacket and slowly raised him above the crowd. He hung upside down and caught eyes with Stacy and Janet. Stacy blew him a kiss. He smiled slightly—enough for her to see. Behind him, the sun made its way closer to the horizon in the pink sky. The smell of reefer hung in the air. Someone banged on conga drums. Pelicans streaked across the sky.

"I don't like this," Janet said. "I feel bad for him." It reminded her of a lynching instead of performance art. The crowd looked like hundreds of Bobbys shouting out and laughing at the black man hanging from chains.

"This is awful," Janet whispered to Stacy.

"It's Key West. We left political correctness on the mainland. Sometimes we have to play the game."

Eli squirmed around to make his escape.

"He has to dislocate his shoulders to do that," Stacy told Janet.

"Why go through so much pain?" Janet asked.

"Because look at the audience, they love it. And ultimately, he loves seeing that."

"But I thought he hated it."

"Not this part. Not this part. This is what he lives for. Look at those little kids up front staring at him in awe. They will remember him forever. Some people laugh a little too loudly, but others respect his work, and he helps them create memories. We get to live here. For others, this may be the only time they ever visit. We are part of the experience. We are creating something that doesn't exist anywhere else in the world."

Eli shed the chains, and the straight jacket dropped to the ground. He spread his arms wide and hung like an upside-down crucifix. Janet understood why they did what they did.

45

B obby woke underneath the trampoline of a propped-up hull of a discarded Hobie Cat. The no-see-ums and mosquitoes feasted on him through the night. The sun already blared down, and he emerged groggy and slightly confused, having a vague memory of getting to the island. A dog trotted down the rocky shoreline. Three people walked down a way collecting flotsam and jetsam in a garbage bag. Fifteen or twenty boats anchored just offshore. The smell of coffee and bacon drifted by. Bobby couldn't remember ever being more thirsty. He had one oxycodone left. He reached into his pocket for it, worked up the spit in his mouth, and swallowed the pill. It hung in his throat briefly before he could get it down, leaving on the back of his tongue a bitterness that tasted like urine smelled. He dry heaved. His stomach ached as he walked back into a wooded area, looked around, and found some crumbled newspaper. He dropped his pants to expel a foul liquid, wiped with the found newspaper, and emerged from the woods. Walking along the water's edge, he passed tents and hammocks hanging from limbs, shelters made from tarps, one with a recliner chair underneath it facing a television not plugged into anything, and a sailboat painted on the screen.

He walked until he found what looked like a community gathering spot. Tarps overhead, lawn chairs and camping chairs and office chairs scattered about, multiple rain barrels lined up together, a bookshelf with tattered paperbacks, towels and blankets hanging from trees, four children, maybe aged five to ten years old, sat around a chess board on the ground. Maybe ten adults, chatting and eating, gathered around a fire pit dug into the ground with a grill. A pot of coffee sat to the side of the grill, away from the hot coals, staying warm from indirect heat. Directly on the heat sat a large iron skillet filled with scrambled eggs. A man with long gray dreadlocks stopped strumming his guitar when he saw Bobby approach. The man, brown and wrinkly, wore only shorts. No shirt, no shoes. If looked at with the right angle, he didn't wear undershorts either. His old, withered testicles hung slightly visible under his shorts.

"Howdy," the man said. The others quieted when he spoke. "Hungry?"

Bobby stared, blinked his dried eyes, and nodded. "Thirsty," he said, his voice sounding like a rusty hinge.

"You're the man that Scotty dropped off last night, right?" the dread-haired man said.

Bobby nodded. A woman wearing a long skirt, white linen shirt, and no bra brought Bobby a cup made from a gourd that she filled with water that drained from one of the rain barrels marked potable. They had attached a generator to it and somehow figured a way to filter the water.

Bobby downed it and thanked the lady. She then brought Bobby a plate of eggs with bacon and an orange. He set the cup on a table made from a tree trunk, held the plate close to his face, and ate the food. He then sat the plate next to the cup.

"Have a seat," the man said, pointing to a camping chair. Bobby did.

"Scotty said he doesn't know you, but you needed a place to crash for a few days. He said you said you were looking for an old friend. Is that right?"

Bobby nodded. "I found her," he said. "I won't be here long. I'll stay out of y'all's way. I appreciate the food and water." He looked around at the camp as the others did their own thing. A pontoon boat approached the shore, and the kids gathered up, slung bookbags over their shoulders, and climbed aboard. Bobby turned his head and followed with his eyes, and the kids said bye as the boat pushed off and headed away.

"School," the man said.

"Y'all live out here? They live out here."

The man nodded. "Too expensive over there." He nodded his head toward Key West.

Bobby eyed a half-filled bottle of George Dickell sitting on a table by the fire.

"Need you a drink?" the man said.

Bobby nodded. "I'm rather dry."

"Get you a sip."

Bobby stood and picked up the bottle. His hand shook as he unscrewed the cap. His mouth watered. Bile rose up his gullet. He took a sip and closed his eyes as his stomach warmed.

"How do I get back over there?" Bobby asked. He took another sip and then screwed the cap on and set the bottle down. He sat back in his chair.

"Somebody'll be heading over. You can catch a ride with them."

"How long y'all been out here.?"

"I've been here thirteen years," the man said. "But people started living out here in the 50s. Currently, I've been out here the longest."

"Police don't bother y'all?"

"Not as long as we don't bother no one."

"They ever come out here?"

"Sure." The man set a small tray on his lap and rolled a joint. "But only when necessary."

He lit the joint, took a puff, and offered it to Bobby. Bobby accepted it and took a long hit until his lungs burned, and he coughed. The lady with the long skirt walked over. Bobby handed her the joint.

"Last time the police came out was because this motherfucker on the other side of the island brought an underage girl out here. She was a runaway. But then he started sleeping with her. Certain things we don't allow."

"So y'all called the cops on him?" Bobby asked.

"Only after we beat the shit out of him. He needed to get to the hospital."

"Who enforces the rules out here? You?"

"We all do."

"Besides sleeping with underage girls, what else isn't tolerated?"

"We don't allow heroin addicts over here. And no thieves. Other than that, the idea is just to be cool. Can you do that?"

"Yeah," Bobby said. He smiled his missing tooth smile, stretched his legs out, and scratched behind his ears. He closed his eyes, the buzz from the whiskey, the cannabis, and the oxycodone enveloping him in a comforting embrace.

46

They arrived at Randall's bar on Duval at nearly 11 p.m. Janet and Eli listened to Stacy's performance at the Hog's Breath, and when she ended, they walked down to see Randall. Stacy locked up her guitar at the Hog's Breath and would get it in the morning before her lunchtime show at Blue Heaven.

Mostly male patrons filled the large round bar. Some older women also sat there, but they were the minority. The bartenders were all younger males without shirts and glistening with glitter.

"What kind of bar is this?" Janet asked. Eli looked at Stacy.

"Just the kind of bar you need," Stacy said. "Should we have a drink before we go upstairs?"

"What is upstairs?" Janet asked.

"It's where Randall works."

But before they could order drinks, the DJ announced the show started in less than five minutes, and all but three men rose from their barstools and headed to the stairs.

"I guess we'll get one up there," Stacy said. She led the way to the front of the line, skipping the others waiting patiently, and an overweight man in fishnet lingerie and a blonde wig quickly led them through the velvet rope. He kissed all three on the cheek, squeezing Janet too long for her liking. All of it a bit too much for her liking but somehow liberating. She knew she would never go back to Bobby. She wasn't sure she could ever go back to Sullivan either. And although she was never religious, her family rarely went to church, maybe twice her entire life. Still, religion seemed prevalent. It permeated in nearly all aspects of society in Sullivan. She wasn't sure where the idea came from specifically. It subsisted there in Sullivan, and the gay lifestyle was considered an abomination from as early as she could remember. Entering a gay bar, filled her with anxiety: was she turning her back to God? Was she crossing a threshold into damnation? Panic rose in her, tightening her chest again, lumping her throat. She stopped halfway up the purple velvet stairs.

"I don't think I should be here," Janet said.

"Fuck that. You're going," Stacy replied, grabbed her by the wrist, and led her up. Eli walked behind them and said to Janet, "She's a bit of a firecracker, huh?"

Janet knew Stacy was already drunk, having watched her drink beer and take shots throughout her three-hour show. It seemed expected of her. Janet drank only one glass of wine while Stacy performed. Eli seemed to be able to drink beer like water, and it never changed his behavior. His voice stayed the same level, and his countenance didn't change. He remained the same even-keeled man sober or after however many beers he drank.

"Is that a man?" Janet asked, referring to a skinny, yet sculpted and sinewy, black woman in a skin-tight spaghetti-strapped evening gown standing on stage.

"Not when she is dressed like that." Stacy said.

"This is too much," Janet said. "I can't be here."

Stacy put her hand up to hush her. "We'll go as soon as we see Randall."

"This is what Randall does?"

"And he's fabulous."

"This doesn't bother you at all?" Janet asked Eli.

"No," he said.

The music started, the singer lip-synched to Cher's "Dark Lady," and the crowd sang along to the line about the fortune queen knowing more about "me than I knew myself." And while that song played, the crowd, while mostly gay, some straight women and a few straight men who were there with their girlfriends or wives, swayed and danced, and Stacy noticed Janet moving too. However, a half smile formed from her lips ever so slightly and barely noticeable but moving. The feeling of unity and love became palpable in that space of personal freedom, where people could be whoever they wanted, free from religious and familial dogma.

The song ended, the crowd cheered and clapped, and the dancer paraded around the stage collecting dollar bills. Then, the bar went dark except for a red light shining on the center of the stage, awaiting the next performer.

"Welcome to the stage, Raven," the voice in the speaker announced.

Randall walked out dressed as Raven. She wore a long green sequin evening gown and a wig of wavy golden locks. The four-inch heels didn't seem to give her any problems. She spread her arms to the crowd, commanding attention like a superstar, and held the pose while the audience clapped and shouted. And when they finally settled down, she blew kisses to Stacy and Eli and wiggled her fingers in a wave to Janet. Janet smiled and waved back.

"He's beautiful," she said to Stacy.

Stacy smiled. "She damn sure is. Look at that sexy motherfucker."

The music started. The classic drag show anthem: Gloria Gayner's "I Will Survive."

Stacy went to the bar and returned with a beer and a Long Island Iced Tea for Janet. Janet looked at her and then smiled.

"Thank you," she said. "What is it?"

"Just taste it," Stacy said, having to shout.

Janet did. Randall spun around on the stage and collected dollars from the crowd.

"Well?" Stacy asked.

"It's good."

"It's a Long Island. Might be the only drink you need tonight."

When Raven finished, Stacy shouted like she stood in the front row of a rock concert. Raven returned behind the bar, and Stacy maneuvered her way up close enough to eventually make room for Janet and Eli to get to the bar, too.

Raven leaned over and kissed Stacy's cheek.

"What did you think?" she asked Janet.

"Unbelievable. You're absolutely gorgeous."

"Little different than a rugged charter boat captain, huh?"

"Not sure I would say rugged," Eli said.

Raven poured four lemon drop shots, and they each took one before she made her way down the bar, talking and pouring drinks for customers and fans. The place became too crowded for them to hang out and chat with Raven, so after the next performance, they left.

47

The entire football team, coaches, and most of the student body were in attendance at Jared's funeral. Randall watched the pretense with disgust. Now that Jared was dead, cremated, and in the ground, people cared about him. The football coach even spoke about his "passion for the game and his commitment to the team." The church provided cookies, finger sandwiches, coffee, and cokes for fellowship after the service. Many stuck around for the free food. Jared's mother sat in the corner and accepted condolences and hugs. His stepdad stood and talked to other dads about the upcoming baseball season. Randall didn't know what Jared's biological father looked like, so he wasn't sure if he showed up or not.

Randall rode there with his parents but was ready to leave as soon as the service ended. His parents talked with some of the other parents. The chatter blended into an unbearable murmur. The acoustics in the banquet hall made it so that people had to nearly yell to one another to hear.

Randall walked outside and stared out over the cemetery. He didn't cry when he learned of Jared's death or during the ceremony. He thought maybe he should, but didn't feel much emotion. He hadn't felt much emotion since the death of his brother. It all seemed so pointless to him. The charades people played. The world felt like a cosmic joke with no punchline. No grand payoff. A shaggy-dog story from birth until death.

"Crazy, huh?" Andy said. He was a DII prospect offensive lineman. He and Randall had known each other since elementary school and started playing football together in the sixth grade. They were never friends but always friendly.

Randall turned and looked at him. His fat, dopey face seemed sincere.

"Yeah. Kid got a raw deal. From the get-go."

Andy wasn't sure what Randall meant by that, but said "yeah" anyway.

Over Andy's shoulder, Randall saw Jared's stepfather walk outside and light up a cigarette. Randall didn't want to talk to him but knew that he should.

"Excuse me," he told Andy and walked that way.

Jared's stepfather eyed him as he walked over. He blew a cloud of smoke above his head and took a flask out of his back pocket and unscrewed the top. He took a long pull as he continued eyeing Randall coming nearer. He returned the flask as Randall approached.

The silence between them hung for too long. A crow squawked in the distance to break the awkwardness. The sun emerged from behind the clouds, and the day got much hotter and brighter. Randall squinted and said, "I know there is nothing I can say."

His stepfather grunted and looked away. He took a drag from his cigarette.

"Then don't."

Randall didn't. He stood there and watched the pain in the man's face.

"Don't say a goddamn word."

Randall nodded. After a couple of seconds, he began to turn but was stopped as Jared's stepfather started to say something. Whatever he intended to say got caught, and he cleared his throat instead. Randall didn't know if it was because he was holding back emotion or trying to articulate a difficult concept. He stood patiently, allowing the man to regain his thoughts.

"You hold some of this responsibility," Jared's stepfather said. "You remember that. Whatever you two had going on contributed to this."

Randall didn't respond. The vein in his neck pulsated, though. His breathing became noticeable. But he stood there to make sure he heard everything this man needed to say.

"He probably would've been better down in Key West with all those other fags," the man said. "You too."

Randall had never been to Key West, but three months later, after he graduated, that was where he decided to go. His parents forbid him. Said if he went to live that degenerate lifestyle instead of going to college, he may as well be dead like his brother. Two weeks after graduation, he packed a bag, said goodbye, and rode the Greyhound bus down to the end of U.S. 1. It wasn't easy being an eighteen-year-old kid down there, but it wasn't easy being an eighteen-year-old kid anywhere. So he did what was necessary to survive. Found jobs at bars and made extra money servicing men and women on vacation. All of it felt slimy, but it was better than the alternative, whatever the alternative was.

48

Bobby hitched a ride to Key West on a dinghy. He found out that Stacy played a lunchtime gig at the Blue Heaven. He wasn't sure how, but he figured that if he kept tabs on Stacy without alerting her to his presence, he could eventually find Janet. Bouncing across the water, he watched the shoreline come closer.

They docked, and he stepped from the dinghy. The day alive with tourists, a little lazier than the previous night, but excitement hung in the air, as if people already looked forward to going to the bars and starting to drink. People vacationed there precisely because it was acceptable to start drinking at 11 am or earlier. Bobby never needed a reason to start drinking at 11 am, and most of the people he knew in Sullivan didn't either. But it seemed like the folks in Key West were closeted morning drinkers back home. They probably held respectable jobs and waited until after work to drink publicly. In Key West, it was expected. It was encouraged. It's what the economy depended on, and it kept people employed, as seen by how most residents were in the service and hospitality industries.

The hostess at Blue Heaven looked at him skeptically as if she knew he couldn't afford to eat there. Even if he could, she kind of wished he wouldn't because of his disheveled look and pungent body odor.

He said he was looking for a friend, and without making eye contact or really even acknowledging the young girl's presence, he stepped a few feet beyond the hostess stand. He looked into the courtyard, and saw Stacy singing on the stage. He was pretty sure that she looked up and saw him. She looked away and then quickly back to him and squinted her eyes as if to make sure what she saw wasn't a mistake. Bobby smiled at her. Stacy looked toward a table, and he followed her eyes to where she sat. He could only see her shoulders and the back of her head, but it was unmistakably Janet. He wanted to walk over and sit at her table and surprise her with his sudden appearance. His heart rate raced. His breathing quickened. He could maintain control mainly because of the two men sitting with Janet. He would've walked over if it was just the one, but the black man with an eye patch gave him pause. He then saw the other man, the one with the shoulder-length locks, lean over and whisper in Janet's ear, and she laughed. His urge to kill came back—this time, not only Janet but also that man.

"Sir," the hostess said, "do you see who you're looking for? Would you like a table?"

Bobby looked down at her, and she stepped back and swallowed. The look frightened her. Bobby left and paced around outside on the sidewalk for a minute. He bummed a cigarette from a passerby. The hostess looked at him and spoke to another man who worked there. Bobby walked across the street, out of sight from the hostess, on the corner of Thomas and Petronia, but he could still keep an eye on the restaurant's exit. He sat on the curb and waited. A gray six-toed cat scurried across the street. A rooster strutted nearby. People entered and exited nearby shops. One guy walked by eating what looked like a slice of key lime pie on a stick.

The long-haired man stepped from the restaurant, lit a cigarette, and headed down Petronia toward Bobby. Bobby stood and approached the man.

"Hey bud," Bobby said. "Excuse me."

The man stopped.

"Hate to bother you," Bobby said. "You happen to have another cigarette I could have?"

The man pulled the pack from his pocket, opened it, and held it out for Bobby. Bobby took a cigarette and put it in his mouth. The man lifted a light to him and flicked it to get a flame. Bobby leaned in and lit the cigarette.

"I'm David," Bobby said. "Just arrived yesterday. I know I look a bit rough. Slept out on Wisteria Island last night."

"You look fine," the man said. "I'm Randall."

"If you don't mind me asking, you don't happen to know of any kind of work for someone just getting here, do you?"

Randall looked at him and didn't attempt to hide his suspicion.

"You telling me that you moved to Key West without a plan for work?"

"Probably not the smartest thing, huh?" Bobby said and laughed a little.

"I wish I could help you, but I've got to get going."

Randall started walking.

"But what about you?" Bobby said, following behind him. "What do you do for work?"

Randall turned his head and looked at Bobby but kept walking.

"I fish, and I bartend. Most people have two jobs, some even three. A lot of folks have to create their own work. I wish you luck."

Bobby kept up with him. "You fish, like for your food?"

Randall stopped. "Hey man, I'm not the person to be answering these questions. I'm struggling to survive down here."

"I'm sorry," Bobby said. "Not trying to pry. I appreciate the cigarette."

"No problem," Randall said. "And no, not for my food. I mean, sure, I eat a lot of what I catch. But I take people out fishing. I've got a boat. But even with my own boat, it ain't easy making a living."

"Gotcha," Bobby said. "Take care. Maybe I'll see you around and repay you for the cigarette."

"It's nothing," Randall said and continued walking.

"What's the name of your boat?" Bobby shouted out.

"The Green Flash," Randall shouted without stopping or looking back.

49

They walked down Duvall Street. The raucous nightlife in full swing. One woman approached utterly naked in a fully painted-on outfit. Janet didn't notice the lack of clothing.

"Look at this lady," Stacy said as they got closer.

"Which one?" Janet asked.

"Right in front of us," Stacy said. "Full nudity. That's all body paint."

"Where?" Janet said. But Janet noticed as she walked by. Nipples clearly visible under the paint, so was her crotch. Shaven but visible. A painted-on iguana's tail ended where her vagina started. The iguana's feet covered her breasts.

Stacy, Janet, and Eli all turned around as the lady passed and looked at the painted-on palm tree covering her ass.

"How is that allowed?" Janet said. Stacy and Eli laughed.

"We should go there," Stacy said, pointing to the Bull and Whistle Bar across the street. A two-story white building with a wrap-around balcony. A building from the 1900s that, throughout its history, was once a boarding house, a brothel, a speakeasy, a gambling den, and a hideout for smugglers and shipwreckers.

"Hell no," Eli said. "I know the only reason you want to go there."

They stopped on the sidewalk.

"It'll be fun," Stacy said.

"I'm tired," Eli said. "I'm going home and getting some sleep. You young ladies, go have some fun."

"He's an old man," Stacy said.

"Damn right, I am."

"I don't know," Janet said. "I probably shouldn't. I think I've seen enough for my first day. I'm pretty tired, too."

"You didn't even drink all of your last drink. Come on. Just one drink."

Eli said, "Y'all be safe. Don't pressure her too much."

Stacy gave him a quick kiss on the lips, and he headed home.

"He doesn't mind you going out alone?" Janet asked.

"No. Why would he?"

"Aren't y'all together," Janet asked. "Like, isn't he your boyfriend?"

Stacy laughed. "Oh, sweet child. I mean, we sleep together if that's what you are asking. But no, we aren't," and she air-quoted "'boyfriend and girlfriend' in that sense."

Janet looked perplexed.

"We enjoy each other's company. I love him dearly. But, well, I like to have a bit more fun than he does."

Janet still looked perplexed.

"It doesn't matter," Stacy said. "You don't have a curfew, you don't have any obligations, and no one will tell you no. You are a woman and free to do as you please—and who you please. You are beautiful, and you will survive."

Janet said, "Just one drink."

"That's right," Stacy said. "Just one drink."

They walked across the street.

"So what is this place you wanted to show me so bad?"

"Girl, I'm so happy you are here. You don't know how much I've missed this. Oh, we're going to have fun. I've been worried about you for a long time." She held Janet's hand, and while it felt odd for Janet, she also felt comforted. She didn't remember the last time she held someone's hand, and she didn't remember the last time she felt like someone cared about her.

"What is this place?" she asked again as they stood at the entrance. The windows were large and open, and you could just make out the sound of the people inside and outside the bar, someone singing and strumming the guitar.

"Come on," Stacy said as they entered.

Downstairs was too crowded, so they went to the second floor. People playing pool. Some young guys played foosball. They ordered drinks at the bar. Two vodka cranberries and lime. They took them outside on the balcony. Three men, maybe in their forties, were shouting at a couple of girls who looked much younger. They were trying to get them upstairs and join them for a drink. The girls said no, and one of the men shouted, "Show us your tits then," and one of the girls did. She lifted her tank top without hesitation. The men about fell over the balcony. The girls kept walking.

"Is it like this every night?" Janet asked Stacy.

Stacy nodded. "Even crazier during Fantasy Fest."

"I'm not sure I can handle crazier."

"You get used to it. Look at those guys." She motioned to the men who were still in ecstasy at having seen breasts. "It's just flesh, but they lose their minds over seeing some titties. Sure hope they aren't married. Their poor wives."

One of the men saw Stacy and Janet looking at them.

Stacy waved.

"What are you doing?" Janet said.

"Drink up. We are about to get two free drinks. These clowns will do anything to see more titties."

The men approached them. Stacy finished her drink.

"Where y'all visiting from?" she asked.

Georgia. They came down to do some fishing. All three married. "But not this week," said the red-faced man with a belly that hung over his belt. They all dressed alike. Golf shirts tucked into too-short shorts and flip-flops. All three wore baseball caps.

One noticed Stacy's empty drink and offered to buy her another one.

"My friend needs one too," she said.

Janet's cup was still nearly full. But the man went off and bought one anyway.

"Y'all going upstairs?" Stacy asked. "To the rooftop bar?"

The two men's eyes nearly bulged from their sockets.

He stuttered, trying to say, "Well if y'all are."

Stacy said they were.

When the guy returned with drinks, the stuttering one whispered in his friend's ear that the girls wanted to go upstairs.

"Oh, hell yeah," the man said.

"Y'all ain't ready," Stacy said, leading Janet to the stairs to the rooftop bar. Janet held two drinks and stopped when she noticed the sign that said, "Clothing optional beyond this point."

"I'm not going up there."

Stacy laughed. "It's okay. We don't have to get naked. Come on. Just take a peek. It's hilarious. I'm going to get those douchebags nude, and then we'll leave."

Janet shook her head and giggled. "You're crazy," she said. "You haven't changed."

"These have," she said, grabbing her breasts in her hands. "Only two years old."

"I thought they were." She grabbed Janet's half-drunk drink at the top of the stairs and set it on a ledge.

"Feel them. They're great."

"I'm not feeling your…"

Stacy grabbed her hand, placing it on her breast.

"Feels natural, right?"

"That's what I'm talking about," one of the guys said as they got to the top of the stairs. The other two guys high-fived.

"Let's see them puppies," he said.

"Fuck off," Stacy said and playfully shoved his head into the wall.

"What the fuck?" he said.

She did it again. This time, harder and with intent.

She walked into the rooftop bar, and the men followed behind like lemmings. The breeze carried the fragrance of frangipani flowers.

There were only four people nude. The others were voyeurs. Of the four nudists, only one was a woman. She wore leather chaps that highlighted her not-so-well-groomed bush. An eagle tattoo across her back and tiny titties that seemed impossible that they hung as low as they did. She danced with an overweight fellow who wore nothing but ostrich skin, Tony Lamas. One would have to really stare to find his penis. It looked like a three-inch pink turtle head trying to poke from beneath a massive hairy shell. Another nudist sat at the bar sipping a red drink in a martini glass. And the last nudist danced by himself, hidden in the far dark corner, a skinny guy with glasses that were too big but an elephant trunk of a cock. Stacy pointed him out. Janet looked to where Stacy pointed and then quickly turned her head. She then looked at Stacy, who started laughing. Janet stole another glance and wanted to laugh, too, but she held it in.

"What are we drinking, ladies?" the man said.

"I'm good," Janet said. She started getting a little tipsy. She knew that because she wanted to look back at the skinny guy with the giant penis.

"Lemon drops," Stacy said. "You'll be fine," she told Janet. "One drink, and then we'll go. I just wanted you to get the full Key West experience."

Janet did the shot, and the alcohol started to taste good. The men bought them another drink, and Stacy ordered two more vodka-cranberries. When she got the drinks, she turned her back to the man and gave her full attention to Janet.

"Why did you get your breasts done?" Janet asked. She looked down at Stacy's cleavage. "Don't get me wrong. They are fantastic."

"I 'dated' a record executive in Nashville," she said, using air quotes with only one hand when she said *dated* because the other held her drink. "Let's be honest. We weren't dating. We were fucking. But anyway, he kept saying he could probably get me a record deal. He offered to buy them for me. I thought, what could it hurt? Tits might be able to sell some music, you know. Well, he didn't get me a deal. We stopped seeing each other. But I got some great tits from it."

"Can we see them?" one of the men buying them drinks said over her shoulder.

Stacy looked back at him. "No," she said. "I'm talking to my friend."

"We're buying you drinks, and we're in a nudity bar. I thought we'd at least get to see your boobs."

Stacy turned all the way around to confront him. "Get naked then," she said. "Stop being chickenshit. Go on. Let's see your dick."

His friends laughed. "Yeah, Owen. Get naked. Show her your dick," one said.

"He's scared," Stacy said.

"Bitch, ain't anyone scared," Owen said.

"Then come on." She tugged at his waistband.

"Shit," he said. He took off his shirt.

His buddies cheered. Others standing around did, too. Those that were already naked didn't show interest. But those who were there strictly for voyeurism got what they came for.

Owen stopped. "What about you?" he said to Stacy. "Shirt for shirt."

"Sure," she said. She took off her tank top, standing in her sports bra.

"Nah, that's cheating," he said. Stacy shrugged and turned back to Janet.

"Okay, okay, okay," Owen said. Stacy turned back to face him.

Janet leaned in and said quietly into Stacy's ear, "Stacy, let's go. I don't like this anymore. You don't have to do this."

"Shorts," Stacy said to the man.

"Don't chicken out now," one of his buddies said.

Some other folks egged him on, too. "Do it, do it, do it," the crowd started chanting.

He slipped out of his flip-flops, undid his belt, unbuttoned his shorts, and dropped them to his ankles. He wore boxer briefs. He lifted his hands as if in celebration of a victory. A beer in one hand.

The crowd cheered.

"Now, your turn," he said to Stacy.

"No," she said. "Not going to happen. Sorry, bud."

His friends laughed.

Owen dropped his arms but kept his shorts down by his ankles as he pouted. "We had a deal."

"No, we didn't." Stacy drank the rest of her drink and set it on the bar.

"I knew you were just a tease. A bitch trying to get free drinks."

Stacy grabbed him by the balls.

"That's the second time you've called me a bitch. Ask to see my tits again? I dare you."

"Wait until the brothers hear about this," his buddy said. The other two were nearly in tears from laughter while Owen stood on his tiptoes to relieve some pressure.

The bouncer, much larger than Owen, then came up, put a hand on Owen's shoulder, and said, "I think it's time you fellas leave. Pull up your pants."

He did, and they left.

Stacy and Janet left shortly after.

Down in the street, the crowd passed by in a blur. Janet's head swirled from the drinks, and the adrenaline from the confrontation became too much for her, and she began to cry.

"Shit. I'm sorry," Stacy said. She put her tank top back on. "I was just having a little fun with those assholes."

"It's not the kind of fun that I'm used to," Janet said, sobbing.

"I know," Stacy said. "Maybe this is a bit much for the first night."

Janet then laughed through the tears. "You think?"

Stacy laughed, too, and they hugged.

On the walk home, away from the crowd, Janet said, "I'm sorry I became distant from you in high school. Bobby didn't want me hanging out with you, and I shouldn't have listened to him. I wish I could go back and do things differently."

"Me too," Stacy said. "I needed you."

"I know," Janet said.

"But why didn't Bobby want you around me?" Stacy asked.

"Because," Janet started to say, but then began laughing and, because she was drunk, laughed more than she probably should have and finally managed to say, "because he said you were a slut."

Stacy laughed, too. "I mean..." She laughed some more. "He was afraid I'd corrupt you, huh? Like I did tonight. Fuck him. No more talking about him."

Back at the house, Janet lay in bed and told herself that when she woke up, she would tell Stacy she was going home. Key West was too much.

50

A week passed as if Janet always lived in Key West. After waking that morning from visiting the Garden of Eden, she told herself that if she could handle that, she could handle anything Key West offered.

Her days consisted of drinking coffee on the front porch, petting the two cats that would come by every morning, reading for an hour, and then painting. She finished nine paintings and set them out on display in the yard for people to purchase. Few people walked by, some stopped, but no one bought anything yet. The street was relatively quiet. When she painted twenty pieces, she would apply for a permit and set up a booth down on the square. She was finishing her favorite so far, the girl on the bike. All of her paintings until then were on eleven by fourteen size canvases, paintings of Queen Anne style homes or shotgun shacks with either a bicycle in the frame or a cat or a rooster sometimes perched on a picket fence or in the street. One painting included all three—a rooster, bicycle, and cat. She felt the art was touristy and folky but knew if that's how she would attempt to make a living, it was what the tourists were buying. And although it was commercial art, she maintained a sense of pride in having created it. But the girl on the bike was different. It meant something more to her, and she painted it on a twenty by twenty-four canvas, focusing on the girl's facial features that she hoped would show the joy of newfound freedom that came with first learning to ride a bike. Besides the folksy Key West art, she painted three from memory depicting Sullivan's swampy landscapes with Spanish Moss hanging from live oaks and of worn-down women sitting on the porch of a trailer, smoking cigarettes with beer cans littered by their feet. Those weren't necessarily painted to sell. They were, for her, a reminder of what she escaped.

She finished reading *The Sun Also Rises* and was surprised by her jealousy of Lady Brett Ashley's sexual freedom. She currently read a tattered paperback of the John D. MacDonald novel *Clemmie,* a story with another highly sexualized woman character written by a man. She slowly realized how Bobby distorted her view of sex. The thoughts of Bobby were fewer and fewer, and the thoughts filled her less with fear and more with anger. She was angry that he preyed on her and angry with herself for not having the strength to deny his approaches. So much so that she married him. She didn't know who that scared, vulnerable girl was anymore. She seemed so far removed from him that she felt it was a different life she had lived in a different world, a parallel world that existed. It took seven months of being away from him to find her strength, but even then, she was almost too afraid to make that final step of leaving Sullivan and waited just before his release from prison to make the move. Bobby was free, she thought. It would've happened two days ago. She nearly gasped at the idea of Bobby walking the streets of Sullivan.

She called her mother.

"He came by your house?" She yelled into the phone. "Mom, what the hell are you talking about? Are you okay?"

Her stomach turned. She felt bile rise. The fear returned. She listened to her mother tell her everything.

"Mom, mom. Stop. Listen to me. He knows where I am?"

The room spun. She held the wall to steady herself.

"I love you, mom. No, you are okay. I'll be fine. Things are good. I don't know when I'll be home. I have to go. I love you."

She hung up the phone, sat on the couch, tried to steady her breathing, and cried. After about ten minutes, she wiped her nose with the back of her hand and stood from the couch. She washed her face and went to see Stacy at Blue Heaven.

During the set break, Stacy sat at the table with Janet and asked, "What are the chances of him actually coming down here?"

"It's Bobby," Janet said. "He's capable of anything."

"I guess so," Stacy said. "We aren't going to let anything happen to you."

Eli and Randall joined them shortly after. Stacy pulled Eli aside.

Janet assumed Stacy was telling him about Bobby.

Randall ordered a beer, and Janet sipped her iced tea. She did her best not to think of the worst-case scenario.

"I thought I was going crazy last night at the Hog's Breath," Stacy said. She worked her long hair into a half-assed bun on the top of her head. "I looked up and saw a man that looked just like Bobby sitting at the bar. He even smiled at me."

"He'll be foolish to try anything."

"You don't know Bobby."

"How well do you know him?" Eli asked.

"We grew up with him. He was crazy even when we were kids. And not too bright which makes him even scarier."

"Goddamn it, Stacy, why the hell did you get involved in this bullshit? I thought the whole reason you left that town was to avoid shit like this?"

Stacy looked at Eli without saying anything.

"I'm sorry," he said. "That was fucked up of me."

"If I escaped, I hoped I could help someone else do the same," she said. "That's what friends do for each other."

"I know. Your compassion is commendable."

"We won't say anything to her until we know for sure."

He bent lower so she could kiss him on the cheek, and then she returned to the stage for her next set. Three songs in, she looked up and saw Bobby standing back by the hostess table.

51

J anet set out her paintings at the house, hanging them from the chain link fence surrounding the yard. She brought the easel with the larger painting she currently worked on to the porch and stared at it. The painting looked complete. She knew it did but couldn't let go just yet. She held on to an unexplainable, irrational fear of finishing it. With a fine point brush, she added hardly visible strokes of white to the bike's chrome, to the girl's eyes, and the girl's toenails, creating the illusion of glinting light. She stepped back and looked at it again.

"Excuse me, mam?" a voice called from the street.

Startled, Janet turned to the gray-haired lady looking at the paintings on the fence.

"Hi," Janet said. She brushed her hair from her eyes and set down her bush.

"These are beautiful," the lady said. "Just unique enough but maintaining the tourist art quality. Are you new here?"

"About a week," Janet said.

"I'm Annalise."

Janet smiled and nodded.

"And you?"

"Right?" Janet said. "I'm Janet."

"Do you have a last name?"

"Yes. Drex..." She paused. "Janet Schroeder."

"Nice to meet you, Janet Schroeder. Would you mind if I came up and took a look at what you are working on?"

"Please do."

Annalise opened the gate latch and walked into the yard. Janet watched her. She walked like a woman with power. Her dress flowed behind her. Although older, the wrinkles visible, she carried an air of royalty, as if age produced strength, having survived. No matter how good or rough someone had it, survival was triumphant, and Annalise knew it.

Janet, only in her twenties, survived plenty, and as long as she continued to survive when she reached the age of Annalise, maybe she could carry herself in such a manner that everyone knew she endured plenty. As much as the world tried, she wasn't broken yet.

"Remarkable," Annalise said as she walked the porch steps and looked more intently at the painting. "That stuff out there will sell all day, but this will sell to someone important. This is what sets you apart. A week, you said?"

"Yes, ma'am," Janet said.

Annalise laughed. "Ma'am? I told you my name already. No need for that 'ma'am' bullshit."

"I'm sorry."

Annalise turned to Janet and looked at her as if Janet were the cutest, most naive little puppy around. "Where are you from?" Annalise asked.

"Sullivan," Janet said.

"Sullivan? I'm just supposed to know where a town named Sullivan is located. Aren't you precious?"

"Well, it's in Florida, ma'am...sorry...Ms. Annalise."

Annalise laughed. "You just can't help yourself, can you? Where in Florida?"

"Up top."

"Up top?"

Janet nodded.

"Near Tallahassee? Near Jacksonville?"

"No," Janet said. "Near Pensacola. About fifty miles north. On the border."

"My lord," Annalise said. "A Panhandler."

"A week?"

"People from the Panhandle always fascinate me."

Janet didn't respond. She averted her eyes away from Annalise. Looked out at the street. The birds sang.

"I can help you, Janet," Annalise said. "You can help me, too. Come see me tonight." She gave her the address on Fleming Street. "I'm having a bit of gathering, and I think you should join us." She told her what time. "And bring that painting."

"I don't think it will be finished," Janet said.

"Bring it however it is."

"I don't have any nice clothes to wear," Janet said.

Annalise laughed. "Oh, darling. I want you just as you are. Stop making excuses, will you?"

"Okay," Janet said.

"A week, you said?"

"Excuse me."

"You've only been here a week. Is that right?"

Janet nodded.

"And you painted all this in a week?"

Janet nodded.

Annalise smiled. "Tonight, my love."

Janet nodded again.

52

"I need you to open this envelope after 9 p.m. tonight, not before," Eli said to Police Chief Sampson. They met at Pepe's. With a handkerchief, the chief wiped the sweat from his bald, pink head.

Chief Sampson accepted the manila envelope and, feeling its weight, said, "I don't have a good feeling about this, Eli. What are you asking of me?"

"Please. I need you to do this for me."

The chief saw Eli's despair. "You aren't planning anything stupid, are you?"

Eli nodded. "I'm sorry, but I'm afraid I am."

"God damn it. Don't put me in this situation."

"I'm sorry," Eli said, and he walked out.

Eli did what seemed to observers his regular routine that evening during the sunset celebration at Mallory Square. He stood under his hanging contraption and spoke to the crowd, already strapped and chained.

"Now, folks," he said. "How many have seen my performances in the past?"

The crowd cheered. A wave of melancholy washed over him. His eye blurred, and he blinked it clear. He would miss the crowd, Stacy and Randall, and Scotty for some stupid reason.

He'd miss the familiarity of walking into his favorite bars and the Cuban coffee. He knew the time had come, though. Dragging it out any longer would only make it more painful.

"Well," he continued. "I'm going to attempt something different. Something I've never tried. Hell, it may fail."

He walked backward until he reached the ledge and asked for a volunteer to help him step up.

"If I fail," he paused. "If I fail, it could mean death."

The crowd's reaction was mixed. Half laughed, and the others seemed concerned.

"Once I perform my trick, some of you may be concerned. But I want you to be assured everything will be fine. Behind me, watch the sunset for the green flash. I have a feeling tonight is the night."

The crowd erupted.

"Now, on the count of three. I need y'all to help me out."

"One," the crowd said together. "Two." And before they could say, "Three," Eli backflipped into the water. The chains sank him quickly, so he worked fast and made no mistakes. Even with two good eyes, seeing was nearly impossible in the dark waters. But he did it without being able to see many times and knew he could do it again.

Once free of the chains and jacket, he still had about a minute of air left and reached into his pants to get his gloves on so he could go for the pier pilings without cutting his hands on the barnacles and then swim to the surface underneath the dock. Under the pier, he worked his way around the large concrete posts that held up Mallory Square until he reached the end. He saw Scotty sitting in his dinghy, waiting for him. He climbed aboard, and Scotty threw a towel over him. Underneath the towel he stripped off the wet clothes, and switched to dry jeans and a hooded sweatshirt.

At the docks, he stepped from the dinghy and thanked Scotty.

"You be good," Scotty said. "If you ain't good, be good at it."

"Don't spend all that money in one place," Eli said. He gave Scotty a thousand dollars to be his getaway driver and never tell a person.

His truck was parked in a nearby parking lot with one suitcase, and he drove it directly to the airport. With twenty minutes remaining before takeoff, he boarded the flight.

When Chief Sampson realized what was happening, Eli was landing in Miami to board his connecting flight to La Paz, Mexico. Chief Sampson would open the envelope and see the ten thousand dollars to cover emergency responses if they sent out water rescuers looking for him. Hopefully, Chief Sampson would open the envelope before that happened and call off the search.

Hopefully, he would also see the envelope addressed to Stacy and get it to her before she heard the news.

From the sale of his rental property, he made enough money to buy a bungalow in Todo Santos. Stacy would wire him money every month for the next ten years, after which she would own the house she and Randall lived in.

Eli would perform barstool magic tricks for tourists at cantinas and, on weekends, take the bus down to Cabo San Lucas. In one night, he would make enough in tips to live comfortably for a week in his small abode and hope his eyesight never fully faded.

53

The distant sirens slightly interrupted her sunset gig at the Hog's Breath. It startled Stacy because sirens weren't usually heard on the island. There was plenty of petty theft, public intoxication, domestic violence, and bar room fights, but not really anything that warranted sirens—multiple sirens. She stopped mid-song.

"Well, shit," Stacy said into the microphone. "Something serious must be going on."

The crowd murmured in assumptions. One person said they heard someone jumped into the water off Mallory Square and didn't resurface. A wave of people left the bar, people who flocked to tragedy, people who wanted a story to take home, to go back after a vacation and tell their friends that they were there when the excitement happened.

In the bar crowd, Stacy spotted Chief Sampson, an odd sight in the bar.

"I think I will take a quick break if you don't mind. Let some of the excitement die down and then recollect ourselves. If you like what you've heard so far, I've got some CDs for sale. Come on up and say hey. And if you'd like to drop a little bit in the tip jar, that's greatly appreciated, too. I'm just trying to raise a cool million tonight. Nothing too extravagant."

She set her guitar in the stand. Chief Sampson walked toward the stage, and a ripple of anxiety flooded through her. She stepped down to meet him.

"Is it Eli?" she asked.

He nodded. Her knees weakened. He held her by the elbow.

"I'm pretty sure he is okay," Chief Sampson said. "Let's go for a walk."

Stacy spoke into the microphone. "I'm so sorry, folks, but I think the break will take longer. I'll be back shortly."

A man stopped Stacy as she stepped from the stage. "Do you mind if I play a few songs until you return?" Stacy was star-struck. She knew the man's music well but never met him personally. His name was Keith, and he wrote songs for many recording artists.

"I would be honored," Stacy said.

As she left the bar with the chief, Keith started into one of Stacy's favorite tunes, "The Coast of Marseilles."

Outside the bar, Chief Sampson told Stacy about the envelope and that he wasn't to open it until after 9 p.m., a little more than an hour away.

"Do you have it?"

He handed it to her. They continued walking at a fast pace toward Mallory Square. Police taped off the area from where he jumped. A crowd pushed as close as they could get to watch. The sun sped toward the horizon.

"Not only have I got this going on, but we just got a distress call from a boat out at Channel Key. Someone's been stabbed and the caller was shot through the gut with a spear gun. I'm telling you, this fucking island makes people do some crazy shit."

"I'm not waiting," Stacy said and opened the envelope while standing inside the circle of yellow tape. Two rescue divers were gearing up on the ledge.

The envelope contained a bundle of cash and a typed letter addressed to Chief Sampson and a smaller envelope addressed to Stacy. She took that envelope out and handed the manila envelope back to the chief.

"I think what's left in there is for you."

The chief held the envelope and looked at his watch.

Stacy opened the one addressed to her and read it. Tears streamed down her face, and she shook her head. Then, she laughed through the tears.

"He did it," she said, looking up at the chief.

"I guess I should read what he left for me, huh?"

Stacy nodded. He read it. "Son of a bitch," he said. He hurried to call off the search before the divers jumped in. A reporter for the *Key West Times* already jotted down what he knew and headed back to the office to get the article published in the morning paper, "Magician Elijah the Great Performs Houdini-like Disappearing Act."

The sun touched the horizon, and the onlookers turned their attention from the missing magician to the water in hopes of catching a glimpse of the illusive green flash.

Stacy said goodbye to the chief and returned to the Hog's Breath to relieve Mr. Keith and continue her set.

At the end of the night, Keith hung around and said his good friend owned a recording studio down by the wharf, an old ice house that he converted. He'd like to take Stacy there to meet his friend and discuss producing an album for her. Mr. Keith and his friend had been catching her shows for the last couple of years and thought it was time to take her act to the next level.

Stacy knew of which friend Mr. Keith spoke.

54

Randall sat on the captain chair of his boat, smoking a joint. He listened to the Allman Brothers Band play "Blue Sky" from his tape deck. Having played that tape so often, the lyrics "you're my sunny day" warbled from being worn, but Randall sang along.

A man's voice startled him from the dock. Randall looked up and then turned the volume down on his tape deck. He recognized the man from earlier in the day when he walked out of Blue Heaven. He had given the man a cigarette, and the man asked him what boat he operated.

"How are you doing?" Randall said. "Twice in one day, huh?"

"Yeah, well, I hate to bother you, but you see," the man said, "I'd like to learn to fish these waters, so when I met you, I thought that was the good Lord giving me a sign, ya know?"

"Man, look, I'd love to help you, but I don't think you've got the right guy."

"I ain't got much money, but I can put gas in your boat and pay you something for your time."

"How much do you have?" Randall asked.

"How long can we go out for a hundred dollars?"

"Shit, man, that barely puts gas in the tank. I've got to work tonight, but I can take you for a quick spin. Wet the line for an hour. Maybe catch a mangrove snapper if we are lucky."

"It would be much appreciated."

"Tell you what. There's a corner store right over there. Go get some beer. By the time you get back, I'll be ready to head out."

"Yes, sir," the man said.

"You can call me Randall."

"You bet."

"Tell me your name again."

The man hesitated. "Daniel."

Randall looked at him. "Daniel?"

The man turned to go to the corner store. When he returned, he carried a twelve-pack of beer with him, and he stepped aboard The Green Flash.

They motored out from the dock. Randall throttled it wide open so he wouldn't have to talk to the guy on the ride to the fishing spot. He drank his beer and enjoyed the wind in his face. He set his sights on Channel Key. He hadn't visited there since finding the bodies but knew it was an easy place for him to pick up a snapper or two.

He slowed the boat as he approached the key. "Hey, David," he said. "Grab this rod here. It's already rigged with a lure." He tapped the rod over his right shoulder. "Step up on the platform, and I'll do some chumming. You'll see them come to the surface. With some luck, we'll be out of here in thirty or forty minutes."

The man walked back to where Randall pointed.

"Daniel or David?" Randall asked.

"What?" the man said. He stopped before taking the rod down.

"Didn't you tell me your name was Daniel on the dock?"

"It's David," the man said. "Why would I have said Daniel?"

"Guess I'm hearing things," Randall said. He walked to the front of the boat and dropped the anchor.

"Hey," the man said. "Can you show me how to use this?" He held a speargun that had been strapped down next to the rods.

"Do me a favor. Don't be touching all my shit. You asked me to teach you a bit about fishing. Spearing is another trip."

"What kind of fish are you spearing?"

Randall sighed. He walked back near the man, grabbed another beer, opened it, and took a long pull. "Hand it here," he said. He put the spear against his hip, pulled the band back, and hooked it. "I use it for mahi, snapper, grouper, hogfish, snook."

"I'll have to take another trip with you to learn that," the man said. He smiled and showed his missing side teeth.

Randall undid the speargun and set it down. The man smelled and Randall sighed thinking of the things he did for money. Taking a borderline homeless man fishing was one of the more mild ways.

"You can stand up on there and start casting. I'm going to step out and take a piss. When I return, I'll throw a cast net to get some bait fish to chop up and chum the waters."

Randall took another long drink from his beer before setting it in the cup holder on the console. Then, he jumped down into the waist-deep water and waded toward shore. A week ago, those bodies were floating on this key, and the thoughts of Jared came rushing back to him. He put that thought away for a while, but for the past week, it returned, and he hated it.

Heading back to the boat, waist high in the water, he looked up at the man on the platform holding the speargun.

"Hey man," Randall said, "I asked you not to touch my stuff."

"I loaded it right," the man said.

"I don't give a shit," Randall said. "We aren't spearing."

"You might not be," the man said.

The slight roll of the tide lapped against the side of the boat. A pelican dove face down into the water nearby and then sat floating on the water.

"This motherfucker," Randall muttered and continued closer to the boat. "Set it down," he said.

"You been fucking Janet," the man said. "I saw y'all sitting together at that restaurant this morning."

Randall stopped.

"I thought so," the man said.

Randall continued toward the boat. "Look, man. I don't know Janet. She just moved down here. I have no idea what you two have going on, and I don't care."

Before he could continue talking, the shaft of the spear gun went into his stomach.

Randall looked down and gripped the shaft but knew it was deep and there was no way to pull the barb out. Blood started fanning out in the water around him.

The man turned to the console of the boat before whipping back to face Randall. "Where the fuck is the key?"

Randall blinked. The pain started registering. The man and the boat seemed farther off than he thought. "I have it," Randall shouted through the pain. He reached down and unclasped the sheath on the fixed-blade knife he kept on his belt loop.

"Well, I need it," the man shouted.

Randall tried to move closer to the boat. He reached for the gunwale.

"Give me the key, and I'll help you aboard," the man said.

"Shut up and get me aboard," Randall said, as blood started to seep more profusely. "I think you are going to have to radio for help. This isn't good."

"Give me the key," the man said.

Randall dropped the steps near the motor and tried to pull himself up. "Give me a hand, goddamn it."

The man stepped from the platform and reached his hand down. Randall lurched forward and stuck him with the knife under his sternum, and the man quickly slumped forward, driving the knife to the hilt. Randall grabbed the man's shirt and pulled him into the water with the same hand. The man flipped forward and landed on his back with a splash. The pelican flew off.

Randall pulled himself back into the boat. Blood covered the floor. The man tried to stand in the water but fell back down. He stopped struggling and accepted his fate. Randall did the same. He reached up and unhooked the radio, telling the person on the other end what happened and the boat's location. He knew it would be too late by the time someone arrived, but he didn't want a stranger to happen across such an unexpected scene.

A frigatebird flew by overhead. The bird songs in the mangroves grew louder before fading. Randall lay back and watched the brightness of day darken before the sunset.

55

S he felt silly lugging the canvas through the streets and in the past would have skipped the invite, but she decided to no longer waste opportunities. What was the worst that could happen? She endured some awful things and was confident that arriving at a party at an art gallery would not be worse than her past experiences. So she went.

Annilese greeted her at the door. A spacious gallery, with a few sculptures on pedestals. One of a man's torso, muscular, veins on the abdominal obliques. One of a hand, also veiny with rugged, large knuckles. Same artist. Another, from a different artist, of a blue heron. The white brick walls displayed paintings of splatters, lines, and circles—nothing like what she painted. She felt like she arrived at the wrong address.

It wasn't overly crowded, maybe fifteen people. The elegance of the crowd took Janet aback. Being underdressed in a blouse and long skirt, she no longer wanted to be there. She made a mistake. The women wore shiny dresses, and the men wore jackets and ties. She was never invited anywhere by people who dressed like that—a moment of anxiety swept over her. Breathing became manual, and her cheeks flushed. A man took the painting from her and leaned it against the wall on the floor. The guests flocked around it and gathered around her as if she were a spectacle. Annilese heralded her as an original. She felt like a fraud.

They spoke about her as if she weren't in the room.

"You were so right, Annilese. It's like you discovered a diamond in a trash pile," one lady said, wearing large dangling earrings. "Only someone who has lived that lifestyle can capture the emotion and the pain of someone longing for freedom."

"I was just painting the girl in the picture," Janet said, but no one listened. She wondered if she said that out loud or thought it.

A young man wearing a pastel suit, blush on his cheeks, and light-tinted lipstick walked by with a tray of champagne flutes. Those around him quickly took drinks, and the young man was gone. Annilese took two glasses and handed one to Janet.

"Tonight, we celebrate you, Janet," Annilese said.

"Why?" Janet asked.

The guests laughed. Janet didn't know what was funny.

"We are going to exhibit your work," Annilese said. "I want ten pieces this size and a few of your small ones too."

"From the Panhandle to Key West," one man with a gray mustache said. "I can't wait to see those Panhandle paintings you mentioned, Annalise. That area is something else. I don't know how people live like that."

"Like what?" Janet said, but again, her question went unanswered.

Outside, police sirens sounded in the distance.

"There is something beautiful about poverty when looked at from the outside," a woman said, shiny black hair down to her mid-back. She looked young, but when examined closely, one could see the age in her features, although she had very few wrinkles. "The struggle. The survival. The sheer energy it takes to get out of bed every morning."

"No, there isn't," Janet said louder than she expected. "Poverty isn't beautiful. The people are, but living in it isn't beautiful."

The guests' eyes widened. They glanced at one another.

"Oh, honey," Annalise said. "You know what she meant." The guests laughed. Janet didn't. "Come here, darling," Annalise said, putting an arm around her shoulders and guiding her from the group toward her painting. "Your painting tonight is going to sell for a lot of money. And then all your paintings will fetch a surprising amount. You have no idea what these people can do for you."

"But," Janet started to protest.

"No," Annalise said. "You paint, and I'll do the selling."

Janet nodded. She understood. This was how the world worked—she could try to fight it or endure it, and enduring it was all she knew.

Acknowledgments

You'd think after writing a couple novels that it would start getting easier. It doesn't. I wouldn't have been able to finish this without my wife, Julie. She is my biggest cheerleader. Without her encouragement, this would've probably taken another five years or longer. My children, another inspiration to keep moving forward. If I quit, they quit, and I refuse to allow that to happen. My mother who made me believe that making up stories was a worthy endeavor. Izo Besares, you've been supporting my work for over 20 years. Sharing what we read and what we are writing is always a joy. Tony Eberhardt, for putting in the time on this thing. A very special thanks to Derek and Katie Smith, true patrons of the arts.

While writing the book was hard enough, publishing it was equally as difficult. The following people made it much easier. I'm forever grateful for your generosity:

Will Searcy	William Robbins	Melanie Pyne
Susan Holtzclaw	Christiana Reed	Casey Ford
David Lewallyn	Jason Simpson.	Marcy Desantis
Ronald Zupinski	Kate Treick	Lori Thompson
Kyle Crawford	Laurel Brownlee	Shelley Lamie
Izodrik Besares	Pat Meusel	Julie Prevost
Derek Smith	Heather Dammeyer	Tammy Ingle
Kelly Motto	Anthony Zupinski	Slater Dance
Anonymous	Jesh Yancey	Kat Walker
Julia Lippincott	Lance Vargas	Ryan Hughes
Michael Zavison	Dolores Daniels	Warren Hanna
Michelle Lamar-Acuff		

About the author

Photo: Julie Schuck

Nic Schuck of Pensacola, Florida teaches high school English and leads historic tours of Downtown Pensacola with Emerald Coast Tours, a company he started in 2012.

Instagram: @nic_schuck

Praise for NATIVE MOMENTS

"Like the Walt Whitman lines from which Nic Schuck takes the title for his debut novel, *Native Moments* explores 'life coarse and rank' with its 'libidinous joys' and passions. With a keen ear for dialogue and a poet's eye for the resonate detail, Nic Schuck creates a world his readers will be eager to enter and reluctant to leave." - Jonathan Fink, author of *The Crossing*

"Schuck does a good job of showing the multilayered cake that is Costa Rica, complete with surfing paradise, dangerous fauna, unlimited vice, all of which is coated in a sweet, ironic icing of Pura Vida. This is a great book to toss in your board bag on your next surf trip." - Drew Sievers, TheWatermansLi brary.com

Purchase Here:

Praise for PANHANDLERS

"Things have changed little in the profound South since the days of Harry Crews and Larry Brown. If you like the gritty South noir that began with *Sanctuary*, you will find *Panhandlers*--from the piney-woods northwest Florida region--very satisfying. Nic Schuck knows his territory and he knows the inhabitants and their mores--cock fighting, dog fighting, beer drinking, shooting, and the never-ending, gut-wrenching age-old art of mere survival--first-hand. If you want the real story, this is it." - Allen Josephs is the author, most recently, *of On Cormac McCarthy: Essays on Mexico, Crime, Hemingway and God*

"As an instructor of literature and the co-owner of an indie bookstore, I have the opportunity to read a number of young authors. By far, Nic Schuck is one of the most talented new writers I've come across in years. With echoes of Hemingway and McCarthy-- as well as newer Southern writers such as Tom Franklin--Nic Schuck adds a unique contribution to both modern Southern literature and the emerging Florida canon, with the truly authentic voice of the Gulf South." - C. Scott Satterwhite, co-owner of Open Books, author of *A Punkhouse in the Deep South*